Dark Angel

Dark Angel

[signature: Ron Baird]

Written by Ronald E. Baird

Writer's Showcase

San Jose New York Lincoln Shanghai

Dark Angel

Writer's Showcase
an imprint of iUniverse.com, Inc.

For information address:
iUniverse.com, Inc.
5220 S 16th, Ste. 200
Lincoln, NE 68512
www.iuniverse.com

ISBN: 0-595-17975-4

Printed in the United States of America

To Aurora, for giving me the story, and to Trisha, wherever you are.

ACKNOWLEDGMENTS

All thanks to Steve Austin, Carla Reardon-Gustafson, Rex Burns, Jeff Long, and many others for braving dangerous fictional territory and/or for encouragement. Thanks to Kevin Rogers for art and inspiration. And especially, I want to thank Nancy Morrell, for believing and making it possible.

CHAPTER I

The big cat ambled along the canyon rim, her lowered head swinging from side to side. She paused every few steps to smell the air, to scan the horizon. The sun was high and it went against her instincts to hunt in the middle of the day, but hunger gnawed at her guts.

Her coat was dark for a mountain lion so the sun took an even greater toll.

If she were a few years older, the lioness would have known to crawl into the cool shadows and rest during the day, to save her energy for the night, no matter how hungry she was. But she was only two years old and hadn't been on her own long enough to be wise in the ways of her kind.

She still had a vague memory of her mother driving her away just two months earlier and the lingering but minor pain where her mother had swatted her on the shoulder with full claws to be sure she got the point; she was on her own.

Farther back, on her hip, was another column of scars, still raw, where an old lion had warned her off his territory. This newer pain still felt like fire, but less so every day.

Despite these distractions, hunger was her main concern and she picked up the scent of a rabbit. But it was faint, void of promise. She stopped and raised her muzzle to the air, nostrils flaring. Nothing that smelled like food and an end to the ache in her belly was on the wind.

Keeping to the thick Douglas fir and brush, she continued to pad cautiously along the canyon, but well back from the rim. Below, she could hear the rushing water of a cool, thirst-quenching stream.

In mid-stride she heard a strange sound float up from the canyon. She crouched flat against the earth, raised her ears and tuned her senses to the presence of potential danger. Her smooth, dark flanks fluttered and her heart raced. While she held her body still, the black tip of her tail twitched, something she was unable to control.

Minutes passed and so, it seemed, had any danger. The cat relaxed, her breathing returned to normal. As she relaxed, the young lioness became curious about the sound and raised her body just inches above the ground.

Young muscles rippled beneath her dark pelage and displayed the power in her body as she seemed to be floating toward the canyon rim.

Once there, she saw a creature standing in the water waving a thin object, and a long, green, flimsy line arced back and forth in the air before stretching out and settling onto the flowing stream.

The cat sank to the cool forest floor, mesmerized by the quiet repetition of the creature, the stick and the line. The scene, although puzzling, lulled the young lioness into forgetting her hunger for the moment. At the point the cat was almost dozing, the creature below uttered a sharp sound.

Within the space of a single heartbeat, the cat was alert, untold millennia of instinct honed to recognize danger. But something was splashing in the water, something the cat recognized as food. Her stomach rumbled, alive now with growing hunger. Juices were flowing in her mouth and throat, her eyes dilated, and she crept down through the brush and fallen trees.

The action from the stream had quieted as the creature dipped something into the water and held up a silvery-gold fish with bright spots on the side.

Emboldened by hunger, the cat moved down to the stream bank, stopping behind a fallen log when the brush no longer covered her approach. She craned her neck over the log to see, and the creature in the stream stood up, looked directly at her and said, "Whoa! Nice kitty, nice kitty."

Hunger drew the young cat on but wariness held her back; she couldn't smell any real fear coming from the creature but neither did she sense danger.

But the fish, still struggling in the net, was most certainly something to eat. The creature locked eyes with the cat, a move that would have been taken by an older animal as a challenge. But the creature and the cat were joined in a mental dance of awe, shock and uncertainty.

As if recognizing the young cat's quandary, the creature backed out of the water. This movement heightened the cat's senses. Her flanks moved in and out like a bellows. The thick hair along her spine bristled and her tail twitched. But she held her spot.

Once on the stream bank, the creature placed the still-flopping fish on the ground and moved away without turning its back on the cat. When it had gone up the stream, out of sight, the cat waited what seemed like an eternity as her stomach tumbled and churned. When all seemed safe, she crept to the stream, waded across and devoured the large fish in a few seconds.

It wasn't much, but it was enough to give her the strength to go on. She would now seek out a place to sleep until darkness brought safety and another chance to hunt.

Back at his old beat up Subaru station wagon, Aaron Hemingway leaned against the fender on shaky legs, looked back down the trail and said, "Holy shit."

In my dream the following night, I'd been up on the mountain hunting for my dog when the flashlight beam reflected off of something in the darkness. A fear born deep in ancestral memory–when ferocious animals stalked the perimeter of campfires—told me these were the eyes of a man-eater. My knees became weak, my bowels turned watery. The eyes disappeared as I reached for the gun in my down vest pocket. But the pocket was small and the hammer of the gun caught on the lining. As I struggled to pull it out, the pocket seemed to fight me for control of the weapon.

Shining with a pale-green fire, the eyes appeared again, closer, much closer. An unseen hand choked the scream in my throat. Something was moving toward me in the dark when a hideous cry ripped the suffocating silence.

Just at the moment my heart was ready to burst, it went 'thunk.'

Thunk?

My heart went 'thunk?'

Deciphering the puzzle of the noise spurred my brain into a higher gear, and sleep-encrusted eyes filled with the familiar scene of my cabin. I realized it had only been a nightmare; there was no demon with green eyes and my heart hadn't exploded.

Then I heard the noise again, only this time it sounded like a tiny bowling ball rolling down the ceiling, striking the wall next to my head.

I lay there and let the fear drain from my sweat-drenched body. The dog, curled up like a 100-pound furball next to the door, whimpered in a dream of his own.

The mouse sauntered down the ceiling into the wall next to my bed, where it began to munch on the piece of dog food it had rolled from its stash in the ceiling. The little bastard had set up a dining room right next to my bed. The noise was gnawing away my skull from the inside. And this was, what, the fifth day in a row? Too goddamn many, in any case.

I should have been thankful because the mouse had rescued me from the nightmare. But I was still reeling from the terror and impotence that enfolded me moments earlier. The mouse had, unwittingly, stumbled into a bad situation. But I decided to give it a chance and slammed my fist hard against the wall.

The mouse was quiet but within seconds it was munching away again.

I reached under the bed, drew out my snub-nosed .22-magnum revolver and raised the gun, placing the stubby barrel against the spot on the wall where the mouse was chowing down. Then I cocked the hammer.

"Okay, you little turd factory, you got five seconds. Should I count out loud or just surprise you?" A second later, its tiny feet pattered away.

I put the gun back under the bed and closed my eyes, but the panic caused by the nightmare lingered. Running into the mountain lion had been frightening but also exhilarating. What had turned that memory into such a horrible nightmare? I yawned, closed my eyes and tried to relax, but a strange glow crept into my consciousness.

I rolled over and peered through the window as the first rays of sunrise painted the undersides of the heavy morning clouds the color of blood.

Somehow, I managed to fall asleep but a short time later reawakened to find the morning sun bright and warm. The heavy clouds had dissipated, and bright sunlight swept gently up the forested slopes across the valley. Behind my cabin, shadows grew distinct on a half-mile long ridge of exposed granite that rose two-hundred feet into the sky. The ridge, which looked like a massive prehistoric spine as it emerged from a fifty-million-year-old grave, was created by an uplift in the Earth's surface millions of years earlier and sculpted by glaciation. Eons of wind and water have stripped away all but the core rock. Its appearance caused the area's earliest non-native inhabitants to call it the Dragon's Backbone, but now was called Dragonback Ridge.

Slabs of stone and boulders, some as big as my cabin, had fallen away and crashed down the mountain, littering the slopes below like beer cans along a Texas highway.

Moments of early morning clarity sometimes swept me up in the geologic time frame that had rearranged my backyard every few millennia. And I wondered if the Dragon would shed a couple-hundred tons of rock onto my cabin and squash me like a bug while I slept.

The telephone jangled.

"This better be important," I growled into the phone, not a pleasant person first thing in the morning and today feeling downright ornery.

"Get out of bed, Aaron," came the grating whine of Abigail Osgood, my editor at the Mountain Miner. I imagined a bullet hole between her aristocratic blue eyes.

"Just what the hell could be happening at 6:30 a.m. in Jack Springs, Colorado, that requires my attention, Abigail? Did the mayor finally get caught wagging his weenie at little girls in front of the bus stop?"

"There's a dead body on the front porch," she said.

What other kind of body is there, my sleep-addled brain was trying to ask?

"It's Stephanie Goldman, or was, I should say," she continued, her voice wavering.

If Abigail had any sense of humor at all, I might have thought she was playing a sick joke on me. But she didn't.

"On our doorstep?" the implication finally getting through.

"Now you're getting the idea," she said.

"Give me thirty minutes."

"Make it fifteen," she said as she hung up.

Stephanie Goldman was a big, tough-as-nails mountain woman who had been raising holy hell about a proposed gold mine in the mountains above the town, and somebody had murdered her and left the body at the newspaper office. Well, hell, that seemed a good enough reason to get out of bed early.

I pulled on my Levis, a checked western shirt and cowboy boots, and hauled ass into town. Speeding down Magnolia Road, the feeling of being at the center of the action once again tingled in my belly, a feeling that had been absent from my life in recent years. But then, I wasn't always a reporter for a weekly, small-town newspaper. I used to be a cop.

CHAPTER 2

I wound down the Peak-to-Peak highway and pulled into town. Jack Springs, once a sleepy little mining town, was bustling these days. Houses were still being built in the anarchic fashion typical of many less prosperous mountain towns. But unlike some, the eclectic styles gave the town a pleasant-if-chaotic appearance. Somehow, the worst impulses of design had so far been avoided. Flower gardens bloomed after the July rains and tiny lawns were neat and green. Stacks of firewood were already growing high for the coming winter.

For all its quaint facade, violence lurked just beneath the veneer of civilization in these old mountain towns and Jack Springs was no exception.

The landscape itself was unforgiving, turning simple lapses of judgment into fatal mistakes. Madness simmered in alcohol during the long, bitter winters, erupting with the light-speed slash of a broken beer bottle, a knife slipped silently from a boot, or the hellish explosion of a large-caliber bullet.

But that violence was born of passion or madness or even greed. The cop in me said to look for the simple answer, but the reporter couldn't shake the feeling that the murder of Stephanie Goldman was something altogether more sinister.

I turned onto Second Street, where a phalanx of police cars had blocked off the area. There were nearly a dozen, from the Boulder County Sheriff's Office, the Colorado State Patrol and a couple of nearby communities, not to mention every old Jeep and car that belonged to the Jack Springs Marshal's office. And every one had their light bars flashing. It looked more like a siege than a crime scene.

Jack Springs' Marshal Harlan Silbaugh was stringing yellow tape around the perimeter of the property. A couple hundred people stood staring just outside the tape. Cops were huddled like conspirators, in hushed conversations. Stopping in the middle of the street, I got out and walked over to where Harlan was joining the last section of tape.

"Morning, Aaron," he said. "Hell of a deal, ain't it?"

"You can say that, I guess." There was black plastic draped ominously over something large and lumpy on the steps. "Is that Steph?"

Harlan nodded.

"Are you sure she was murdered?"

"Yeah, well, I guess it could be something we ain't thought of," he said, stroking his chin. "But a bullet hole in the back of the head seems to rule out most of 'em."

"Dumb question," I admitted. "Talking to Abigail first thing in the morning can be traumatizing."

Harlan smiled but declined to comment.

"What you got so far?" I asked.

He looked around to see if anyone could overhear.

"Usual deal. Whatever I give you is off the record. The only thing I want to see after my name is 'no comment.'"

With his thinning brown hair combed straight back under a rolled brim cowboy hat, ruddy complexion and big belly on a body like an oak tree trunk, Harlan was the spittin' image of Hoss Cartwright—one of my favorite childhood TV cowboys. Hoss looked like a real cowboy. And Harlan looked like a real Old West marshal.

"Besides, the county has already taken this over. This is just too big for our little department." He gave me a wink that meant there would-n't be any jurisdictional disputes over the investigation. Harlan was about as interested in conducting a murder investigation as he was in having an impacted wisdom tooth pulled without anesthesia. He knew his limitations.

"Let's go over to Bob's for some donuts and coffee," he said. "We can't do any more here until the crime scene gets done."

Coffee and donuts. After working in the uranium mines at Uravan for fifteen years, Harlan Silbaugh wasn't a man to let something like a murder disrupt the important things in life—like a ritual involving something edible.

He took a can of snuff out of his back pocket, pinched a large wad and packed it inside his lower lip. He grunted a little as we walked up the slight hill towards Bob's. His equipment belt, laden with a holster, handcuffs, Mace, baton and PAC radio, squeaked as he walked. The hol-ster, holding a long-barrel .44 magnum, slapped his leg every other step. As we reached the highway, a convoy of TV news satellite trucks came speeding into town. We had barely made it across when the first one sped by.

"Well, that settles it," I said. "We got a real live news event on our hands here, Marshal Silbaugh."

"Hell fire, Mr. Hemingway, I could have told you that," he said and launched an arcing stream of tobacco juice against the shiny side of the last news van as it passed. Like most cops, Harlan wasn't a big fan of the media—present company excepted, of course.

In Bob's Bakery, Harlan rebuffed questions from a few of the citizens who had heard about the murder but had better things to do than stand around the crime scene. He grabbed his two personal mugs off the wall. Bob's police scanner was humming with the news, anyway, so Harlan turned down his PAC set. He bought six small cake donuts and carried them, along with two steaming mugs of coffee, to the booth in the corner. I had one donut and a small cup of coffee.

For a man of his girth, Harlan had to be one of the most fastidious eaters in the world. One cup was for dunking, one was for drinking. After each bite of a coffee-soaked donut, he wiped his mouth with a napkin. It was hard to see how he could keep his weight up without eating twenty four hours a day.

Harlan and I had a lot in common. We were about the same age and had held our present jobs about the same amount of time. I coached his daughter's basketball team. And I had been a Denver cop before leaving that city's finest under somewhat strained circumstances. He'd returned to Jack Springs from western Colorado to work in a local small-time gold mine. The town council hired him because they figured he would go easy on the locals and generate some income by going after out-of-town drunks and speeders. That proved to be wrong, however. He was serious about his job and that meant being fair, much to the council's dismay.

As a result, Harlan was popular with the citizenry, especially after arresting the town manager for drunk driving. The council members knew they couldn't fire him without losing their coveted jobs.

After the fifth donut disappeared, I'd had enough. "Are you going to fill me in sometime this century?"

He raised an eyebrow and said, "I have to keep my blood sugar up or my mind doesn't work right. You wouldn't want me to leave anything out, would ya?" At last, only the sixth donut remained. It had pink icing and little chrome sprinkles—almost too pretty to eat. But Harlan ate it anyway, then took a slow sip of his drinking coffee.

"Before we go into that, I was wondering if there's something we could do to get the girl's free-throw percentage up before next season?"

Such leaps in thinking weren't unusual for Harlan. From the look on his face, you could tell this was something he had been worried about for a while. Since I was the Jack Springs High School girl's basketball coach, it was only logical that he ask me. The "girl" was his daughter, Tresha. Still, it seemed a little odd considering the circumstances. But I knew Harlan wouldn't budge until the question was answered, which didn't keep me from scratching my head for a while, giving him a little pay back. He started to squirm.

"Well, Harlan, she needs to keep her elbow in when she shoots. That's the physical part of it. But for the most part it's mental. She freezes up when there's nobody trying to jam the ball down her throat."

I knew what he was waiting to hear. "Tell her we can go up to the gym sometime this week and work on it."

"That'd be fine, Aaron. It surely would. You know how bad we need to get her a scholarship if she's goin' to college." The marshal's job barely paid enough to keep her in high school, which is to say not very damn much.

"Anyway, Billy Estill got to the feed store about 5:00 a.m., just as it was getting light. He saw something lying on the Miner porch and thought ol' Joshua had passed out drunk. When he went over to check, he saw it was a woman. He called us. I was already on my way in so I got there first. It was Stephanie Goldman. Somebody shot her."

"That's it? I waited through six donuts to find that out? Hell, Harlan. You could have told me that on the walk over here, three times."

He shrugged. "That's what we know so far. But what I'm thinkin' is a mite strange is that she was killed someplace else and dropped on the steps to your office. I'd say that makes things kind a curious, wouldn't you? Besides, I don't like to eat alone."

"What do you mean curious?" I asked

"If the killer had to move the body, why didn't he drop it by the road somewhere or up in the woods?" Harlan said. "Why take a chance on being seen dropping it in the middle of the town?"

It was a good point.

Stephanie lived by herself in a little cabin a few miles west of town that she built after moving from New York in the late sixties "to get back to the land," as she liked to say. She was a tough old broad who wasn't very happy with the immigration of yuppies to her mountain town. But when she found out about the plan to mine a half-billion dollars worth of gold in the high valley above her cabin, she had gone ballistic. On more than one occasion, she had threatened the mine's supporters.

Nobody believed Stephanie's threat involved filing a lawsuit. She was talking about kicking ass. But why kill her? She wasn't going to stop the mine. Hell, my editorials weren't going to stop the mine either. Greed was powerful motivation. Projects with that much money to be made assume a life of their own, beyond reason or sanity. Even so, killing Stephanie to stop the mine didn't make any sense at all.

The screen door to the donut shop slammed, and Abigail stood over the table, glaring. Her body language spelled t-r-o-u-b-l-e. Her face was flushed under the curly blonde hair that was always swept tightly up into a topknot—giving her a perpetual sneer. She had a camera slung across her body like a Nazi sidearm. With her khaki shorts, her "save-the-wolf" T-shirt and Banana Republic safari jacket, she looked like Barbie-gone-bad, Wicked Wanda on safari. She did indeed look like she wished she had a whip in her hand.

"Harlan, they won't let me into the goddamn office," she said, hands on her hips, the toe of her expensive hiking boot tapping like a machine gun. "I got a paper to get out. This is the biggest fucking story this burg has ever seen. And I can't get in my office."

"Aaron, talk him into being sensible," she ordered. "We need to get to work."

Harlan patted his lips with a napkin one more time for good measure and looked up. "Abigail, when the crime lab boys get done, we'll move the body and you can get in."

Her nostrils flared slightly as she caught the evil spoor of sexism.

"Harlan, the goddamn crime lab 'boys' are here, and two of them are women," she said, tightly.

That threw him a bit because his wife and daughter had strong feminist leanings. He went along with them, but his acquiescence didn't extend to accepting a woman cussing like a diesel mechanic. I knew what was coming.

"Well, you know what I meant. If they're here, we should be able to get you in pretty quick. Anyway there's no need to be profane, young lady."

The 'young lady' rankled the hell out of her, I knew, but for once she kept her mouth shut. She must have wanted to get in real bad. I wasn't watching just a clash of wills but a clash of cultures. Harlan represented the old and Abigail the new.

Jack Springs had always been home base to a population of ne'er-do-wells, miners, ranchers, loggers, students, hippies, drifters, athletes and tourists; a veritable slumgullion stew of humanity. But all had existed on a relatively level economic playing field—just a cut above poverty. In the last few years, Jack Springs and all the mountain towns had been invaded by immigrants from the East and West Coasts who wanted to buy a little chunk of Shangri-la before it was all gone.

They brought their money with them and raised property values and taxes. But their money also helped rescue an ailing town. Some of the old-timers now had visions of their children staying around home.

The newcomers did not want their quaint little mountain town to change, even though they were changing it simply by moving here. Some of the old-timers thought it had changed too much already. And others were ready to ride the boom-and-bust tiger wherever it would take them as long as it paid well.

So far, all the groups had gotten along pretty well. The tolerance that had existed since the town's outlaw days had survived even the onslaught of yuppies. But the mine threatened to change all that. And now Stephanie had been murdered.

Harlan stood, brushed all the crumbs into his hand and emptied them into the trash basket. He rinsed the cups and hung them on hooks behind the counter. And he swished the balled up napkins into the trash can. "Let's go."

As we crossed the highway, Harlan dug the wad of chew out and flung it into the road where it rolled a few times before coming apart. Abigail saw him do it and looked like she was going to be ill. Again, she kept her mouth shut.

"Harlan, how do you keep from swallowing that stuff while you're eating?" I asked.

"It's an art, boy," he said, smiling wickedly. "It's an art."

CHAPTER 3

The crowd was still hanging around in nervous anticipation of the body being removed. Harlan scanned the scene. "Now Abigail, you and Aaron stay out here until I talk to these boy…uh…these folks," he said. "We'll get you in as quick as possible." He left to join a group of officers who were talking inside the tape. TV cameras formed a semicircle facing the body on our porch. Vans and even motorhomes were parked in the street. News people were preening and posturing in front of the cameras. The mini-cams' dish antennas were fully extended, pointing at some spot in the heavens. Heavy cables crisscrossed the street.

"When we get in, call Al Bartholomew and somebody at Canaus Minerals for comment," Abigail said, her irritation gone in anticipation of knocking out a big story. Bartholomew was the local mouthpiece for a group that agitated for more jobs from logging, ranching and mining—especially mining. He'd almost come to blows with Stephanie Goldman more than once. Nobody, including Bartholomew, was sure how that would have come out. People told jokes about the threat behind his back and even teased him a little. He acted like it wasn't a big deal, but I thought it was. But was it enough to make him kill her? It didn't seem likely.

Canaus Minerals—a Canadian mining company owned by furtive New York deal maker Robert Gottlieb—held a patent on the gold. Everybody knew the company was helping to finance Bartholomew's group, the Western Jobs Coalition. But what the hell? Jobs were jobs, and paychecks came out weekly. Never mind that a reservoir holding a few million gallons of toxic soup would be perched above the town for a thousand years.

Abigail was fired up, running on adrenaline. Of course I would call Al Bartholomew. Still, it pissed me off when she treated me like a rookie.

"Gee whiz, boss, why didn't I think of that?" I wondered aloud. "You want me to interview the man-on-the-street, too. Grab a few tourists for good measure and ask 'em what they think about the murder?"

"Just this once, Aaron, don't give me any of your shit," Abigail said. "Just do it."

It was time to slow her down a little. "Harlan thinks that whoever dropped Stephanie's body on our front step was sending us some kind of a warning, although he won't come out and say it," I told her. As she turned, it was clear the thought had occurred to her too.

"Screw 'em. I won't be intimidated by any goddamn rednecks," she said, not quite convincingly. That was pretty cavalier of her since it was most likely my ass that would end up in the crosshairs, but I kept my mouth shut. Instead, I scanned the faces of the crowd pressed up against the tape, people who wanted to see a tragedy from a distance.

A few stood farther back, not so sure they wanted to see, or maybe already knowing what it was going to be like. I recognized three or four of them, including Joshua, a Vietnam vet who got caught in an Agent Orange drop during that war that killed his sense of smell and his body's ability to regulate his temperature. Consequently, he wore a parka, even in the warmest weather and was blissfully unaware of his sometimes ripe body odor.

The medical examiner pulled the plastic off of Stephanie's body and the crowd gasped. What had been her lined, scowling face was now an unrecognizable mask of torn flesh, splintered bone and dried blood. A few vomited. Someone started crying. Even I looked away.

A close look at violent death is like that—a million miles from the daily images you can switch on and off with the flick of a wrist or the tap of a finger.

Both of Harlan's deputies were standing just inside the tape, keeping an eye on the crowd. Toby Echoheart, a Jicarilla Apache, looked like a young Michael Ansara, who played Cochise in the 50's television series. He had long black hair and was trim like a Marine drill instructor, with narrow waist and broad shoulders.

Toby often came off as a joker. When I wrote about him being hired as a deputy, I asked him whether I should refer to him as a Native American or an Indian.

"I'm an Indian, man. You know, just like them redskins that took all those white men's scalps back in the olden days," he said, grinning.

But something told me there was another a side of him that few had seen. Call it cop instinct.

Ray Hesperus, a young black man, was a thinner, shyer version of Toby. But he had survived ten years as a beat cop on the mean streets of Baltimore. He sported a shaved head and wire rim glasses. He was serious and intense, which had earned him the moniker 'perfessor' from the locals he got along with. People he didn't know well just called him "Sir." Both were good, conscientious cops, single and shared a small house in town.

Needless to say, they were popular with the ladies. We worked out together at the Peaks to Pecs health club, where I hoped some of the female attention would come my way. But it was hard to compete with these guys in the weight room.

Everyone wondered how Harlan had convinced them to work in Jack Springs.

"I needed a job," Hesperus said.

"Me too," replied Toby Echoheart. "Besides, Marshal Silbaugh said I wouldn't have to cut my hair."

Like a comedy team, Ray Hesperus chimed in with, "He told me I wouldn't have to grow mine."

There seemed to be something incomplete about their explanations; in Toby's case because he had graduated at the top of his police academy class in New Mexico and could have gotten a cop job just about anywhere he wanted. For Ray, who had been twice decorated for bravery in action, it was assumed he just wanted off the streets. The truth was both were well-liked in town and people were glad to have them here, even if it didn't make a lot of sense.

Despite what was going on in front of us, the nightmare was still fucking with my mind, so I explained what happened to Toby.

"I'd just hooked this big brown, and there he was watching me. He had this little head and skinny neck and he looked half-dead from starvation. And his coat was dark brown, nothing like the pictures I've seen of mountain lions."

Toby didn't seem particularly interested in the story, so I told him about the nightmare. At that, he dropped the loopy grin and looked at me with an indecipherable expression.

"What do you think it means?" I asked.

He recovered his smile. "I think it means you need to stop nibbling on those little red mushrooms that grow along the trail up behind your homestead." And he laughed again.

As I turned back to the action, crime scene techs were hovering around Stephanie's body, shooting photographs. Abigail, too, was shooting pictures, throwing sharp elbows to part the crowd to get a better angle on the action.

I wondered if anybody else noticed that Stephanie's body lay beneath the newspaper's sign: "The Mountain Miner. Searching for nuggets of truth." As we waited, a wall of dark clouds started to slide off the peaks and into the valley above town like a slow-motion avalanche. The lightning and thunder made it seem as if a terrible battle were underway in that barren landscape.

CHAPTER 4

We got in the office about 10:30 and, wanting to get the nasty stuff out of the way and Abigail off my back, I called Al Bartholomew. He owned the mine where Harlan had worked before he became the town marshal. Batholomew's mine had never been more than marginally profitable and when the EPA caught him releasing mine waste into Jack Creek, he shut it down rather than comply with an order to clean it up. The feds were trying to fine him $250,000, but the case had been in court for two years with no end in sight. Meanwhile, he had run for the town council and had lost—but not by much.

When the Western Jobs Coalition organizers came to town, Al Bartholomew was the perfect candidate to organize a local chapter. He had a big grudge against the government, blaming it for his lack of success at the mining business. Rumor had it a pretty good chunk of money came along with the job, but I thought he was just kissing ass, trying to get an important job if the mine opened. Not too many people cared for him personally, but his continual ranting and raving against the government had struck a nerve with folks who were frustrated with the way the world was going and needed somebody to blame.

Bartholomew picked up the phone on the fifth ring.

"Al, this is Aaron Hemingway, at the Miner," I said.

"I think by now I know who the hell you are, Hemingway. Whadda ya want?"

"A comment about Stephanie Goldman's murder," I said.

He paused. "So what?"

"So, do you have any comment?" I said, dispensing with the pleasantries. Again, he hesitated. When he did answer, he didn't pull any punches.

"She was a mean bitch. She was an outsider and she stepped on a lot of toes in this community. I'm not surprised somebody shot her."

Bartholomew had opened the door and I was going to push him through it.

"So, Al, let me see if I got this straight. If somebody's an outsider and they step on too many toes, it's okay to blow their head off? She stepped on your toes more than anybody's. She threatened to kick your ass and there was even-money around town that she could do it."

It was a low blow, but I was on a roll and couldn't stop my mouth. "So maybe you got tired of her hassles and shot her yourself. It wouldn't be the first time something like that happened in this wacky little burg of ours."

"Hemingway, you sonofabitch, are you accusing me of murder? If you are, I'll have a libel suit filed so fast, you won't know what hit you."

"First off, Al, you can't file a libel lawsuit until something is published. But I just asked you a question. So don't call your lawyer yet. Wait till you answer and see what we print."

"No, mister big shot fucking reporter, I didn't kill her. I'm sorry she's dead. But I'm not surprised. You can print that."

"Then how about this, Al? Do you think one of your so-called followers killed her? You accuse people like Stephanie of trying to destroy a way of life. That's pretty inflammatory language. Some of your people might not understand that that's just overblown bullshit trying to scare the hell out of the politicians and grab some headlines. Some of those guys aren't too smart, Al. Maybe they took your bullshit seriously."

Bartholomew's silence suggested I might have thrown him a curve. To be honest, I hadn't even thought of it until he got me going.

Something about his pause bothered me. But he never gave me the time
to figure it out.

"Fuck you, Hemingway! Where do you get off asking questions like
that?"

"You're just not used to dealing with a reporter you can't sweet talk,"
I said. "Tough shit, Al."

"Then go fuck yourself. That's off the record. All of this conversation is."

"Sorry, Al. It doesn't work that way. The rules get set before any conversation. Otherwise, it's all on the record."

"Fuck you!" he yelled as he slammed the phone down. I held it away
from my ear and blew on it to cool it off.

Abigail stepped out of her office. I knew she had heard my side of the
conversation because I'd almost been yelling. And I reckoned there was
no way in hell she was going to let most of that get in the story. Not in a
small-town newspaper. Bartholomew had too many friends in the business community.

"Was that what you had in mind?"

For once, she wasn't scowling. "That was pretty goddamn good,
Aaron. Of course you realize—"

"Yeah, yeah, I know."

"I've just talked to the printers. We're going to put out a special edi-
tion tomorrow," she said. "When Terri gets in, I'll have her call
Stephanie's friends and some of the other people who oppose the mine.
You stick with the cops. Oh yeah, and don't forget to call Canaus
Minerals. I doubt their response will be as colorful as Al
Bartholomew's."

Abigail glided back into her office and fired up the espresso maker.
She was going to run with the story. There were moments when I felt
like I might get over my dislike for her. They were few and far between
and never lasted long. But she really was a news hound—albeit a
frustrated one. The special edition would cost a couple of thousand
right out of the budget. There wouldn't be any advertisements in it. Of

course, she never missed a chance to rub the town's nose in any dog shit we dug up.

The battle lines were drawn right after Abigail took over the paper. When the town council realized she intended to publish a real newspaper, not just an ad sheet full of fluff, they called the publisher and told him they didn't think her "style" was right for Jack Springs.

He told them he'd keep an eye on things, and he did; he kept an eye on the bottom line. As Abigail turned the Mountain Miner into a real newspaper, the profits surprisingly went up. But she never forgave the town fathers for what they tried to do.

I looked up the number for Canaus Minerals, called and asked for their PR department. Christine McDermott, their number-one flack, took the call.

"Hello, Aaron. How can I help you?" As if she didn't know.

"I'm sure you've heard that Stephanie Goldman was murdered last night. Would your boss like to comment? She wasn't a big fan of your gold mine down here, if you recall."

Christine was ready, as I knew she would be. "Yes, we heard about the unfortunate incident. First, we dispute any suggestion that her murder had anything to do with her opposition to the mine. And any allegation like that in the newspaper would be actionable. However, having said that, let me say this and you can quote me: We regret that an effective voice in the debate about the mine has been silenced. After all, it's the debate that allows us to proceed with everyone's best interest at heart."

At first I thought a breeze had just blown a whiff of eau-de-feedlot in the window. But the nearest one was seventy miles away and downwind. Then I checked my boots. Nope, they were clean. Had to be Chrissy baby.

No matter who killed Stephanie, Gottlieb and his crew were tickled to death she was gone, out of the "debate" as Christine called it. Stephanie had been a real thorn in their collective ass. By now, I had almost got control of my mouth.

"Thanks for the comment, Christine. Once again, I am overwhelmed by the corporate conscience and your eloquence in expressing it. By the way, I got some interesting court records here from Canada. I'll be calling you in a few days for comments."

"Records? What records?" she asked, her voice rising. I hung up just as she was starting to say something else about "actionable."

Multiple lawsuit threats in one morning—was it two or three? Either way, it was a record. It was going to be a hell of a story. I left messages for the coroner's office, as well as Detective Earl McCormick of the Sheriff's Department, who would be in charge of the investigation, and reached Harlan on the second ring.

"Got anything for me?" I asked.

"Let's have lunch. How about Annie's at one? I've got a hankering for some of those baby spud hash browns."

"Sounds good."

The message light on my phone had been flashing all morning and I punched in the access code. It was a call from my daughter—the second in a week. "Dad, it's Cassie. Just trying to get a hold of you."

A chasm opened and threatened to swallow my heart at the sound of her voice. But I forced it closed, once again, and tried to call. An answering machine asked me to leave a message, but I didn't.

As the message ended, Terri Smith walked in. She looked like she had been crying.

"I heard about Stephanie on the radio on my way up the canyon," she said, shaking her head. "I just can't believe it. We had a long talk last week." She sat down at her desk and put her head in her hands, running her fingers through her thick red hair. She turned away from me.

Her reaction to the news reminded me that Stephanie's death was more than just a story, an easy trap to fall into in this business. Stephanie Goldman was a vital presence in the community, although not always a pleasant one.

She was one of the first wave of '60s immigrants to hit the Rocky Mountains, people who for the most part were determined to blend in, not remake the community the way they thought it should be like the more-recent arrivals. But Steph took it a step further; she would out-native the natives. She built her own house, lived without electricity or a phone. She hunted deer and elk to stock the larder. When the snow was deep, she would snowshoe in to her cabin rather than drive a snowmobile.

As a result, the community made her one of its own, the same as if her family had lived here for several generations. That is, until the Dark Angel Mine plan came to light.

Terri had woven her fingers through her loose mane of red curls, keeping it out of her face. Today it was down, but she often wore it pulled back. When she did, wisps of curls escaped, framing her face and highlighting her delicate, long neck.

We had been romantically involved for a time and it hadn't gone well, but lately she'd been loosening up a little, kidding around and throwing some of my innuendoes back at me.

There was no kidding around today. "Cassie left another message," I told her, trying to get her mind off of Stephanie's murder.

She raised her head and looked at me with those big emerald-green eyes. "Is something wrong?"

"It didn't sound like it. It was just another message asking me to call her. I tried but she wasn't there."

"Isn't there any other way to get a hold of her?" she asked.

"I'll just keep trying."

"Yeah, that's probably a good idea," Terri said, in a way that told me I had failed to make the grade, again. She got up and went into Abigail's office.

I looked out the window and saw Joshua standing in the same spot he'd stood while Stephanie's body was being removed. The old hermit survived in the mountains for the last twenty years by catching and selling fish to supplement his veteran's disability check. On his good days, he could carry on an intelligent conversation and even had a sense of humor. On his bad days, he ranted and raved and scared the bejesus out of the tourists.

The merchants wanted him hauled off and locked up in a psych ward someplace. When it got bad, Harlan would buy him some food and take him to the mountains to mellow out.

Today, Joshua was still staring at the Miner porch, as if some drama was being played with actors only he could see.

CHAPTER 5

Despite the line at Annie's, Harlan was allowed to go inside and get a table. It was one of the few perks he accepted. After all, when town business was pressing, the marshal couldn't be allowed to waste time standing in line.

I suspect it was also because Harlan was such a good customer. He was passionate about the new red potatoes, baked, lightly fried and then doused with herbs. Even I, at 6-1 and two hundred pounds, with a full head of hair and beard, couldn't command a presence like Harlan. I liked to think it was the big pistol he carried.

Whatever the case, I followed in his wake. Harlan made each trip into Annie's seem like official business, and in a way it was.

We took a table inside the front of the windows and Annie herself waited on us. Harlan put his PAC set on the table and turned the sound down.

"I'll take a cheese, bacon and ham omelet," Harlan said, and after a thoughtful pause, "...double meat and a double order of spuds."

Annie turned to me. "I'll have the spinach salad."

"Heaven's sakes, Aaron, you eat like one of them Boulder crystal gazers," he said. To Harlan, Boulder was another planet. For the most part we agreed, but I appreciated Boulder because it was so weird it made Jack Springs seem almost like a normal, All-American place.

Annie smiled and walked away. She'd heard this before.

"Harlan, don't harass me about what I eat or I'll write an article about what you had for lunch today. The headline would be something like 'Jack Springs' Marshal consumes a lethal dose of cholesterol and lives.' I'm sure your wife would be interested."

He gave me a hard look, but he knew he was had. Hattie had been trying to get him to eat better since his last checkup revealed his cholesterol level was 320.

"Okay already," he said, shaking off the unpleasant prospect of Hattie's scolding. "Anyway, I went up to Stephanie's cabin with Earl and his boys. It was pretty bad. There was blood and flesh and bone on the kitchen floor."

He paused, shaking his head. "That place was a mess—I mean besides the murder. How the hell anybody could live like that is beyond me. The sink was so full of dirty dishes, you couldn't a pissed in it. There were cat boxes plumb full of shit. But no cats."

I gulped. "Jesus, Harlan, you could be a little less graphic considering we're getting ready to have lunch. Besides, where do you come up with disgusting sayings like, 'The sink was so full of dirty dishes, you couldn't a pissed in it?'"

He shrugged. "My family was from Oklahoma," he said. "That's just the way Okies talk. Anyway, as I was sayin', it looks like the killer dug the bullet out of the floor with a knife or some kind of tool. And her cabin was tore up pretty bad, like they were looking for something."

I thought about that. "What the hell could Stephanie have had that got her killed?"

He shrugged and said. "We don't have a clue."

"Harlan, you said 'they'. Was there any indication it was more than one person?"

"Naw, that's just the way I talk, Aaron. The footprints indicate it was one person, size-ten shoes. And they got some tire tracks. None of it will help us find the killer unless something else points the way."

Harlan was right. You can't go around checking people's shoes or tires unless you know where to look.

"We're questioning her friends and people around town. So far it seems like the last time anybody saw her was when she bought some food at the co-op yesterday afternoon."

There were some advantages to investigating crime in a small town. Everybody knew everybody else and their business too, often as not. So far, it didn't seem to be helping in this case. The rule of thumb is that any murder not solved in the first 48 hours is likely to remain unsolved for quite a while. The next statistical spike for murder arrests comes about two years later, when criminals who are locked up for some other crime start shooting off their mouths to other inmates.

"One thing, though," Harlan said. "Stephanie might have had a regular visitor lately. Maybe it was a boyfriend. You know how her cabin is situated—you can see it from the road, but barely. Besides her old Volkswagen bus, a few people say they think they saw a newer pickup with a camper parked up there a few times.

"Nobody recognized it, at least nobody we've talked to so far. It was a light-colored four-wheel drive with a dark camper shell. That's all we know. Ol' Steph played her cards pretty close to her ample bosom."

"A boyfriend, huh? That seems worth looking into."

"Oh, we'll look into it all right. But it hasn't been going on for long. Still, in a town this size, you'd think somebody would know something."

"You would," I agreed.

Harlan went to work on his omelet, potatoes and coffee and said no more. In light of our agreement, nothing he told me of this could be used in the story, but it was good to know. It made it easier to question other law enforcement agencies. That's the thing about cops. They'd rarely volunteer any information, but if I had a question, sometimes they'd give me an answer.

My contact with the Boulder County Sheriff's Department had not been extensive. But I had a history with Lt. Earl McCormick, who had recently been promoted to head the Detective Division. It wasn't something we talked about, but it went back to the days of the North Metro Drug Task Force. One of those things when cops look out for each other after a tough situation goes bad.

Generally, though, the cops seemed to treat me better than some reporters. The story of how I was drummed out of the Denver Police Department, while it never made the papers, had certainly made the rounds of the cop shops in the area. To most cops, it was probably an honorable separation since I got fired for shooting up a lawyer's office—while he was in it.

Yessiree, that shyster had done a right passable version of the boot-scootin' boogie.

Cops hate lawyers almost as much as they hate criminals and in some cases even more. No doubt the story had even grown in the re-telling.

Lt. Earl McCormick was not one of those who talked about it. In fact, Earl was one of the most tight-lipped son of a bitches I'd ever met. And under the circumstances, I wasn't going to complain because he accepted my phone calls, even if he couldn't give me the information I wanted.

Back at the Miner, Abigail was engaged in a high-volume telephone argument with someone and Terri was busy tapping her computer keyboard. She looked up and almost gave me a smile. She had apparently stored away her disappointment at the way I handled my daughter's phone calls with my other shortcomings too numerous to dwell upon.

"Aaron, would you look at this before I turn it in?" she asked. We often edited each other's copy before we gave it to Abigail. It saved a lot of screaming at deadline.

"Sure. Let me make a couple of calls first."

John Warshawski, the county coroner, told me only what we already suspected. Stephanie had been shot between 8 p.m. and midnight, execution-style, with a medium-caliber gun, probably a 9 mm. She had been struck in the side of the head and knocked unconscious before she was killed. There were splinters in her face from the blowback of the bullet entering the wood. Blood alcohol was negative and drug tests were pending, but no one expected anything there. It was well known Steph hated drunks and druggies. And she hadn't had sex recently or been raped.

At least she never knew what happened unless, before she was hit, she realized she had been betrayed by someone she had trusted, maybe even loved. And she hadn't trusted many people. But it seemed she had trusted someone enough to turn her back to them. There weren't many who would take her on face to face.

Earl McCormick told me about searching the house and finding evidence she was killed there. And that was all. The rest of what Harlan had told me would obviously be used as "hold-backs" or as Earl called them, "Aces-in-the-hole." That information would be used to determine the veracity of any tips or prospective witnesses. He never mentioned anything about a boyfriend. There were no suspects and the investigation was continuing. He hadn't interviewed Al Bartholomew yet but was planning to. The scene around the Miner office held no apparent clues. And the reference to Bartholomew was, of course, off the record, he added.

When I had finished my notes, Terri stopped typing and surrendered her computer to me. In the story, she quoted a neighbor as saying Stephanie might have had a frequent visitor.

"That information about the visitor is dynamite, " I told her. "Harlan told me, but it was off the record. Put that in the lead paragraph. You'll have to call Harlan and Earl for comment. They'll decline, but we've got to get it in there. Good job." Terri beamed at the praise.

Abigail came out of her office and appeared shaken by whatever had just happened.

"That was our esteemed publisher Arnold Escamilla. He agreed to let me put out the special edition, but I have to pay for any lost revenues out of my own pocket if we piss too many people off," she said. The flush in her cheeks was slowly fading.

"So the special is out?" Terri asked.

"Hell, no! Get to work. I want to see something by five o'clock."

We turned the copy in at 5:00 p.m. on the dot. Abigail took the disks to her computer and read them. We could hear her make a few changes but she asked no questions. "Good enough," she yelled through the door, grudgingly it sounded to me.

Terri was gathering her things and getting ready to leave when she turned toward me. She looked sad again, now that the distraction of knocking out a story had passed.

"You know, last week when I talked to Stephanie, she seemed kind of, I don't know, deflated. She's always been such a ball of fire. It was strange. And when I walked in, she covered something up on her table so I couldn't see it. She was definitely not acting like her usual self."

"What were you talking to her about?" I asked, my curiosity piqued.

"Background for a story; why she came to Colorado, what her life was like before she came. Sort of a profile of an activist. You know, the typical crap I write. She wasn't very interested, though. But she tried to be nice about it."

That didn't surprise me. Steph had always been a private person. But something occurred to me.

"Did you talk to anyone else about the story?"

"Yeah, couple of people whose opinions I wanted to get in the story."

"Who did you talk to?"

"A couple of members of her group," she said, "and Al Bartholomew, you know, to get balance in the story."

It alarmed me that Bartholomew knew Terri had talked to Steph, but I tried to keep that alarm to myself. As far as I was concerned, he was a suspect. Or at the very least, he knew more about Stephanie's murder than he was letting on. The disturbing questions remained, however.

What if something was going on that somebody didn't want Steph talking about? That didn't necessarily mean Terri was in any danger. Still, it was possible someone thought she now had some dangerous information, even if she didn't realize it. What if dropping Steph's body on our porch was a warning to Terri, and not me, as I supposed? My imagination was running away with my good sense. Nothing was said. Nothing was printed. It just didn't add up that Terri was in any danger. Until there was more, it was pointless to add another meaningless detail to the investigation.

And speaking of meaningless details, something Harlan said at lunch popped into my head. "Terri, were Stephanie's cats around when you were there?"

"Yeah, they were all over the place. Why?"

"Just wondering. Harlan said there weren't any cats there when they did the crime scene." It seemed like something Earl and Harlan should have picked up on. Terri scrunched her forehead, and I could see she was considering the problem of the missing cats. But she didn't pursue it.

Still, it was a good day's work. In the old days of a big city newspaper, I would have broken out a bottle of whiskey from the bottom drawer of my desk and we'd have celebrated right there. But it wasn't the old days, and this was a small town newspaper. But the buzz from the day's excitement hadn't worn off. Maybe Terri would have a drink with me before she went home. It was worth a try.

"Do you want to go out for a beer?"

"Sorry, Aaron. I have to pick the kids up before 6:30 or get penalized on my day care fees. If we can find a place to live in Jack Springs, maybe I can do that sometime."

Well, that was a rain check of sorts, wasn't it? But I still felt like a runner who had won a big race only to learn the awards ceremony had been canceled. Instead, I stayed around and helped put the paper together. Abigail's photo of the coroner's investigators examining the body took up about one fourth of the front page. A cop was mercifully blocking the view of Stephanie's face, but it still captured the grim reality of what had happened. My story about the murder itself was the lead. And Abigail had left in more of Bartholomew's quotes than she might have. We played down the significance of Stephanie's body being left on our porch. And no one speculated, on the record, that it meant anything.

Terri's story, leading with the mysterious visitor, took up the rest of the page. Harlan and Earl's "no comments" about the mystery man were featured highly in the story. There were references to Stephanie's opposition to the mine and many people said they would carry on with renewed vigor.

Work done, I went home and celebrated with an old friend—Evan Williams. He was from Kentucky and always willing to party if you had the price.

CHAPTER 6

That morning I stayed in bed and ran over what had happened the past two days: Stephanie's murder, the phone call from Cassie, the nightmare, the mountain lion itself.

The fact that Steph's body had been moved suggested a certain degree of planning. But why drop the body on our porch? The Mountain Miner and my articles and editorials in particular had been hard on the proposed mine. Maybe somebody had gotten wind of our intention to write about Gottlieb's schemes in Canada, and they were trying to scare us off the story. But who could have known? And wouldn't there have been a warning note or a phone call or something?

Or was it something unrelated to the mine? Maybe the killer placed her body on the newspaper's porch to deflect suspicion. Anyone who would do such a thing had to be smart enough to know it could backfire.

But what if, as I had suggested to Al Bartholomew, it was somebody who wasn't very smart? In some ways, that made the most sense.

If there were anything to that theory, tonight might be a good chance to find out since Al Bartholomew had scheduled a Western Jobs Coalition meeting on the mine. Someone stupid enough to kill Stephanie would be unlikely to brag about it. But little things give big things away. As much as I disliked covering those meetings, there was a chance to learn something about Stephanie's murder.

The volatile political situation in Jack Springs as a result of the Dark Angel Mine made it unlikely the investigation would begin with those with the most obvious motive—an approach that would, without a doubt, be called harassment.

That wouldn't stop me from pursuing it, but caution was not a bad idea. I had already jumped the gun on the court documents. Copies of the rulings were supposed to be on the way, but unlike what I told Christine, they had yet to arrive.

A "friend of a friend" in the British Columbia Provincial Court system said Gottlieb had been sued twice, accused of defrauding investors in his gold mines. But the same court had also sealed the records from the press. Because of my big mouth, Gottlieb might have got to the court records in time to be sure they really were sealed. But sometimes it's hard to resist turning the screws on those mealy-mouthed corporate assholes.

Too many thoughts were bombarding my brain so I decided to go for a run. The sun was just cresting the ridge behind my house and it was still cool. Dressing in shorts, a sleeveless sweatshirt that said, "I fish; therefore I am," and running shoes, I took a long drink of water and went outside. Roscoe, my Great Dane-Chow mongrel, had developed an uncanny ability to read my mind and was waiting at the foot of the steps to join me.

"Run, boy?" I asked.

"Whuff," he answered, rumbling like thunder.

We took off down the driveway on a six-mile loop to Gross Reservoir and back. About half way through our run, I was soaked with sweat and Roscoe was slobbering like a mad dog.

It was tough but we completed the loop. As I staggered up the trail to my cabin, an artist friend's description of it came to me—a plywood space ship crashed on the side of the hill. It did look like that, if you squinted a bit. But it was home and that made it beautiful to me.

The sun was warm and drawing resin from the ponderosa pine needles. I got to the cabin rejuvenated, ready for a new day. Roscoe slurped in his water bowl, drinking half of it and splashing the rest on the floor. Then he disappeared outside looking for a shady spot to spend a long day guarding the homestead.

After a quick washing from the wooden barrel of tepid rainwater on the deck, I put on my work uniform; a denim shirt, Wrangler jeans, roughout cowboy boots. In front of the tiny mirror over the sink, I snipped a small forest of errant gray hairs from my bushy beard and the ends of my hair, which fell almost to my collar. Neither made me look any more respectable; I needed a professional hair cut and beard trim.

Roscoe was nowhere to be seen when I tramped back down the trail to my '78 Subaru wagon.

The sun was already high as I drove down Magnolia Road.

When I got to the Miner office just before noon, it was open but empty of working bodies. There was, however, a fat brown envelope postmarked Vancouver, B.C. with no return address on my desk. I breathed a sigh of relief and opened it.

From a quick glance, it looked like there was not only the record of decision, with a finding of facts and claims for monetary damages but also financial statements from Gottlieb and his corporation. One section in particular caught my attention and I got a tingle of excitement reading it. One of the mines went bankrupt and when the operators pulled out a tailings pond had overflowed. As a result, the cyanide and acidic mine runoff had killed about forty miles of river in the surrounding wilderness. It was for the most part the same kind of operation Gottlieb had planned for the Dark Angel Mine.

Somebody took a big risk to send me these documents. The contact in the B.C. court system was reportedly an animal-rights activist friend of Stephanie's. Animal lovers are a sneaky bunch, because you can never tell who they are. They make perfect spies.

Before doing anything else, I had to verify the documents were authentic. It wasn't out of the question that this was a set-up, but if it was, I wasn't going to fall for it. How to verify the documents was another matter. Putting it off for now made sense.

I called Harlan instead. "We on for lunch?"

"Huh? Oh, Aaron. No, not today. I'm going to go home. Seems somebody snitched me out yesterday. You know, I've lived in small towns all my life. But sometimes it gets damned uncomfortable."

"Especially when you've got a wife like Hattie," I said.

"All right, all right, what do you want? By the way, lecturing me isn't the best way to get it."

"Anything new on Stephanie's murder?" I asked.

"Nothing you don't already have. McCormick has started questioning some of Stephanie's friends. Members of the anti-mine group, Al and his cronies and everyone who might have been around at that time of the night are next."

Terri came in, nodded, and went to her desk. She had on a cream-colored, low-cut T-shirt, tight designer jeans and huarache sandals. Her hair was pulled back in a ponytail, gathered with a green velvet hair tie. Harlan was still talking, but I missed some of it while thinking Terri looked pretty good today.

"Harlan, listen, thanks a lot. Are you going to be at the moron militia meeting tonight?"

"Al's little shindig? I wouldn't miss it for all the *Skoal* in Copenhagen."

"OK, I'll see you there." I hung up. "Terri, you look great." The silver-tongued devil strikes again.

She smiled as if to say "Nice try" and continued to look through her notes.

"Oh, by the way, the court file on Gottlieb got here."

"I know. I picked up the mail." After a pause, she asked, "Have you called your daughter?"

Damn, so that was it.

"Not yet," I said and shrugged. "I will."

The message from Cassie didn't sound like an emergency but we hadn't talked in two years so something was up.

Up until that time, I had called her every Thanksgiving, Christmas and birthday. Then two years ago I missed the call at Christmas because I was drunk on my ass. The picture in my mind of Cassie waiting there by the phone has haunted me since.

On my desk, a photograph showed her in a YMCA soccer T-shirt, Umbro shorts and soccer shoes, holding a black-and-white ball on her knee. Her hair was cut short, like an athlete's. No nonsense bangs. It might have been my imagination, but there seemed to be a hint of pain in her eyes. She was 11 years old when the picture was taken. How much pain would be in those eyes today?

As the weight of this tried to settle on me, I shrugged it off, called and got the message machine again. My hand was shaking. Did I have the guts to call her mother at work? The worst that could happen would be Madeline's trying to dump two years worth of guilt on me. At least it would be a one-shot deal.

It was becoming clear, however, there would be no slack in Terri's attitude until I talked to my daughter. It was still lunch time in Kansas City, but I suspected Madeline would be eating in, trying to impress the partners with her dedication, so I called there. The utter silence at Terri's desk told me she was listening.

"Bronfman, Bluitt and Garcia," came the clipped but somehow still nasal greeting.

"I'd like to speak to Madeline Hemingway," I said. Madeline had kept her married name not out of any sentimentality, but her maiden name was Polish and had so many consonants that it was unpronounceable. An up-and-coming lawyer couldn't afford to have an unpronounceable name any more than she could afford to leave for lunch.

"She's not available. Would you like to leave a message?"

"Do you know if she's going to be back today?"

"She's out of the office for a few days. Would you like to leave a message…sir?" Her voice dripped with scorn born of the conviction that all men are scum.

"Please tell her Aaron called," I said, trying not to sound like the scurvy dog she took me for.

The receptionist uttered a dismissive "humph" as she hung up. Being polite apparently didn't work.

The noise level from Terri's desk picked up. She said, "Well?"

"She's 'out of the office' for a few days, whatever that means. I'll try them at home again later. If there were really something wrong, Madeline would have called," I said, not quite believing it.

Abigail walked in and slammed a copy of the Rocky Mountain News down on my desk. "That son of a bitch misquoted me," she bellowed. "I'll have his ass for that."

We both grabbed the thick tabloid and looked at the banner headline, which read, "Mine activist murdered in Jack Springs" Beneath it, the drop head said, "Newspaper editor worried the killer was sending a message." We scanned the story itself, but it only quoted Abigail as saying she was "concerned, of course," but she didn't believe it had anything to do with the newspaper.

So the headline was wrong, not the story. Nobody hates seeing their name in a news story worse than a journalist, and when it happens, we're just as blind as any reader. But Abigail was not in a listening mode at the moment. We could hear her yelling into the phone at somebody.

I looked again at the stack of documents, and they seemed to be whispering my name from a dark doorway: "Psst, Aaron, come on, have another peek. Good stuff in here." In the news business, documents were often the smoking gun, the hard evidence of wrongdoing. They were the currency of our business. Legal documents were even better.

Because they were going to be scrutinized and challenged, they were for the most part factual. And eventually ruled upon. Legal documents, to a journalist, were like the cops finding fingerprints on the smoking gun.

We already had some newspaper clips reporting problems at his mines, but the coverage stopped abruptly when the cases got to court. The part of the story about the liner failure and subsequent pollution damage hadn't been reported. The fact that Gottlieb got the files sealed suggested there was something he didn't want anyone to know, and walking away from an operation that killed an entire river would fit the bill.

There may have been more. Sometimes the devil is in the financial details. Numbers weren't my strong point, but in legal documents reams of figures were often summarized so I didn't think there would be any particular problem with them. They could, however, present an opportunity to consolidate my recent gains with Terri.

"There's a lot of information here. Would you be interested in going over it, too. Then we could compare notes and write the story together."

"I wouldn't think of it," she said. "That's your story, you should do it. I know how much it means to you."

But a gleam in her eyes told me she was interested. "I'm serious about needing some help. It's going to take a while to get it together. "

"This isn't some kind of ploy to worm your way into my good graces, is it?" she asked, an eyebrow arching slightly.

"What do you mean? I'm not back in your good graces?" I said, feigning innocence.

"Well, you are, for now," she said, still sounding a mite suspicious. "Sure, I'll help you with the story."

Gotcha, I said to myself.

Gottlieb's engineers estimated that $500 million worth of gold could be extracted from the Dark Angel mine before it was played out. At first, they would go into the old shafts and try to get the remainder of the medium-and low-grade ore. Then they would dig up and pulverize most of the valley and extract the remaining trace gold through heap leaching. When it was done, nothing would be alive in that valley. It would be as alien and inhospitable a landscape as Mars.

But about a hundred people or so would be employed for the expected ten years it would take to get all the gold. Those jobs would pay about twenty bucks an hour.

It wasn't hard to see how appealing that would be to the out-of-work miners in town. Few of them were basking in the town's economic resurgence. Bartholomew assured everyone that those jobs would go to Jack Springs' residents first. But there were no guarantees about that, as he well knew.

It was going to be called the Park Angel Mine, named after one of the earliest and largest claims on the mountain. In the headline on one of my editorials, the typesetter had erroneously called it the Dark Angel Mine.

Abigail was furious. She accused me of having a hand in it. I didn't, but I have to admit I loved it, and the name stuck; at first among some of the mine's opponents and finally among almost every one but the mine's staunchest proponents.

In the pages of the Mountain Miner, however, it was still called by its official name—the Park Angel Mine. But to my way of thinking, Dark Angel was the more fitting of the two. It conjured an image of something evil and deadly sitting on the mountain, just waiting to unleash its mayhem upon the town.

CHAPTER 7

Drinking on the job is not, as a rule, a very good idea. But there are exceptions to every rule, and attending a meeting run by Al Bartholomew and his ass-kissing cronies on the town council was one—I needed to brace myself. That some relatively normal people showed up, people who felt control of their lives slipping away, didn't help much to make it tolerable.

Take away the mine-company money and there would be no Western Jobs Coalition.

The big companies don't give a damn for the miners. And they don't give a damn about the communities. All they're interested in is slurping big profits at the public trough. But they've done a slick job of combining the three.

So I slipped into the Jackass Inn for a couple of quick, ice-cold Dos Equis before wandering up the street to the town hall. They did the job, as it turned out a little too well.

The street outside the town hall was jammed with parked cars and trucks. But one in particular stood out. I was pretty sure it belonged to Wiley Agnew, one of three Colorado hillbilly brothers who owned a played-out mine near the timberline in Gilpin County, southwest of Jack Springs.

The truck was a war wagon—a four-wheel drive one-ton Chevy painted in camouflage colors, with big tires and an assault rifle resting in the back window. Its presence lent an ominous tone to the meeting. I hadn't been to all of the group's meetings, but I'd been to several and the Agnews had never been there before.

There were rumors about their involvement with a militia, but they kept to themselves and didn't come to town often so the rumors never meant much to the locals.

The same rumors had their mine turned into a fortified camp with twelve-foot fences topped with concertina wire. Neighbors said they heard automatic weapon fire coming from the place at times.

Other, normal, four-wheel drive trucks were also parked in the lot in front of the town hall. There were toolbox-sided work trucks, neat and clean, colors as solid as their owners, with compressors and jacks and diesel fuel tanks. Many had bumper stickers that said, "If you can't grow it, you have to mine it. Save mining jobs," in red, white and blue and adorned by American flags.

People were standing around in groups waiting to go in, but it looked like a smaller crowd than normal. Joshua was lurking in the street, holding a couple of fishing poles in one land and peering darkly from inside the hood of his parka, his long sandy beard hanging out the front and down his chest.

George Gunther, a long-time town council member who owned the equipment rental company and a lot of property in Jack Springs, stood well away from those waiting for the meeting to start. George could, at some point, make a lot of money from business with the mine, but he was one of its more vocal opponents—the odd-man out on the council whenever a vote came up.

George had recently found a young wife and, in the flush of matrimonial success, word was he planned to run for the Board of County Commissioners. His opposition to the mine was seen as playing for the strong environmental vote in the county.

I walked over. "What's up, George? You going in?"

He gave me a hard look before answering, "No, Aaron, I don't believe so. I like to keep an eye on things, but Stephanie Goldman's murder has left a damn sour taste in my mouth. It's hard to believe her opposition to the mine would get her killed, but I can't for the life of me think of any other reason for it, either. I'd worked with Stephanie some in the past year and she was a damned decent woman. I'm going to keep my distance until this thing gets sorted out."

I nodded. The sun hung low over the Indian Peaks Wilderness. A faint, waning half-moon was suspended high in the still-blue sky. The light was on in Harlan's office and his door was open. At the deli next door, Fat Jack was selling coffee, sandwiches and ice cream to the tourists who were hanging around, wondering what the hell was going on but too embarrassed to show their ignorance by asking.

As I walked up, some in the crowd turned to look and then returned to their whispered conversations. The Agnews—Merle, Wiley and Davey—walked over and stood next to the door.

The oldest and youngest brothers, Merle and Davey, had pinched little pig faces beneath flattop haircuts. Wiley didn't look much like the other two, except for the desert-tan camouflage clothes and the hair. He looked more like a stand-in for the banjo player in Deliverance, though taller and older.

The difference between Wiley and his brothers made me wonder if Momma Agnew hadn't been diddling out behind the ore-crusher. Who or what she had been diddling was another matter altogether.

The crowd seemed tense, which was understandable in light of the murder and the fact that not a small percentage of the citizenry suspected somebody in this crowd might be behind it. Bartholomew, with his severe steel gray hair cut to about an inch in length, splotchy face with a two-day growth of beard, bloodshot eyes and nose with the bluish cast of a heavy drinker, snapped his cigarette hard to the ground sending up a shower of sparks and waved everybody in. Just as I started

join the line, Merle and Wiley stepped into the door and blocked my
way. Davey stood off to the side.

"Hey Clark Kent, this here's a private meeting. No noospaper
reporters allowed," Merle said. He and Davey looked at each other and
chortled. Wiley's mouth was twisted in a grimace as if he had something
fun, like tearing the wings off a butterfly or stepping on a baby bird, on
his mind. But his eyes burned with a simmering hatred. He didn't laugh
at his brother's wisecrack. Wiley and Merle had their hands on their
hips, elbows out, leaving no room to pass. Merle was standing relaxed
with his weight back on his heels. But Wiley was leaning forward, flex-
ing his fingers, ready for action.

Reading body language was one of the first and most important
things you learned as a cop and Wiley's spelled trouble. So I dropped
my hands and left my palms open, ready for him.

"Merle, you just don't get it, do you. This is the town hall. It's a public meeting place. You can't have a private meeting in a public place. It's
against the law."

Of course, that wasn't technically true, especially in a small town
where political favors were the currency of choice. But I wanted to give
Merle something to occupy his limited brain power.

He scrunched his face, considering the information before he said,
"Too fucking bad, Clark Kent. Unless you got a big S under that shirt,
you ain't gettin' in." They snickered again. Wiley looked at him and said,
"Shut up, Merle. You're making a goddamn fool of yourself." Merle's
face darkened and he stuck out his jaw. But he did shut up.

Wiley turned back to me and said, "The point's that Al don't want
you around. So we done took it on ourselves to keep you out." Done
took it on themselves? Was I getting something here? We stood there for
a tense minute.

Some were already inside and others were waiting behind me to get
past. I leaned toward Wiley, "Say, Wiley, did your momma visit the zoo
about nine months before you were born? She must have been fucking

a giraffe because that's the only way you could have turned out so ugly."
Some in the crowd snickered. Wiley's angry eyes darted around and the
snickering stopped.

Then, in a calculated risk, I turned away. Astonished, he said "Hey!"
and he grabbed my shoulder to try and spin me back around.

That was a mistake I was hoping he would make. I pinned his hand
to my left shoulder with my right and took a hard shot at his ribs with
my left elbow. It connected; something snapped in his side. He grunted
and crumpled to the ground.

Merle reached to open his belly pack and I faked with my left. As he
hesitated, I caught him on the bridge of the nose with the heel of my
right hand. A stream of blood spurted onto my denim shirt, and he
brought both hands to his face. I grabbed his shoulders and kneed him
in the balls. As he was bending forward, I kicked him on the inside of his
knee and he collapsed onto Wiley.

Davey, finally spurred to action, managed to shove me to the side. As
I staggered, Toby Echoheart appeared out of the crowd and cracked
Davey behind the knee with his baton. He went down hard. Wiley was
reaching inside his belly pack, his fingers on the black grip of a semiau-
tomatic handgun, when Toby caught him on the elbow with a short
swing of the baton.

Wiley's arm went slack and he yelped in pain. "Goddamn you, you
red nigger. You're going to pay for that," Wiley snarled.

Toby brought the baton up but held back. Harlan gently grabbed his
arm, said, "Tobias," and stood over Wiley.

"Maybe he should have let you pull that gun out and then had to
shoot you, you dumb bastard," Harlan said.

Wiley fell back and groaned. Toby was not grinning. His hands
gripped the baton loosely, pointed toward the ground. It looked like a
Kendo fighting stance.

Harlan surveyed the scene, anger on his face. "What the hell was this all about?" He paused to spit a long, dark stream of tobacco juice near the rubber sandals of a tourist, who yelped and jumped away.

Wiley leaned up on his good elbow and tried to point at me. His arm barely cooperated. "I want that motherfucker arrested. He assaulted us."

Harlan just shook his head. "You're a piece of work, Wiley Agnew. You come into my town, loaded for bear, and you try to interfere with this man…" Harlan nodded toward me, "…doin' his job, something I know he didn't look forward to doin' in this particular circumstance. If I arrest him. I'll have to arrest all of you. We'll figure out the charges later, but you boys come down here looking for trouble, carryin' concealed, are going to get the worst of it. Of that, I guarantee. On the other hand, we can all walk away from this right now. Your choice."

By now, the crowd had formed a solid wall of people in a semi-circle around the entrance to the town hall. A few brave tourists had muscled to the front. One with a Colorado Rockies hat, jersey and red Bermuda shorts covered with Budweiser logos was even videotaping the scene. Harlan saw him and yelled, "Get that goddamn thing out of here or I'll stick it up your butthole—sideways!" The man bulled his way through the crowd holding the camera to his chest like a fullback.

Harlan turned back, "What about it, Wiley? You wanna press charges?"

"No charges," Wiley wheezed between tight-clamped teeth.

"All right, that settles it. Let's break this shindig up," Harlan said loud enough for everyone to hear. Ray had showed up and he and Toby walked into the crowd asking people to leave. As Toby approached with the baton held across his body at thigh level, they parted like the Red Sea for Moses.

"This is outrageous," Bartholomew screamed, stepping up behind Harlan. "This man disrupted our meeting." He jabbed his blunt, liver-spotted finger, nails chewed to the quick, into my chest, looked at my eyes, and pulled it back like he had touched a hot woodstove.

Harlan wheeled to face him. "Al, shut…the…fuck…up."

Bartholomew backed away. The crowd had thinned out but some were still watching. Davey reached down to help Merle. When Harlan had turned away for a moment, I leaned over and whispered to Wiley, "Is it true your mother had to tie a pork chop around your neck to get your dog to play with you?"

Wiley stiffened then smiled malignantly, "You better watch your ass, hippie boy, or you're going to end up like your Jew bitch friend." He said it like he would take great joy in seeing that it happened.

Hippie boy? Nobody had ever called me a hippie before and I went for him again, but Harlan stepped between us.

"That's enough, Aaron." He shoved me back. To Ray and Toby he said, "Get them out of here." Rather than deal with Toby again, the Agnews got up and staggered to their truck.

When the way was clear, I went inside, bloody shirt and all and waited for the meeting to begin. A few people came in and stood around but ended up leaving before anything happened.

Bartholomew was still fuming. As he folded up his papers, he looked up and said, "Hemingway, you're making a big mistake. You're getting in way over your head."

My adrenaline was surging. "Al, are you talking something besides a lawsuit? Something like what happened to Stephanie? Your boy Wiley just said something similar."

"Just watch your ass, that's all." Al was trying to be tough, but the past couple of days had been hard on him, harder than he wanted to let on. I walked away.

Harlan was waiting for me when I came out. He grabbed my arm and steered me to the front of the deli, which was closed. Fat Jack was inside cleaning up, and the tables out front were deserted. The look on Harlan's face told me something was indeed amiss.

"You fucked up, my friend. That Wiley is more dangerous than a cross-eyed sidewinder," Harlan said. "What in hell possessed you to get into a scrap with those boys?"

"Those guys aren't that tough."

"I didn't say tough, goddamnit. I said dangerous. There's a pretty good chance they killed their pappy some years back. It was way before your time, and they was never charged. But there ain't many around here believe it was anything other than murder."

He told me the story.

"Old man Agnew was killed about fifteen years ago when he got pinned by a bulldozer while he was cleaning up some mine property," Harlan said. "He died of shock and blood loss. But think about this; it took him a day and a half to die. The autopsy revealed the old man had destroyed his vocal cords screaming for help. And the boys were right there on the claim the whole time.

"They said they never knew anything about it till they found him dead, that the emergency brake must of come loose and the 'dozer had rolled back and crushed him. The investigation revealed the emergency brake was working properly and some of the detectives thought it might have been released on purpose. But there was no way to prove it, so the old man's death was ruled an accident.

"Davey was still a young-un, about eight when it happened. Merle was in his twenties, and Wiley was 16. About two months earlier, the old man had brought Wiley in to the hospital with head injuries. The doctor thought he had been beaten. But nobody would volunteer any information, so they patched him up and sent him back home." Harlan's face was filmed with perspiration telling me the story. He removed his gray Stetson and mopped his brow with the blue bandanna he kept in his rear pants pocket.

"They've built up quite a reputation in the last few years. But they've mostly stayed out of trouble. Merle and Davey are followers, tagging along on Wiley's shirt tails. I do believe that Wiley is dangerous. But he's also a coward. That just means he's more likely to sneak up on someone than face 'em square. You better watch your backside for a while."

I had been holding my breath for the last few moments and sucked air into my lungs.

"That's the third time I've been told that in the last half hour. It's starting to seem like good advice. By the way, did you hear what Wiley said to me about my 'Jew bitch friend?'"

"I heard," Harlan said.

"Well?"

"It's certainly worth looking into."

George Gunther, who had remained inside the town hall, walked by, slowed and caught Harlan's eye.

"It sure ain't like the old days, is it Harlan?" he said, and left without waiting for an answer.

"What was Gunther talking about?"

"That ol' boy was the town marshal when I was comin' up," Harlan said. "About all he had to worry about then was me and my friends drinkin', drag racin' and fightin' and the like. It's a fact he didn't put up with any nonsense. I still got a couple of dents in my skull to prove it."

Yep, them were the good ol' days, I thought.

In the time-honored journalistic tradition, I repaired to the Jackass Inn for a few more drinks to savor my victory in the skirmish with the Moron Militia. For some reason, most of the old-timers looked edgy when I took a seat at the bar. Then it occurred to me it probably had something to do with all the blood on my shirt.

"What'll it be?" asked Alvie, a biker who had tended bar there it seemed like forever. He wore a tight Harley T-shirt, a sleeveless Levi jacket, greasy jeans and had a full red beard and hair pulled back into a thick braid. His ears sported dangling crescent wrenches and his teeth had enough gaps to look like a military grave yard. A good number of teeth he had left were gold capped.

One of his dark eyes was just off center, giving him the maniacal look, when he smiled, of a pirate ready to commit unspeakable acts on unsuspecting swabbies and their wenches. He was well over six feet tall and weighed about two-hundred and fifty pounds. Altogether, Alvie's appearance relieved the owner of the need to hire a bouncer. It was said that his smile could sober up a near-catatonic drunk, right on their bar stool. I thought that was a bit of an exaggeration, though, in light of the hardcases that frequented the Jackass.

Alvie was cool, though, you had to give him that. He never even raised an eyebrow at my bloody shirt.

"The usual," I said, trying to sound like a tough guy.

"And what the hell might that be?" he boomed, leaning over the bar toward me, the off-kilter eye causing a ripple of discomfort to the barflies on my left because you could never be sure who he was looking at.

"Damn, Alvie. Cut me a little slack here."

"OK, so you want a Coors Lite. Am I right?" he asked, smiling.

I gave up. "A shot of Jamieson's and a Dos Equis." Nothing but the best for the victor, even if he had to buy it for himself.

"Fine, a Mick-Spic," he said, showing not a smidgen of cultural sensitivity. "Coming right up." Before he got the booze, he hesitated, "Say, are you any relation to that writer fella that blew his brains out with a shotgun?"

It was a running joke between us. He'd asked me dozens of times. I wasn't up to playing but knew I wouldn't get a drink until I did.

"Yeah, Alvie, he was my great uncle."

"No shit?" he said, shaking his head in wonder as he brought me the beer and whiskey.

I loved the Jackass Inn, really the Jack Springs Inn, but renamed by the locals to describe the behavior that often took place inside. The bar had its own popular history which, true or not, was faithfully passed on to each new generation. My favorite story was about a couple of miners who got in a fight in the bar. One left and got an ax and stood outside the door in ambush. When the other guy came out, he whacked him in the chest with the blunt edge of the ax, then went back inside the bar for a few more beers.

The ax-wounded fellow got his pickup truck, waited until his assailant staggered outside drunk and ran him down in the street. When the deputies arrived, the combatants declined to press charges against each other, "being friends and all."

Returning to the bar after a trip to make room in my bladder for more beer, I noticed a woman sitting in a booth in the rear. I couldn't see her very well, thanks to the dim lights and my fuzzy vision. But she was wearing a cowboy hat and a sleeveless Levi jacket. Long dark hair was pulled back in a pony tail. She was drinking beer from a brown long-neck bottle.

And she appeared to be staring at me. It was kind of unsettling. Then I remembered my bloody shirt.

Things started getting a little hazy towards the end of my fourth beer and shot, and my muscle control went out the window. I couldn't get over the feeling that people were watching my every move. At one point, my shaky hand knocked a shot glass off the bar. It sounded a little like a gunshot, and five drunks were halfway out the door before they realized I'd meant no harm. Hesitant to leave the smoky womb of the Jackass before they had to, they inched sheepishly back to their seats. The cowgirl stayed in her seat, however. She might have even been smiling.

The adrenaline had worn off and I was five Dos Equis and five shots of Jamieson's to the wind by closing time. At some point, the cowgirl had slipped away. But in one last flash of alcohol insight before somehow finding my way home, I wondered if I had, indeed, gotten in way over my head.

CHAPTER 8

The young cat crawled out of her cave as the sun slipped behind the mountains, the stirring of hunger awakening in her stomach. But this was just regular hunger, not the yawning starvation of a week earlier.

She had returned to the place where the strange creature had left her some food, but nothing was there. Since then, however, prey had been more plentiful, hunting easier. She needed to eat an average of one fourth of her weight every day to be satiated. And that's why deer are such natural prey; a kill will last a lion three or four days.

She had yet to bring down a deer. But rabbits, grouse and even a coyote had fallen beneath the young cat's paws. Each required more energy than is optimal, but optimal is a concept unknown to a large predator. Her luck was getting better, as was her skill.

The cave was high in a rock wall above the stream. Behind it was a large forested mesa interspersed with small dry meadows. A game trail wound down from the trees to the stream.

The cat crawled out on a ledge and watched the trail below. With the maddening hunger gone for now, she could afford to be patient. She stretched out on the warm rock and surveyed the trail. As the sun dipped below the mountains and the shadows lengthened, she saw a movement at the forest edge.

An old doe emerged from the trees and started down the trail, stopping to munch on grass along the way. The cat became instantly alert. Her body tensed and the tip of her tail twitched like a dying snake. Staying close to the rock, the cat started down the ledge to a point where her path would intersect the doe's. Within a few minutes, the cat was perched restlessly in a notch between two boulders. She couldn't see the doe, but she had a view of the trail and soon would if the doe continued on the path.

Not long after the lioness settled into position, the doe wandered into view. The cat's body became taut, her rear legs bunched beneath her, ready to spring. Even the tail stopped twitching, lest the movement frighten her quarry.

When the doe was within easy striking distance, the cat launched her body, covering the distance in three strides. Sensing the movement, the doe tried to bolt sideways, but her old legs were arthritic and instead she stumbled. The cat was upon her, using powerful jaw muscles to grip the deer's neck. With a wrenching movement, she snapped the deer's spinal cord. The doe's body shuddered once, powerfully, and then relaxed. Her bowels and bladder emptied on the ground.

The cat sought a better grip with her jaws and started dragging the deer's carcass off the trail, up the hill to the base of the cliff, where she fed. She was so caught up in filling her belly for the first time since she left the mother cat, she didn't smell or hear the old male, upon whose territory she had infringed.

With battle scars on his face and side and a couple of toes missing, he was well past his prime. But he outweighed the lioness by sixty pounds and was a veteran in the animal kingdom, having survived a full eight years.

Once he had assured himself there was no danger nearby, he crept up behind the young cat and pounced upon her back, swatting her with a powerful paw. Caught off guard, the young cat rolled away and came up on her feet, waving one paw, claws extended, snarling and spitting, ears back and white teeth bared in the dark face.

But she was already full and had nothing to gain by standing up to the old lion. And the male, who normally wouldn't kill a young lioness unless he were starving, didn't press the attack. But something else about the

lioness put him off and he maintained his aggressive stance until she was
well out of sight.

While feeding, he would stop every few minutes, twist his head with
alarm in the direction she had escaped and snarl a menacing growl.

With a hangover banging away in my brain, I tried to sleep a little later than usual but Roscoe had other ideas. He put his huge paws on my chest and rumbled what passed for a growl. As I opened my eyes, a dribble of saliva spilled off his purple-splotched tongue and onto my chest. It wasn't the best way for a person with a queasy stomach to start the day.

I tried to push him off but he was having none of it. And he was big enough that I, in my weakened state, couldn't do it. His growl became more insistent, but his eyes were on the wall like he knew if he looked at me in my dissipated state he would have to take pity and leave me alone. More drool. More growls punctuated by little yips began to run together and sound like a D-9 Caterpillar demolishing a hillside.

Subterfuge was the only tactic left. "All right, goddamn it. I'll get up." His head tilted sideways and one miserable excuse for an ear perked up as if to run a doggie-version lie detector on me.

"If you want me to get up, you goddamn overgrown collection of leftover dog parts, you'll have to move your paws," I grunted.

He woofed a happy bark and stood beside the bed waiting for action. When I threw the blanket back, he wiggled and shook his miserable excuse for a tail.

"You wanna go for a walk, huh?" He jumped up and down, shaking the cabin floor and walls. "Okay, let's go," I said, trying to sound enthusiastic. He bounded out the open door and I jumped up and slammed it shut and locked it. I looked out the window and he was standing there, expectantly watching the door. I swallowed a handful of

Advil and vitamins and jumped back in bed. Naturally, he would make me pay for my deception, but there are some things a dog just doesn't understand—things like a vicious mind-warping, stomach-churning hangover.

After a while, the drugs made me feel a little better. At least the mouse hadn't come back, or if it had, I was sleeping too soundly to hear it.

I hadn't come to terms with the mice because mice have no sense of boundaries. Not only will they eat your food, they leave behind little mouse turds to rub it in. But nearly every other critter in the vicinity was welcome.

For four years, my cabin had served as a small wildlife refuge. The first spring, a family of mountain bluebirds built a nest under the eaves of my roof. For a while, watching the birds come and go with grass and twigs was entertaining. Within days, however, there was a cacophony of squawks that started at daybreak and continued every four to five minutes all day long—each time one of the parents brought a juicy morsel.

It drove me nuts because the noise was about twelve inches from the head of my bed. There wasn't much to be done about it short of boarding up the crack and killing the fledglings so I moved out of the loft and set up a bed in the living room where the noise wasn't so bad. Having birds using my cabin for their nest made me feel less like an interloper in their domain, so the next year I pried more facing loose, and soon little tendrils of grass and other nesting material hung from all the cracks. Every spring now, the roof sprouts a scraggly beard. A fringe benefit is that almost all the flying insects around the cabin have disappeared.

But bluebirds aren't my only avian neighbors. Red-tailed hawks perch in the tops of nearby trees and scout for rabbits and field mice, trumpeting their "Screeeaawws" when they take wing, sending any small critters nearby scurrying for cover. Sometimes I lie in the grass and watch as they ride thermals high above the Earth, until they are out of sight.

During the winter, an elk herd shows up from time to time and beds down in the meadow. Coming home and seeing twenty-five tons of elk flesh milling about, steam rising off their bodies in the bright winter moonlight, with grunts, moans and heavy breathing filling the crystalline silence of winter nights, is an awe-inspiring experience.

Roscoe doesn't see it that way and is positively beside himself when it happens. When he barks, they just tighten the group and dare him to come closer. Roscoe is no fool, and after a series of half-hearted "whuffs" he comes inside to sulk.

After being a cop for all those years and realizing there is no particularly redeeming quality to the human race in general and virtually none to the larger human enterprises like government, business, and society, I've made peace with the critters around the place. They were here before I was, before any of us were. Any inconvenience they cause me is much less than people have caused them. How could I not provide a small sanctuary in the growing madness?

But at the same time, I'd become less tolerant of people, as last night demonstrated—especially fools, hypocrites and ignoramuses—into which blurry categories the Al Bartholomews and Agnews of the world somewhere fell. But ignorance and spouting bullshit aren't crimes. And spurred on by some momentary madness or brain glitch, I had taken a chance of losing my job by overreacting. In most circumstances, a newspaper couldn't afford to have a maniac who assaults citizens working for it.

The only thing in my favor was that Abigail was acting a little recklessly herself these days. And after all, it's the Mountain Miner we're talking about here—not the New York Times. Lawlessness had a history in Jack Springs. Hell, it was a tradition. Maybe she could tolerate one minor—well, maybe not so minor—breach of professionalism.

While batting around these ideas in my aching head, the phone had the audacity to ring. It sounded, in my condition, more like a chain saw than a telephone. And if that wasn't enough to piss me off, the call could only mean more bad news.

"Aaron, this is Abigail," she said.

"What a surprise," I said, before it sunk in that she didn't sound like a hard-assed editor for a change. "Sorry, let me get a drink of water." I staggered to the sink and drank deeply.

"Okay, Abigail, what's up this fine morning in paradise?"

"Somebody blew up Gottlieb's headquarters last night."

"No shit? Wow," I said, unable to keep a proper level of gravity in my voice. "Right in the middle of downtown Vancouver?"

"No, not the one in Vancouver," she said, irritated. "The more modest one up at the mine site. And I don't care for that tone of voice. Which reminds me, I've been getting some angry calls about last night. We need to talk." This was more like her.

"Sure thing, Abigail. You want me to come in for an ass-chewing first or go up to the site?" I asked, half trying to be serious because, so far, my job situation appeared to be intact.

"Get up to the site, of course. There'll be plenty of time for an ass-chewing, as you so colorfully put it." She hung up.

The headquarters, a double-wide mobile home, had been empty since Gottlieb's crew finished the survey work. Just property damage, huh? No blood, no foul was the way I looked at it.

Then, remembering the blood on my shirt and the evil in Wiley's eyes when he threatened me, I put my .22 magnum snubnose revolver in the pocket of my wool sport coat. It was small, held three more cartridges than most revolvers and was accurate up to about forty feet. The magnum loads gave it a hell of a punch and a sound that would loosen your sphincter.

As I walked down the steps, it didn't take long to figure out how Roscoe was going to deal with my deception—the old "invisible" treatment. Ace reporter Aaron Hemingway no longer existed. It was chillingly effective and I knew from previous experiences it could last for days. At least he didn't attack me. But I walked down the path to my car glancing over my shoulder to see if he was sneaking up behind me to end our partnership once and for all.

While driving to Gottlieb's double-wide headquarters, it began to sink in just how badly the shit had hit the fan. A murder and a bombing, both likely in some way related to the Dark Angel Mine. The mine's opponents were not a bunch of granola-crunching, trust-fund babies, although there were a few of those up from the university in Boulder, along with a healthy smattering of new residents.

But the most dangerous of the lot were hard-core mountain people. Some of them were ex-drug smugglers, Vietnam vets, and more than a few fugitives who were hiding from the past. These mountain folk were fighting not so much for ideals as for their piece of ground and privacy; strong motivation because many of them knew there was no place left to run.

Steph was their leader because she was willing to be out front. The others didn't want the exposure.

Now that it had happened, the bombing didn't surprise me much. But it sure raised the stakes and was bound to attract some big-time attention. If things weren't settled quickly, the rhetorical "war" that Al Bartholomew was so fond of expounding upon could heat up real fast. Abigail picked up on it quicker than I did. But of course, the hangover and all.

Canaus "headquarters" was parked in a high, remote area of the valley that was already covered by mine tailings. It was on the far side of the valley, just over a ridge, as if those plotting its destruction couldn't stand to look at what would be lost.

Once again, the Boulder Sheriff's Department officers had the area sealed off. Earl was walking toward the roadblock as I pulled up, stopped, got out and waited.

He nodded and came over. A couple of deputies were nearby. "We've got to stop meeting like this," I told him. Earl's sense of humor, such as it was, had obviously worn thin in the past few days, and he looked at me like, "What the hell's that supposed to mean?"

"Look, Aaron, we don't have squat yet," he said. "The ATF is sending a crew up. We're not touching anything until they get here. So you might as well go back to town. I'll call you later."

"Where was the blast site?" I asked, only knowing the location of the property from my story reporting on the county commission hearing to approve it. There was a scorched depression in the tailings not a hundred yards away but no evidence that a structure of any kind had existed except a few unidentifiable chunks of refuse scattered about and a couple of heavy axles lying askew.

Earl, his voice tight with tension, said, "You're looking at it."

"There's nothing larger than a tin can lid out there, Earl. It looks like ground zero at Hiroshima."

"Yeah, well, I guess we can conclude this wasn't done by an amateur with a lead pipe full of match heads."

"Did anybody hear it?"

"We got a few calls," he said. "We just assumed it was a sonic boom." He didn't look happy about the revelation. "And if you print that, I'll kill you."

I was right. He wasn't happy about it.

We looked at each other. "Who the hell could put together an explosive device that would obliterate something from the face of the earth?"

Earl said, "Up here, it's going to be a lot easier to figure out who couldn't do it. I know something like this goes against your grain, but try to play this down a little. Tell the story but don't get too graphic about the site or speculate too much about what it means. We've got to get this under control before it blows up in our faces, no pun intended."

With my blood pressure rising, I drove into town. The sky was deep blue, the sun warm and the smell of mountain air had yet to be contaminated by exhaust from the swarm of motor homes, busses, cars, trucks, campers and motorcycles that flooded the town on warm summer days. Dark clouds were forming up over the Continental Divide, but they wouldn't hit town until early afternoon, if they made it at all. Most of the people around appeared to be enjoying themselves, oblivious to the trouble that was brewing.

Inside Abigail's office, the town mayor, the town manager and Al Bartholomew were in a shouting match with my boss. Harlan was sitting down, with his big arms crossed over his chest, his dark brown uniform shirt pressed neatly but discolored by perspiration in his arm pits.

Mayor Bill Brill, known as Brillo to his detractors due to his wiry hair, was a quintessential mountain-town nut-case who maintained his position by suing other council members and even some citizens when they opposed some of his lunatic schemes. After enough people got fed up and charged him with filing frivolous lawsuits, a county court judge ordered him to cease and desist. Brillo promptly filed a defamation of character suit against the judge and was even more promptly thrown in jail for two weeks for contempt of court. Today, he looked like a demented Albert Einstein in a leisure suit.

Gary Fontaine was the Jack Springs town manager. For my first six months on the job, I would have bet a year's worth of whiskey that he wore a toupee made from the hide of a dead possum. Learning that it really was his hair caused me no end of ribbing in the office for a few weeks.

He used breath spray so often I told Harlan that he ought to confiscate it and have it analyzed for illicit substances, but he refused. Gary walked on the balls of his feet, his nose to the wind like the hood ornament on a '53 Buick Roadmaster, as if he were a going-places type of guy, always sniffing for a shift in the political winds. But the effect was that he looked like he was going to fall on his face at any moment.

Gary Fontaine's main qualification was that, as the town's previous sewage-treatment plant operator, the excrement had backed up only a half-dozen times in two years—a considerably better record than any previous plant operator. After the last manager left town like a thief in the dark of night, Gary's competence was rewarded with Jack Springs' top job. Fontaine was the kind of guy you loved to hate because he provided the good citizens of Jack Springs with so much amusement.

Al Bartholomew's face had a yellowish cast to it and dark bags under his eyes. Dressed in a clean, white western-style shirt and new Roebuck jeans with the cuffs turned up about three inches, he looked like a dead man ready for his own funeral. It was almost enough to make you sorry for the guy.

And it appeared these pillars of the community wanted my head on a platter.

After the shouting and arm waving subsided, Abigail sat down and the group filed out. They avoided me like a coiled rattler when they crossed the room, refusing even to meet my eyes. But even at that distance, Al reeked of sour sweat and moldering cigarettes; the odor of pure fear, but fear of what? Harlan walked past and mouthed: "Call me."

As they were leaving, Abigail crooked a finger, which looked like it had been dipped in fresh blood, and motioned me into her office.

"Can you guess what that was all about?"

"I can guess."

"What the hell happened last night?" she asked, shaking her head.

"They blocked my way into the meeting. And as I turned to go, Wiley grabbed me. So, I hit him."

"And that's all there was to it, right?"

"Well, I might have said something," I hesitated, pondering my options. As an undercover cop for several years, I could be as sneaky as they come. But as a suspect, there were no moral grounds upon which to rationalize deception so I decided to fess up. "Actually, I speculated on the trans-species nature of his parentage."

Her mouth looked like she had just taken a bite out of a wormy apple in polite company and didn't quite know what to do with it. She fought back a smile, tried to look skeptical. "You were drinking before it happened." It wasn't a question.

"Two beers, Abigail. And I would have done the same thing without 'em."

"You suckered Wiley was how I heard it. You knew exactly what you were doing."

My head bobbed in a sort of nolo contendere plea on the accusation. Finally, Abigail couldn't suppress the smile any longer. "Goddamn, that was the funniest thing I've heard since…well…It was all I could do not to laugh in their faces. Until they pissed me off, anyway." She did laugh, then, the first time I had heard her do so in a while, but it came out sounding like a whinnying horse.

The time seemed right to ask, "Do I still have a job?"

"You do," she said, calming down. "But it can't happen again. I've used up all my aces on this one. The next time anyone tries to keep you out of a meeting, we'll call the ACLU or somebody. You are not to engage these idiots in any physical confrontation."

"Sure thing, boss, and thanks."

"Don't thank me. If I let them pressure me into making any changes, they'll eventually cut the heart out of this newspaper. But you're getting too involved in this story, Aaron. Just to give you an idea of how these things can be used against you, Al Bartholomew even suggested your fight with Wiley might have indirectly led to the explosion at Canaus Minerals."

"Boy, is that brilliant logic on Al's part, or what? I guess my whipping Wiley's ass got everybody so riled the mine supporters went and blew up their own headquarters in the confusion."

"That's enough, Aaron," Abigail said, closing the discussion. She paused and picked up a paper from her desk as Terri came in.

"By the way, Gottlieb is offering a $5,000 reward for information leading to an arrest in Stephanie's murder and a $10,000 reward for information on the bombing. And they've bought $1,500 worth of advertising to publicize the rewards. He also sent a statement accusing eco-terrorists of being responsible for the bombing."

What she was telling me slowly sunk in. "Five grand for a human being and ten grand for a goddamn stapled together piece of tin and particle board. At least, they're not afraid to show where their priorities are," I said, disgusted.

"You think they're trying to buy us off?" Terri asked.

"Maybe. I don't know and don't care," Abigail said. She relaxed and went into her newspaper mode. "What happened at Gottlieb's place?"

I told her. It wasn't much.

When I walked out of Abigail's office, Terri followed me. She had on a short summer dress, tan with little blue and brown flowers on it. It was v-cut in the front and showed freckles all the way down to where it got interesting. Her hair was down and red curls fell all around her face, with two gold barrettes holding it back out of her eyes. She was wearing clogs that made her almost as tall as me. She looked good, but she didn't look happy.

Terri walked over to me and searched my face for some hidden clue to what I was about. Her green eyes looked a little hazy. "Aaron, are you all right?" she asked.

Abigail was pressing coffee through a desktop steamer and the aroma of espresso seeping out of her office. It was churning my empty stomach.

A quick check list ran through my head. "I still have my job, I'm not injured. So I guess I'm okay," I shrugged. "Wait a minute, my dog hates me."

"Jerk," she said. "Why am I not surprised?" After that, she ignored me by looking through her mail. Once again, I had become the invisible man. First Roscoe and then Terri. The day wasn't off to a very good start. Not that I didn't bring it on myself. When I hung my sport coat on the back of the chair, the gun bounced against the chair frame, but nobody noticed.

After licking my psychological wounds for a few minutes, I tried to focus on the day's work. The court papers on Gottlieb were enticing, but I needed to confirm their authenticity. Besides, the bombing would be the big story this week, whether Earl liked it or not. The investigation into Stephanie's murder, barring significant progress, would be the number two story.

Taking a long shot, I called the provincial court in Vancouver, British Columbia, asked for the court records office and explained that I needed to confirm some information about a court case that had been settled. The woman who answered sounded like she was going to try to be helpful. I read the number on the court file and asked her if she could confirm the settlement. She took the information and put me on hold. In about three minutes, she came back on the line.

"Well, sir, it seems that this file has been sealed by the court. The information you need is not available. According to a notation in my computer, I'm not even supposed to confirm the existence of the file," she said. "That seems kind of silly. But I'm sorry, that's all I can tell you."

"Actually, you've been very helpful. Thank you."

"You're welcome, sir," she said.

Bingo! I had a story. Sometimes it's that easy.

Harlan called. "How you doin'?"

"Fine," I said. "Look, Harlan, that deal last night wasn't the smartest thing I've ever done. Sorry about any problems."

"Hell, Aaron, I got no problems. Brill, Fontaine and Bartholomew wanted me to arrest you until I explained that them boys was packing concealed weapons and I would've had to arrest them too. None of them three could stomach the idea of the Agnews having a grudge against the town. So they decided to get you fired. Since you're still there, that must not of happened."

"No, Abigail didn't fire me. But I've been put on notice." Terri got up and left in a hurry. What the hell did I say this time? "Have you heard anything from Earl about the bombing?"

"Nothin' since he first went up there," Harlan said. "But I understand it's a lulu of a job."

"Harlan, there's nothing left of that trailer but little pieces. If somebody sets off a bomb like that in town, it isn't going to make any difference which side people are on. There's going to be a lot of folks killed."

"Don't think I ain't thought of that," he said. "I only hope that blowing up such a remote location means that the bomber doesn't want to kill anybody. Maybe they were just making a whaddayacallit, one of them there political statements."

"Well, what else would someone against the mine blow up? That's the only place Gottlieb has, around here anyway."

"I was thinking of Al Bartholomew's place," Harlan said. "I believe Al might have had the same thoughts. His face was yellower than a sucker's belly in that meeting this mornin'."

"Good," I said. "Maybe he'll tone down his rhetoric a little."

"He might at that," Harlan said. "As a matter of fact, I'm going to suggest it, just to make sure he has thought of it."

"Anything new on Steph's murder?" Outside, the clouds had built up quickly and pushed a cold wind into town from the west.

"We got a better description on the truck that was seen at up at Steph's place—a light-colored Ford pickup with a dark camper shell. That pretty much fits about one out of every six vehicles in town, though. The mystery visitor might or might not be the murderer."

"What about questioning Wiley?"

"I told Earl, and he's been trying to get a hold of them. So far, they haven't answered the phone."

The line of dark clouds that seemed benign just a few hours earlier was now sweeping down the mountains. Lightning was flashing over the valley where Gottlieb wanted to build the Dark Angel Mine and the ATF had a bombing scene to process. Thunderous drops of ice-filled rain began smacking the roof. I told Harlan thanks, hung up and went out on the porch to absorb the violence of the storm. By the time I went back inside, patches of blue sky were oozing through the clouds.

CHAPTER 9

Abigail was pulling sheets off the fax machine. "What a day. We get the ad from Canaus Minerals, and now a coalition of environmental groups is placing an ad asking people to maintain their opposition to the mine. All in all, we're about $2,000 ahead unless somebody else pulls their ads. By the way, any progress on the investigation?"

"Not much."

"Well, hell, maybe it would be a good time to let things simmer down a little," she said looking at the latest ad.

"Abigail, I don't think things will simmer down much when the people realize what happened up at Gottlieb's trailer." She shrugged. "We got a confirmation on the court papers from Canada, though."

"That's great. What's in them?" Abigail liked to cut to the chase.

"I haven't taken a detailed looked at them yet. But it appears to be the hard evidence of what we heard. A couple of Gottlieb's mining deals have fallen through. He got sued. And there's something in there that we hadn't heard. A tailing pond blew out and killed an entire river in the Canadian wilderness. Somehow he got the court to seal the records."

What I had just told her didn't seem to sink in and she was already walking away. "Try to get it together by next week's paper. I'm not sure I'm going to be around much longer than that."

She closed the door to her office and picked up the phone. The remark puzzled me but before I could think anymore about it, Terri came rushing in, wet red curls plastered against her head.

"I was at the memorial service for Stephanie," she said. "A woman there told me she had seen a truck parked at Stephanie's house several times. It was a newer model four-wheel drive, light-colored Ford with a dark camper shell. She said Stephanie didn't have many visitors, and most of them owned VW busses or old cars and trucks, so it kind of stuck in her mind. She was out of town until yesterday, and didn't know what had happened." Terri's face was flushed. She appeared to have forgotten about last night in the excitement.

"Great. Harlan told me, but it was off the record, as usual. It could be important to the investigation."

"Do you think we should run it then? I wouldn't want to interfere with the investigation."

"If somebody told you, it'll be all over town tomorrow when the paper comes out whether the cops want it to or not." She looked pleased for a moment, then a cloud came across her face. "Maybe you should put it in your story. You're covering the investigation."

"Yeah, but you've got the real news in the story. Let's write it together."

She was wavering, a grin trying to break out, but she held back. Taking advantage of what could be a moment of weakness, I asked, "You want to have lunch? We can, uh, talk about the story on Gottlieb's lawsuits."

"Sure," she said and resumed typing her notes. She sometimes wore a pair of granny glasses when her contacts were bothering her. Since they didn't seem to fit very well, they slipped down to her button nose and made her look something like a librarian or an old-fashioned school marm. Every so often, she would absentmindedly push them back up. It was funny as hell, but I usually didn't laugh. Today it just seemed to slip out.

She turned her head slowly, looked at me and said, "Are you laughing at my glasses?"

"Huh? Not me. No way." I looked quickly at the court papers and heard her resume typing.

The phone rang, and Earl McCormick was on the line. "We're still waiting for the ATF people, so there's not too much I can add. If you need something for the record, I can tell you we suspect it was set by someone with detailed knowledge of explosives. And we'll be investigating it as a possible retaliation for Stephanie's murder."

I whistled softly. It would make good copy for tomorrow's paper. "So much for playing it down," I said. "Got anything new on the murder?"

I could almost hear him thinking it over. "Harlan's probably told you about the pickup truck seen at Goldman's cabin, off-the-record. Am I correct?"

"I can't confirm or deny that."

"We'll, I'm telling you the same thing—off the record, of course."

"It's too late for that. The woman who saw the truck has already talked to Terri Smith—the other reporter here."

"Goddamn it, I suppose she's told everybody else in town too."

"It's safe to assume it will be common knowledge before sundown."

Earl was silent for a few moments. "All right, I'll confirm it. Maybe we can start to make someone nervous; give the tree a shake or two and see if any rotten fruit falls off. You can say we'll be checking the truck's description against all the trucks owned by residents of Jack Springs. That's on the record. Off the record, we'll be focusing on people associated with the Western Jobs Coalition. That should tickle the shit out of you."

"You heard, huh? By the way, you're going to find out when you check the trucks that Al Bartholomew has a light-green Ford Ranger with a dark-green camper on it."

With a small groan, he said, "Thanks for the tip. One last thing, Stephanie Goldman was in the initial stages of some kind of lymphatic cancer when she was killed. But you'll have to call the coroner to confirm it. He'd have my ass for releasing the information."

"Do you think it's significant?"

"With as little as we have so far, anything is significant."

"That's pretty honest for a cop talking to a reporter."

McCormick grunted something like 'Go fuck yourself' and hung up.

Terri was looking at me. She had heard my end of the conversation—one of the advantages, or disadvantages, of working in a small office. "What was that all about?" she asked.

"Let's talk about it over lunch," I said, shamelessly exploiting my advantage of knowing something that she didn't. Looking at the clock, I added, "A late lunch."

When Terri first came to work at the Miner, she wore coordinated, bright outfits and squarish glasses that look like they are on upside down. Her hair was barely shoulder-length and styled in a way to play down its natural curl. Since then, she had let her hair grow into a wild mane of red curls. Somewhere along the line, the glasses were replaced by contacts.

She was tall and thin—too many angles and not enough curves. And she moved as if she were treading on an ice-covered lake. It was also the way she thought. Life was not going to spring any surprises on Terri Smith, not if she had anything to say about it. She had the high cheek bones that give a face an open, honest look. Freckles and green eyes heightened the effect. She was a package that was more than the sum of her parts.

It was a package I liked, but history had conspired against us.

She had left her husband right before she came to work at the Miner. For a while, we tried to keep our particular demons at bay by becoming lovers. But her husband suspected what was going on and threatened to use that to take her two kids. So we killed our budding romance. Since then, her divorce had become final and she got custody of the kids. But the resolution of her marital problems didn't bring us back together because her ex-husband was a violent drunk, and she was afraid I was too much like him.Whether I deserved it or not, she had given me a temporary reprieve.

Standing in line at Annie's waiting to get a table, the transformation of Terri Smith was nearly complete. Her bare shoulders were showing some muscle definition. In the short dress, her legs looked athletic. Other men had noticed, and their surreptitious glances were getting on my nerves.

When we got a table, I ordered two eggs basted medium, potatoes, whole wheat toast and coffee—a good hangover meal. Terri ordered a bowl of Annie's beef stew, a large garden salad, a French roll and ice tea. She seemed to have the metabolism of a hummingbird; there wasn't a visible ounce of fat on her entire body.

"So, what was that phone call from Detective McCormick about?" she asked, cocking an eye brow ever so slightly.

"He said they were still waiting on the ATF to process the scene so they didn't know much beyond what was obvious; somebody blew the hell out of Gottlieb's trailer. And he confirmed on the record about being interested in the owner of the truck, so we can add that to the story. He also said that she was in the early stages of lymphatic cancer when she was killed."

"Is that important? The cancer I mean." The news appeared to deflate her somewhat.

"Who knows? But it's something new to add to the story."

"Do you have any theories about why she was killed?" she asked. "After all, you used to be a police officer."

"I don't know, nothing about this makes much sense to me." I could see she was a little disappointed. As the incorrigible reader of too many mystery novels, the temptation was too great to resist, "But I can't help thinking there's something real obvious that everybody is missing." At that she brightened. The thing was, it could be true. But my real motivation was drawing Terri into my web.

At first, a spark came into her green eyes then a smoldering flame. You could see something akin to the "Pulitzer Syndrome" taking over her mind. Future headlines danced in her brain. Something like, "Investigative reporter solves murder that baffles police." In truth, that rarely happens. But the motivation wasn't such a bad thing. And she had gone out and dug up some information that everybody but the cops had missed. So I wasn't being completely disingenuous.

Then she slipped on her game face.

"So what, exactly, do you want me to do with the Gottlieb file?"

"You've studied some business and economics in college?"

"Yes, three years of business as a major. Journalism was my minor."

"To be honest, I'm not very good with financial information. And there's a lot of it in those court documents. I'd like you to go through it and be sure we're not missing anything important."

"I can do that," she said, breaking into a smile. "But when I hear you say, 'To be honest,' it makes me want to check and see if my wallet is still in my purse."

So much for subterfuge. But, hey, she didn't say 'no,' did she?

Annie brought our food and we ate in a comfortable silence. We finished off the food and split the check.

Terri seemed preoccupied as we walked back to the Miner office. Instead of going in, she stopped on the porch. "I've got to check on something," she said. "I'll be back in a few minutes."

At the time, I figured she was going to sneak a smoke. If I had any idea where she was really going, I would have tried to stop her.

CHAPTER 10

Inside, Abigail was laying out the paper. Most of the copy was already in. Freelance writers had sent their gardening columns, features, opinion pieces, letters and a host of community and society news early in the week. They were pasted up. The news hole was still open but it wouldn't be for long. A freelance photographer brought in some long distance shots of the spot where Gottlieb's "headquarters" had previously stood. You couldn't tell much, but the photo would take up much of the front page.

I typed up the story, as it stood, on the explosion and put my notes on the murder on a disk. Terri came back about twenty minutes later, looking like a cat with a canary in her mouth. But she kept her mouth shut about whatever it was she had been up to.

I gave her my disk and she added the information to her story, leading with the fact that investigators were trying to establish the identity of the owner of the mysterious truck. Then she quoted the neighbor who had made the report. It wasn't blockbuster stuff, but it was good.

Harlan called about 4:30 and asked me to take a ride with him. Since my work was almost done, I offered to return by 5:00 and help polish the story.

He picked me up out front, and we drove for a while without saying much, but I knew he wanted to talk. The sky had cleared again. The pre-weekend tourist crush was in full force and the town was buzzing with activity. Fumes stunk up the air and there was a continual hum of engines rising above the town. The sound of saws and hammers punctuated the air as carpenters rushed to finish up the day's work.

As we drove past the town park, we saw someone with a big straw cowboy hat standing motionless in the grassy area in front of the picnic shelter. He started moving, his hands cut soft arcs in the air, his body turning in slow motion. We drove closer, but he ignored us and continued spinning an enormous, invisible spider web.

Harlan turned my way with a look saying the world was moving way too fast for a simple country boy, becoming strange in ways that were unimaginable just a few years ago.

"Oh Lordy, what do we have here? Have you heard anything about some new drugs in town?" His voice was doleful, asking if surely the town had not suffered enough this week.

"Hold on a second, Harlan. Let's sit here a little bit." The cowboy continued his strange ballet. "I think he's performing T'ai Chi. It's an ancient form of a martial art—believe it or not."

"It's not drugs then?"

"I don't think so." But I had seen T'ai Chi often during my time in Saigon. "Actually, he's pretty good, if you can get past that hat."

"Well, thank God for small favors," he said in a tone that indicated it wasn't all that much consolation. Harlan sighed. "Damn, normal people in this town are gettin' harder to find than a Wyoming state trooper on a Sunday morning."

Harlan let out a stream of brown tobacco juice and slowly backed the Jeep out of the parking lot. As we drove away, he started chuckling, his lips pulled tight over his teeth. His chuckles turned into laughs. Then walrus-like guffaws filled the Jeep.

"What the hell is so funny?" I asked, fearing he was losing his mind.

"Oh, hell, I just got a picture in my head of that feller getting into a scuffle at the Jackass. Can you imagine the look on Alvie's face if he starts squaring off with somebody, all that wrist flippin' and those cute little turns?"

Harlan was near hyperventilation between laughing and describing the scene. His belly was slapping the steering wheel as he tried to get a breath, and then he started hitting the dashboard with the heel of his hand. Tears were streaming down his red face. If laughter is infectious, this was more like an epidemic and soon we were both laughing like mad men. After I settled down, it didn't seem all that funny. But if anybody needed a laugh after the three days we'd just been through, it was Harlan. He was quiet for a few moments and then dropped the bomb.

"Before I let you off, I thought you'd better know that Earl ran a check on the Agnews in the FBI's data base and Wiley's name came up as a suspected associate of some militia outfit up in Blackhawk. These are some real bad boys up there, according to the feds. We're having a meeting with them tomorrow. They said they should have more information at that time."

Wonderful.

When we pulled back up to the office, someone was sitting on the porch in almost the exact spot Stephanie's body had been found. It was a young girl wearing dark blue, octagonal-lens sun glasses. Suitcases, a duffel bag and a sleeping bag were piled around her like a fortress. She hugged her knees to her chest and stared at the sidewalk. Probably just a runaway or something I told myself and started to go around her and up the steps.

She looked at me with eyes full of uncertainty, started to speak, then hesitated. I stopped on the step and looked down at her. She looked at my face again and said, "Daddy?"

CHAPTER II

A maelstrom of emotions tore at my heart as I stood there. I hadn't even recognized her, my own daughter. Not that I should have. Unlike the picture on my desk, her hair now looked badly cut. She was wearing baggy overalls, an oversized flannel shirt and purple Converse high tops. Her ears had been pierced in several places but she didn't have any earrings on. Her fingernails had flecks of different colored polish; quite a difference from the little girl wearing a soccer uniform in the last picture she had sent me.

I was stunned.

But a warm wind of love blew away the storm clouds around my heart. My daughter, my kid, was here.

"Cassie, what are you doing here?" Tears welled up in my eyes and before she could answer, I reached down, swept her into my arms like holding a baby bird to my chest, its heart beating wildly. Or maybe it was my heart.

"Oh Daddy," she whimpered. Then the dam burst and she cried—huge, breath-robbing sobs as she held me tighter and tighter. Abigail, Terri and a couple of the ad people looked out the window at us. Some people gathered in the street, watching. I saw them, but they weren't really there at that moment. There were only the two of us, Cassie and me. Finally, I let go and looked deep into her eyes, cloudy pools of fear, confusion and relief.

"Where's your mom?" I asked, wondering if she had run away or something worse had happened. The pile of baggage she had with her made it unlikely that she had hitchhiked, anyway.

"She drove me here," Cassie said, looking away. "I think she went right back to Kansas City."

I moved some of her stuff out of the way and sat down next to her. "I assume you had a little falling out."

"Did we ever. The kids I was hanging with got in, like, some trouble. She said I had to come live with you, that I was ruining her career."

I could see Madeline being slightly sensitive about Cassie running around with a bad crowd. But dumping her here like this seemed a bit extreme.

"Drugs?"

"Sort of, yeah, and some other stuff," she said, looking away.

"OK, we can talk about it later. What did your mom say about leaving you here? Is she coming back?"

"She said maybe you'd know how to handle me with, you know, the drugs and all. But she didn't say much besides that. She was pretty mad all the way from Kansas City and didn't talk much. You know how she gets."

Oh yeah, I knew. And I figured Madeline had driven instead of flown just so she could stretch out the punishment. Then I remembered Cassie didn't like to fly. "Okay, here's the plan," I said, trying to sound in charge, like a father is supposed to. "I have to finish some work inside. It won't take long. Then we'll eat and go to my cabin. Do you want to come in?"

"No. It's kind of nice, just sitting here."

"Okay."

"Dad, I'm glad she brought me. I missed you. And she was really driving me crazy."

We hugged again and I went inside. Abigail had gone back into her office, the ad people were working away, busier than usual. Screw 'em if

they were embarrassed by what they had just seen. But Terri was looking at me, her eyes softening.

"So that's what the phone calls were about," she said. "If you want to
leave, go ahead. The story is done—"

"Thanks, but let me look it over for a couple of minutes. It'll give me
a chance to gather my thoughts."

"It's not my business, of course, but do you know what happened?"

"Not exactly. Cassie has gotten into some trouble with her friends. I
suspect her mother sees this as some ingenious kind of punishment,
maybe for both of us."

She nodded. With a ten-year-old son and an eight-year-old daughter,
she probably understood such things better than me.

Neither of us felt like eating so we headed for the cabin. Cassie's eyes
were wide as we rode through pine and aspen groves that hugged
Magnolia Road. The sun was still high and the sky was as blue as a sap-
phire. A coyote was nosing around the meadow on the Reynolds' place,
poised, resting on his haunches with front paws extended, to pounce on
some unsuspecting critter in the tall grass. His mouth snapped up
whatever it was, then he tossed it in the air before settling down for the
snack. Cassie kept her eyes on it until we were around the bend. She
looked better, more relaxed. I could imagine what a ten-hour drive with
her angry mother must have been like.

"Was that a coyote?"

"Yep, it was. There's all kinds of wild things running around up
here." She looked a little worried at the thought. "But it's not dangerous.
The animals and people try to stay out of each others' way for the most
part." It wasn't the time to tell her about the mountain lion.

Speaking of wildlife, Roscoe was standing at attention near the top of
the driveway, and he started to shake appreciatively as the Subaru
stopped. He must have gotten over my duplicity that morning. But
when he saw Cassie, he looked a little surprised. He wasn't used to seeing strangers around the homestead.

"Dad, what is that?"

"That's Roscoe."

"Oh, wow! Does he bite?"

"Only fleas and bad people. You're safe." When she got out of the car, Roscoe summoned all the dignity he could muster, strolled over and sniffed her leg. His chow tail curled like a donut. Cassie froze. Roscoe thought about it for a moment, decided he liked what he smelled, and jumped up, knocking Cassie to the ground.

"Hey!" she yelled. Then he began licking her face. "Oh, yuk," she gasped between sloppy tongue lashings. Then she started to giggle and finally laugh. It was music to my ears, but I had to put a stop to it.

"Roscoe! Get off!" He obeyed and started doing the Roscoe rhumba, instead.

Cassie got up, used her sleeve to wipe her face, brushed herself off, and said, "Whew! That's some serious bad breath," then laughed some more. We walked up the path and Cassie stopped when she caught her first glimpse of the cabin.

"I know it's not much," I said, my heart dropping. It wasn't much, that was the truth. But you don't always notice the truth until you see it through someone else's eyes.

But she didn't look upset. "Not that, I mean, like, what's all that fuzzy stuff hanging down from the roof?"

"Oh, that," I said, relieved. "Well, those are birds' nests. Some blue-birds and swallows use my house to build their nests." The explanation seemed incomplete, so I offered lamely, "It helps keep the bugs away."

"Bugs?" she looked around suspiciously.

"No, no bugs, the birds keep them away."

She smiled, shook her head and started walking again. We muscled her stuff inside the cabin. She did a quick scan of the place. The bed and couch sat across from each other, with the small table at one end and the sink, stove and refrigerator at the other. The rug was old, as were the furniture and appliances. But everything was for the most part neat and clean. Eyes still moving, a shadow crossed her face.

"Dad, like, where's the bathroom?"

"Yeah. The bathroom. It's over there in the trees," I pointed out the door.

"No kidding around, Dad."

My finger remained in place. "No kidding around, kid."

She sat heavily on the couch, not in her wildest imagination having anticipated this turn of events.

"But there is electricity. See." I turned on the dilapidated console stereo, and it blared out Dwight Yoakum singing about guitars, Cadillacs and hillbilly music.

"Oh God," she said and we laughed. The music of her laughter was the sweetest song I'd ever heard. Right then, Stephanie's murder, the Agnews and the Dark Angel Mine were all a million miles away.

CHAPTER 12

That morning a wet gray mist clung to the meadow like a soggy down comforter. It was the kind of weather that made you want to go back to bed. Fat chance.

Cassie stayed asleep on the couch, however, with Roscoe curled up protectively on the floor. Her head was buried in the sleeping bag, and she showed no sign of waking so I tidied up the cabin. It seemed like a fatherly thing to do.

Last night she had fallen asleep before we could talk very much. And I realized, hoped anyway, there would be plenty of time to catch up on the last four years and to tell her my side of the story. It wasn't pretty, but she needed to know the truth. Who knew what Madeline had told her?

With the cabin straightened and a handful of wildflowers stuck in a vase in the window, it was time for breakfast—a pound of hash browns fried with onions and grated cheddar cheese sprinkled across them just before they were done.

It had been Cassie's favorite a few years ago and I was counting on the fact that kids' food preferences don't change very much. The aroma filled the cabin and she stirred. After some wriggling around, she peeked out of the sleeping bag. Roscoe had been watching carefully for the first sign of life from the sleeping bag and his ecstatic face was the first thing she saw.

"Uunnhh," she said and started back into the goose-down cocoon.

Opening the bag a peek, I said, "Good morning, sleeping beauty."

Her eyes were still closed and she wrinkled her nose. "Is that what I think it is?" Roscoe watched her expectantly, beginning his mini-earth-quake routine.

"Yep, time to get up, the world awaits your presence."

She threw the sleeping bag open and Roscoe pounced, slathering her with his tongue.

She crossed her arms over her face and said, "Oh, God, not this again." But then she started to giggle.

"Roscoe!" I yelled. "Get out of here." He ran for the door, jumped down the steps and stood attentively facing the small back porch.

We ate at my tiny table, and she hadn't lost her appetite. She covered the concoction with catsup, which was not easy to look at in light of recent events. Cassie took her first trip to the outhouse without any major trauma, but she did look a little squeamish when she returned. I heated some water so she could clean up. The mist was burning off and weak sunshine was fighting its way through.

After she washed her hair in the sink, she rummaged through one of her suitcases and pulled out a little box, extracting seven earrings and calmly put them in her ears—two in one and five in the other, a random mixture of hoops, gold studs and dangly things. I might have frowned, but when she looked up, my face was a mask of indifference. At least she didn't have one in her tongue or eyebrow.

"What are we going to do today?" she wanted to know.

"Go to work for a while, then take the marshal's daughter to the high school gymnasium and help her with her freethrows. You can stay here—"

She looked at me like I was crazy.

"—or you can go with me and hang around town."

"Can I go to the gym with you?"

"Sure. You can meet Tresha. She's a real character. You two should hit it off pretty well."

Her expression said, "What does that mean?" She disappeared behind the partition that served as a walk-in closet and came out wearing a tank top, a jog bra, some baggy green shorts and a pair of Reebok pump hightop basketball shoes. Then she pulled a basketball, a skateboard and a University of Kansas sweatshirt with Co-ed Naked La Crosse Team written on it from her duffel bag. She surveyed her equipment, then nodded as if to say, 'Ready.'

It was cool so I put on my moth-eaten wool sport coat. The gun was heavy in the pocket, and it seemed kind of foolish to have it now that a couple of days had passed so I slipped it onto a high shelf in the closet.

The dog was still watching the door. "You want to go to town, Roscoe?" With that, he bolted down the hill and launched himself into the back seat through the open window with a furious scratching of claws on the old oxidized green paint. The Subaru was shaking as if the engine were running on three cylinders when we walked up.

"Does he always do that?"

"What?"

"Wiggle like that?"

"Only when he's around a beautiful girl."

"Oh, brother," Cassie said, letting me know, I suppose, that being beautiful wasn't high on her list of important things in life.

As we pulled out of the driveway, she looked over her shoulder at the stone formations on the ridge above the cabin. The mist had dissipated, but enough remained to suffuse the massive rock in a soft light.

She looked back at me. "That's really beautiful. I don't remember much about Colorado from before. Isn't that weird?"

"Probably just as well."

A troubled look slipped across her face. "Dad, you don't owe me any explanation, you know? I know how Mom is."

This fifteen-year-old has done some growing up in the last four years, I realized.

"We'll see."

She shrugged, 'Whatever.'

We drove along in silence after that. Maybe she had the right idea.

Passing the Jack Springs' shopping center, the only place where there was enough unbroken asphalt for a decent skateboard ride, Cassie asked me to drop her off. Already, a group of scruffy-looking boys were slamming off the curb in front of one of the empty shops. It was tempting to stay around and be sure she would be all right. But she didn't seem even a little hesitant so I kept going. Roscoe watched forlornly as we left her behind.

The Miner door was open. There was nobody around at the moment, but all the machines were humming. The newspaper was sitting on every desk and the top-of-the-fold headline said, "Explosion levels mine company trailer." The drophead said, "Cops seek link with activist murder." The second story headline read like something out of a tabloid, saying, "Investigators seek truck owner in local murder," then added, "Murder victim had cancer." The Denver Post was next to it, and a near-banner headline reported, "Governor concerned with violence in mining town," followed by, "May call in the national guard." Ouch. We missed that one, but then it was understandable. A reporter for The Post, out of the loop on the local inside stuff, dug up a story by calling the governor's office and asking, "What are you planning on doing about that situation up there. Don't you think this could hurt the economic boom in the region?"

And the governor did what politicians do best–made noises like a man of action.

Shaking my head as Harlan pulled up out front, I walked out to his Jeep.

"Hear tell you got company," he said.

"Her Mom just dropped her on the steps and left. I don't know exactly what brought that on."

"Expect you'll find out soon enough. Before I forget, we still haven't been able to get a hold of the Agnews."

"That's pretty suspicious, seems to me."

"They're not official suspects in Stephanie's murder, Aaron. So we can't make them come in. Another way of looking at it, and I ain't sayin' this is right, is that if they were involved, they'd be more cooperative to throw off suspicion," he said. "But knowing them, it's hard to tell." He took his hat off and scratched his head. "If I ever appear to have figured out the Agnews' minds, take me out and shoot me.

"One thing, though, we got a list of the locals who own a truck fitting the description of the one seen at Steph's. There are forty seven and about half of them are Fords, but Earl isn't putting much stock in the fact that it was for sure a Ford. We're running background checks on all the owners anyway."

My car was parked in the street in front of Harlan's Jeep. Roscoe rolled over, causing the shock absorbers to squeak, and stuck his paws in the air. They were just visible over the back of the seat.

Harlan looked away and was silent for a few seconds. "By the way, a guy from the Federal Bureau of Investigation and a woman from that Jewish, uh, group are coming up this afternoon. Earl will be by if he can get away. Those lab boys…er, uh, them people from the ATF arrived early yesterday evening. Haven't heard anything though. We decided to double the number of officers on patrol up here this weekend, although for the life of me I can't see that it'll do a pile of cow plop's worth of good.

"Earl said we should do it anyway, just so if something happens, we can say we did. To my way of thinking, if something happens anyway, seems to me it would be even more embarassin'."

As usual, Harlan had come up with an interesting way of looking at the situation and was probably right on the money. The twisted logic of public relations was just too much for a simple country boy, as Harlan would say.

There didn't seem to be anything else to discuss at the moment.

"Tell Tresha to meet me at the school about 1:30." As Harlan started to drive away, he said, "See ya' later, if those folks have anything interesting to say about the Agnews."

"I'd appreciate it."

Back inside the Miner, I found the Gottlieb file on Terri's desk. She'd apparently gone about half way through it. Picking up the stack she'd already written notes on, I returned to my desk. Cassie's soccer picture sat there facing me.

It occurred to me that my life had gotten pretty goddamn complicated in the past twenty-four hours. One of the things I had figured out since leaving the Denver cops is I don't like complications. Keep it simple, stupid. It's even our team motto. But that's easier said than done.

I walked out and checked on Roscoe, who was still sleeping. Momentum kept me moving until I was at the shopping center and watching—from a discreet distance—Cassie riding her board. She stumbled once, shooting her board into the path of a car, and my heart missed a few beats. The car stopped, Cassie retrieved her board and made another run. After about five minutes of spying, I returned to the Miner office feeling just a little guilty.

Inside, Terri had the phone sandwiched between her ear and shoulder and she was typing away, nodding, saying, "Yes, yes, that's right. Sure." She was animated and I had a feeling I was going to learn what she had been up to the day before when she disappeared just after lunch.

After listening for a minute or so, she said, "Thank you, thank you very much," and hung up. "Oh boy, I got a story."

"Yeah?"

"It was your idea," she continued. "You know, what you said at lunch yesterday about there being something that everybody was missing. I found it, sort of."

"Well, can you tell me about it, since it was my idea and all?"

"Sure, but for now, you have to promise not to say anything about it to anyone."

My hand raised in a three finger salute, I pledged, "Scout's honor."

"Do you remember when I said Stephanie was looking at something and covered it up when I went in to talk to her?"

"Yeah, I remember."

"I went up there yesterday and found it."

"You went into a secured crime scene?"

She shrugged off the implication and the question.

"It was a travel brochure to Mazatlan, Mexico," she said, appearing quite pleased with herself.

"Yeah, so?"

"Stephanie was planning to take a trip to Mexico. "

"So what's it mean?"

"By itself, nothing," she said. "But how about a reservation, paid in full, for a round trip flight to Mazatlan with an open return date?"

She got me, there. That was a tough one to explain, because Stephanie didn't even like leaving her cabin to come to town.

"Well, you might be on to something if you can figure out why she was going. "

"The reservation was made this past weekend," Terri said. " And the flight was leaving Denver tomorrow. She could have been planning to go to a cancer treatment clinic there. They have a lot of cancer therapies in Mexico that aren't allowed here in the United States."

"But so far, you're just speculating."

She sagged a little. "So far, but when I get a list of clinics, I'm going to call and ask if she's registered."

The clinics were legal in Mexico, but they were still controversial. They'd want to protect their patients' privacy. Assuming, of course, that was why Steph was going. It wouldn't be easy, but there was a way she might be able to get that information.

"See if they'll tell you about the money first; how much they charge, if a deposit is required. Make a separate call to see if Steph is registered—you'll probably have to use a ruse of some kind. Since Steph didn't show up this weekend, try that call on Monday—say you're her and you're going to be a little late and ask if you should send more money to hold your spot. If they don't know what you're talking about, then she wouldn't be registered there. If they do, then you've got your story."

"The money's important, right?"

"Maybe, because if Steph came into a lot of money recently, and we can figure out why, it might give us a motive in her murder. Think about it; where did she get it and where is it now?" She nodded and scratched some quick notes.

"And don't you mention this to anyone, either. You got that? Anyone."

She looked puzzled. "I wouldn't, but what's the big deal?"

"Terri, look, trust me on this," I said, and wondering if Earl should be told after all.

"Don't be so melodramatic, Aaron."

"Melodramatic, huh? Somebody killed Stephanie, shot her through the head. And we don't know who did it or why." I put my hands on her shoulders. "Think about it, goddamnit! And once you find out if she is registered and if she paid any money or how much she was supposed to pay, we're definitely going to Earl with the information. Once the cops have it, there won't be any reason to—"

She looked up at me with alarm because I was shaking her.

"I don't want anything to happen to you, that's all. This may be a game to us. But it's not a game to somebody out there," I said and walked to the front door, where I turned and asked, "What about the cats? Did her cats come back?"

"No, there weren't any cats around," she said, shrugging her shoulders as if she didn't understand why it mattered. But then, neither did I.

Outside, a ragged procession of teenage boys came up the street with Cassie in the lead—kind of a skateboard posse. When she saw me she dismissed her troop of baggy-trousered admirers and came inside. They milled around for awhile, then walked away with boards tucked under their arms rather than negotiate the gravel street.

We went up to Fat Jack's for bagels and cream cheese.

CHAPTER 13

By the look on her face while we ordered lunch, I surmised Cassie had something besides food on her mind.

"So, Dad," Cassie said while slathering honey cream cheese on a walnut cranberry bagel, drawing the words out like she was broaching a delicate subject, "Are you a basketball coach, or something?"

She took a bite and gave herself a cream cheese mustache.

"I'm the varsity girl's basketball coach at the high school."

"Wow. I didn't even know you played basketball. You must have played to be the coach, right?"

It really hit me how little my daughter knew about me, since she didn't know how much basketball meant to me. "Not necessarily, but yeah, I played."

"Tell me about it?" she asked.

Sure, a nice, safe topic. Glad to.

"I made varsity as a freshman in high school because I was big. My specialties were defense and rebounding, not scoring, but it was enough to give us a winning record for the first time in 20 years. I had a certain zest for contact, as my coach used to say.

"After that year, my father sent me to camp at Mesa State where my shot came together."

She finished her bagel and asked for another.

"The next year we made it to the first round of the state playoffs and people started paying attention to me. When my father realized basketball could pay my way to college and he couldn't, he built a small court inside the barn. It was tough because practicing upset the horses, and the ceiling was too low for long shots. Still, it allowed me to practice when it would have been too cold and snowy outside."

"In the barn?" she asked, huffing a chortle.

"What's wrong with that?"

"Nothing," she said. "It's just...never mind."

"Our team took second place in the state tournament my junior and senior years—the only times Dolores High School had ever made the playoffs. And I got a full ride to Colorado State.

"In college, the coaches could never seem to figure out what to do with me. Not big enough to play post or quick enough for a guard, I became a utility player—getting my minutes when someone else was injured, sick or in foul trouble. When everything was going well, I sat on the bench. And things went real well my junior year."

She nodded, as if understanding the injustice of that situation, and finished off her second bagel.

"After that I lost my motivation and dropped out of college to join the Army, just in time to get sent to Vietnam just before the shit really hit the fan in 1975."

"You were in Vietnam? We studied that in American History."

"Well, yeah, military police. Some of the guys put up a basketball hoop by headquarters. We ringed the court with a four-feet-high wall of sandbags. It wasn't much help against snipers, but it would give us some protection against mortars and grenades unless it was a direct hit."

Her eyes were wide and her mouth, half full of chewed up bagel and cream cheese, was hanging open.

She swallowed hard. "They were, like, shooting at you?" she asked, incredulous.

"Cassie, it was a war. That's what happens in a war." She didn't need to hear about the time a sniper nailed the ball on my last-second three-point shot during a big game against the Marine embassy guards, because it turned out to be a Marine sniper, not VC.

"Playing basketball was the only time I wasn't scared to death in Vietnam. And I kept playing at the Y while I was a cop. When the high school girl's basketball coach quit to take another job just before school started two years ago, the school offered me the job."

"That's way cool, Dad" she said, "because I've got a basketball jones."

I choked on a sip of coffee and sprayed it across the table.

We walked through town to the high school and got there just before 1:30. Tresha, who had her mother's looks, with the widest smile west of the Mississippi and a halo of frizzy brown hair, and a body with her father's strength, was waiting in the parking lot.

Like me, Tresha, whose team nickname was Tree, had a zest for contact. She could mix it up with the boys—whom we scrimmaged for a while during the season until we started playing too well. Then they didn't want to play any more.

Her only problem was that she froze up on the free-throw line. Without somebody trying to take her head off, with nothing but blue sky between her and the basket, she could barely hit the backboard.

"Hey, stud," I said as she stopped dribbling. "This is my daughter Cassie. Cassie, this is Tresha—the star of our basketball team." Tresha smiled. Cassie nodded. It was a tense moment or so, but I got things moving by opening the door into the gym and turning on the lights. Both of the girls started shooting, at different baskets. I wondered if my daughter wasn't a little jealous.

Cassie dribbled the basketball between her legs, drove on the basket and shot a respectable pull-up jumper. It went through the hoop without hitting the rim. She did the same thing three or four times, missing only once. After grabbing the rebound, she dribbled away from the basket along the baseline, did a spin move, and went for the basket, hitting a short jumper off the glass.

Since Cassie seemed to be in her own world, we went to work on Tresha's free throws. She walked up to the line, checked her position, tucked her elbow in and shot, holding her follow-through. It was a good-looking shot but the ball hit the back of the rim and bounced out.

"Remember, start with your legs and finish with your wrist," I told her for the hundredth time. "And keep your elbow in."

She shot eight or nine more times and hit twice.

"Tresha, there's nothing wrong with your shot except you miss the basket. It's just lack of concentration."

"But I am concentrating," she said, frustrated.

Cassie had stopped and was standing at half court watching. She walked up and said, "Can I, like, make a suggestion?"

Tresha, nearly defeated, shrugged her shoulders and said, "Sure, I'll try anything."

"Just as you're starting your shooting motion, say to yourself, `down the middle, follow through.'"

"Down the middle, follow through?"

"Yeah. It's a basketball mantra. To help you focus and block out distractions. You could probably say something else if you wanted to."

"A mantra?"

"It's a meditation technique, you know?"

"Sure, I know all about manta rays. We studied them in biology," Tresha said, giggling. "Say, where y'all from, anyway?"

Cassie grinned and went along with the joke. She moved under the basket to rebound. Tresha's face was fixed in concentration. She swished the first shot and looked surprised. She almost made the next two.

"Look, don't, like, concentrate so hard. Let the words do their job." Tresha smiled, took a deep breath, let it out and nailed the next six shots. Both Cassie and Tresha were smiling now, and they became like a machine—shoot, rebound, pass back, shoot, rebound, pass back.

Tresha kept shooting and was hitting seven or eight out of ten shots consistently. I just sat on the bleachers and watched. When they took a break and walked over, Tresha was beaming.

"Where did you learn that?" I asked Cassie.

"Off a basketball video I bought."

"Oh," I said, glad that it wasn't another coach.

Cassie was going to be a sophomore, and visions of the state playoffs were dancing in my head. They got a drink and went back to the basket. Tresha posted up and Cassie shot little bounce passes into her. She'd do a drop step and shoot, or turn and face the basket going into a shot fake, cross-over dribble and pull up and swish a jump shot. Then, about every other pass she would kick back to Cassie, who would shoot a long jumper. Most of them went in. Finally they played one-on-one. If Tresha guarded Cassie too close outside, she'd fake and drive to the hoop. If she backed off, Cassie would shoot a straight jumper.

When Tresha got the ball, she'd use her dribble to back in to the basket and muscle up a shot. Before long they were "high-fiving" each other after good moves.

Watching this, I recalled something Henry Miller wrote about living on the beach at Big Sur; that there are a few moments in life that are so illuminating, so rewarding, that you can say, "It's okay to die now because, after this moment, I have lived."

It sounded good, but I wasn't quite there. What with people being murdered, bombs blowing up and a maniac possibly on my trail, danger was a little too real to be so philosophical about dying. So I sat back and watched two of my favorite people in the world becoming fast friends.

After a while, the play got sloppy. They were laughing all the time and talking about something besides basketball. I wasn't sure I wanted to know what it was.

"Hey, that's enough for today. Let's wrap it up."

They walked over.

"Can we do it again tomorrow?" Cassie wanted to know.

"Sure. I'll give you guys the keys and let you come over on your own. You'll have to stay out of trouble, though."

They looked at each other and smiled.

On the way back to the office, the realization that I should call Madeline nagged me. She'd probably be back by now, but the truth was I didn't want to talk to her. Nothing she could tell me would be better than things were now.

Harlan pulled up about that time and spared me from further procrastination. Roscoe was in the office, looking expectantly through the door.

"Cassie, would you go on inside and get Roscoe. Take him for a walk then put him in the car." For some reason, Roscoe was a perfect gentleman when he was in the Miner office, silently passing occasional gas his only social transgression. I think my big, tough dog was scared of Abigail.

"Sure, Dad." Twenty-four hours and we hadn't had our first argument yet. My success as a father was so far unblemished.

As I climbed in, Harlan said, "The FBI and a profiler from that Jewish Defense League were here." While he let this bit of news sink in, he pulled out a pinch of Copenhagen and put it under his lip. "Get this, Mrs. Glickstein wouldn't let the FBI look at their file. She brought it along and answered questions, though. The skinny is that they don't know much about the Agnews except that Wiley has been seen with a couple of these guys, and they don't know what this group is doing in Colorado. An informant in Idaho, who said the group packed it in up there a year ago and moved to here, has since disappeared.

"Special Agent Conroy said they were suspected of several murders, bank robberies and abortion-clinic bombings while they were in Idaho. Of all the hate groups in the country, these yahoos are about the worst, so he says. They believe in Armageddon and that they will be the only ones to survive. Conroy and Mrs. Glickstein agreed on that point. But there's never been enough evidence to charge anybody. She did offer to take some aerial photographs of the Agnews' mine claim."

"Aerial photographs? Who the hell are these people?"

"Special Agent Conroy told me afterwards Mrs. Glickstein's group is funded by the Israeli government, kind of a private intelligence agency."

"That sounds like some serious clout," I said.

"Bout as serious as gum disease," Harlan agreed, squirting a viscous brown torrent onto the curb.

"Anything else on Steph's murder? Things seem to have stalled, if you know what I mean." Then realizing we were withholding a possible lead, my righteous indignation leaked away.

"Don't get your bowels in an uproar, Aaron. We've got the FBI, the Jewish Defense League, the Sheriff and the Jack Springs' Marshal's office working on this. Not counting the ATF on this other deal. That's about as much scrutiny as the situation can stand. At least that's what Earl says. Me, I welcome all the help we can get. Besides, your problem is you put the hurt on them Agnew boys and now you're scared of the consequences. It don't have nothing to do with Stephanie's murder."

He was right. I was trying to build a federal case against the Agnews because I had been stupid and let them draw me into a fight.

"Oh hell, Harlan. I'm sorry. I've just got myself in a bind here."

"That's all right, Aaron. I understand. What to do about it is a bird of a different color."

A wisecrack about mixed metaphors was on the tip of my tongue but I squelched it. Instead, I told him about Tresha's freethrow shooting. Just talking about something normal calmed things down.

Harlan nodded, satisfied that at least one thing was going right. Over the course of the afternoon, the town had become eerily quiet. News of the bombing was having an effect. As we were returning, Harlan swung past the town hall where a number of news crews were setting up cameras. This time they left their tractor trailers behind, but that was little consolation to Harlan, who said, "Lordy, Lordy" mashing the accelerator and speeding away. His face was pale.

"My guess is they want to ask you about the possibility of war breaking out in the streets."

"They're gonna have to find me first," he said, as he pulled up in front of the Miner. I got out of his Jeep and went around to the parking lot. Harlan turned the corner and was gone.

Terri was standing next to a pile of sleeping bags, cooking gear and clothes, and I could feel another curve ball coming my way.

"Going camping?" Boy, that was brilliant.

She looked uncomfortable. "Oh," she said. "Yeah, the kids and I are going up to Lake Granby with a neighbor, Bill. He's our insurance agent," she added, as if that explanation cleared something up.

The news hit me like a jab to the gut. I stood there a few seconds and said, "An insurance agent?"

"Yes, Aaron, an insurance agent. Is something wrong with that?" Her tone of voice was shifting to annoyance.

"Wrong? Nothing's wrong. Insurance is good." I wheeled around and walked to the Subaru.

"Aaron? Aaron!" her voice was rising, but I didn't stop. I got in the car, started it and made a U-turn.

Roscoe had his head lodged between the seat backs, whining softly.

Cassie looked over at me, "What's wrong?"

"Nothing."

She kept her eyes on me a little longer then said, "You like her, don't you?"

Roscoe woofed.

"Great, I get to spend the evening with a couple of mind readers."

CHAPTER 14

On the drive home, Cassie seemed distracted, not even noticing the scenery that had been so interesting a day earlier. Soft breaths punctuated long periods of silence. After a few tense moments, she asked, "Dad, is it, like, you know, all right that I'm here?" The brave front she had shown so far was gone. She was like the little girl I found on the porch, the lost little bird sitting in her nest of worldly possessions.

"Cassie, since I left, there's been a part of me that's missing, a hole in my life that nothing else could fill, not drugs, not booze, not anybody else. Right now, that hole is all filled up."

My throat was tight and my heart heaved. I wanted to stop and grab her and pull her to me, to hold her so tight nothing would ever hurt her and she'd never go away. If only life were that simple.

She let out a long breath and put a hand up to her eyes, like she was shading them from the sun. But the sun was sitting above the mountains behind us. Then I saw a tear trickle down her face. Just one tiny, salty rivulet like the death throes of a desert stream. She dropped her hand and looked over at me. There wasn't any false bravery. Just a sense of vulnerability and a weak ray of hope.

"Dad, could we maybe go ahead and have that talk?"

"That's a good idea," I told her.

Roscoe sighed in the back seat like he'd been holding his breath. It was so dramatic we both laughed.

When we got to the cabin, I fixed a big bowl of dog chow for Roscoe and a couple of buffalo burgers for Cassie and me.

I turned on the radio, found a rock station and set the volume low so it provided some background music but didn't intrude. Roscoe left in a huff. He didn't like rock music. He was strictly a country-western fan. With country music playing, Roscoe would sleep with his head almost in the speaker. He liked Chris LeDoux and George Strait but seemed ambivalent about George Jones. He would often whine when the "Possum" sang. Of course, maybe he was trying to harmonize with Jones, who was something of a whiner himself. But rock drove him right out of the cabin.

Speaking of whiners, I reminded myself once again of my resolution to call Madeline. Tomorrow, I told myself. It's too late tonight. What is it, an hour later in Kansas City? Too late tonight for darn sure.

"So, who goes first?" I asked.

"You," Cassie said. "You're the dad."

"No, you go first. I'm the dad and I'm ordering you."

"Let's flip for it," Cassie said.

I shrugged, fished a quarter out of my pocket, flipped it and said, "Call it, Turkeybutt."

"Tails," she called. It was tails. "Turkeybutt?"

"That's what your little butt looked like then you were born. Bare and red and dimpled like the butt of a plucked turkey."

She rolled her eyes—the time-honed signal of teenage disdain. "That's so—" unable to complete the thought. "I'll go first if you promise to never, ever call me that in front of anyone."

"No way, going first is my penance for being crude."

"Dad," she stretched it out, like her patience with a senile parent was nearing an end.

"All right, all right. You first."

Any seriousness was by then nearly impossible. From the look on her face, I could see she was giving it a shot.

"My friend and I were arrested for being accessories to armed robbery," she said.

If I had been hit broadside by a Mack truck, I wouldn't have been any more shocked. She had to be kidding, so I decided not to rise to the bait.

"No wonder your mom was a little worried about her career, after something like that."

As it turned out, she wasn't pulling my leg, but it sounded a lot worse than it was. A couple of guys she and her friend had just met asked them if they wanted to smoke some dope. They said sure and the guys tried to rob the convenience store with a pellet gun to get the money. The old black guy working there kicked their butts and called the police, who rounded up Cassie and her friend sitting in the car around the corner. Cassie claimed they didn't know the guys were going to rob anybody, just assumed they were going to borrow some money from a friend. The guys backed them up and charges were dropped.

But Madeline had had enough.

Then it was my turn. But how do you explain the rationalization, the justification for the ultimate failure in life—walking away from one's child?

Rather than become swallowed up in a morass of an unanswerable question, I simply began talking. First things first; get the big one out of the way.

"Cassie, I'm sorry about not calling you at Christmas two years ago. I was dr—"

She looked surprised and then interrupted, "But Dad, we weren't even home that night. Mom had tickets to the Nutcracker and made me go with her. I tried to call you the next day, but you weren't home either."

Oh, Jesus, two years of torturing myself about something that never even happened. But any relief was short lived, because I never held up my end of the deal and then let my guilt interfere with straightening the situation out.

But she was here, now, that's what mattered. "I guess there's enough blame to go around," I said.

She was on the couch with her legs tucked under her, a blanket wrapped around her and then came up with what had likely been on her mind for four years.

"How come you and mom got divorced?"

"What has she told you?"

"Not very much. Just that your lives went, like, you know, separate ways."

It didn't sound like Madeline, who I figured had painted me as the bad guy.

"Your mother wanted me home at nights. But being a cop, even living and working in Fort Collins, didn't always allow me to do that. Then I got a better-paying job with the Denver police and it kept me away even more. After four years in patrol, they asked me to go undercover in narcotics. That was when things began to come apart."

Her forehead wrinkled, trying to understand.

"This is hard to explain to someone who hasn't been there, but the role consumed me. Nothing seemed as important as convincing the dealers, because, you see, I wasn't one of them. I was one of the good guys. But they say to be a good undercover cop, there has to be a criminal element to your personality. And there is to mine.

"In order to be successful, you have to take it right out to the edge. But in order to survive, you have to know when to pull back. It's a thin line and not always real clear.

"It was the most incredible high you can imagine. You've smoked dope, maybe done some other things, I don't care. But there's never been a drug more addicting than adrenaline. And probably never will." My blood pressure was shooting up just talking about it.

"Anyway, we were working for a big sweep, with suppliers and dealers all rolled up at once. Then one day, I recognized a guy I used to play basketball against. He was hanging out with some of the dealers we were working. My teammates had all been cops when I played against him. Our jerseys even had a picture of a pig on them so there was reason to be worried.

I should have told my supervisor. But we were close to bringing down the whole drug network, and they might have pulled me from the bust. But it kept preying on my mind. Your mom couldn't understand. There was no way anyone who hasn't done it could understand. So I started using a little speed to keep going. At first it got me charged up, but eventually, the fear and loneliness overwhelmed me and the speed made it worse. So I started using heroin."

Cassie's eyes widened in surprise. Whatever she thought, she didn't interrupt. But she got up and let Roscoe back inside.

"Going up and down like that fractures reality; you don't even know what's real and what's not. And you start making bad decisions.

"Then the guy I had seen with the dealers came by my apartment and tried to rob me. And that's when he remembered. He tried to kill me, but his gun jammed. Mine didn't. Another cop helped me dump the body in the rail yards because we knew reporting it would blow my cover and the bust. As it turned out, the guy was just a rip-off artist. At least nobody missed him or connected him to me."

Cassie shivered, her eyes probing mine.

"Maybe I shouldn't have told you that," I said.

She paused a moment, then shook off whatever she had been thinking. My heart nearly stopped. But she said, "If it was him or you, I'm glad it was him." Tears of relief were forming in the corners of my eyes. We sat in silence for a few more moments.

Roscoe had curled up near the door and fallen asleep. He must have been having a dream or a nightmare because he started whimpering and scratching the wall as if he were chasing a rabbit. Cassie had sunk deep into the sleeping bag and had her arms wrapped around herself.

"It was about then that your Mom told me she wanted a divorce. And I crossed over the line. A week later, the Lakewood Police found me sleeping in my car on West Colfax. My mind is a total blank for that period of time. But I had an arm full of needle tracks, four guns and a pile of money."

Cassie's eyes were staring off into space like she was trying to imagine what it had been like. Roscoe was awake, listening to something outside.

"There was this rehab program for cops. Things started to get a little better. But then the divorce papers and a restraining order arrived and everything went to hell. I walked into her lawyer's office and emptied a gun into the floor and wall behind his desk. And that was the end of everything. I lost my job and your mom divorced me. She got custody."

We seemed to have reached a space where things needed to end, at least for the night.

Cassie was fading fast. She had been yawning for the last few minutes. But Roscoe was wide awake, his ears erect. He let out a low growl. I don't like to let him out at such times. There's too much chance of a bear or a mountain lion being near. But I had heard an engine idling nearby a few minutes earlier. And Roscoe's bark does a great job keeping intruders away.

He continued to growl, then got up and walked to the door. The growl became more insistent, and dropped a register or two. Cassie sat up, her eyes big and fearful.

"Dad, what's wrong? Why is he doing that?"

"He heard something on the road. It's nothing serious. Roscoe is very protective of the cabin."

She looked into the darkness outside the windows. "Dad, he's scaring me. Shouldn't we do something?"

Roscoe pre-empted all discussion by charging through the door and disappearing into the night. Cassie started to sink back into the folds of the sleeping bag. Roscoe had been outside about fifteen seconds when his barking signaled he was ready to attack. Within a heartbeat, three gunshots split the night and Cassie bolted upright. "Was that—?"

"Yeah. Get on the floor."

I pulled her down and switched off the lights. In the dark, I reached up on the shelf and found my gun. It's hard to describe how comforting that little pound-and-a-half chunk of cold steel can be when you need it.

"Dad? Is Roscoe all right?" She started to cry.

"I don't know. But I can't leave you here to go look for him."

"But he might be hurt." Goddamn, this was killing me. I wanted to find him, but I couldn't take her and couldn't leave her. A car roared away.

Before the noise of the engine had receded, Roscoe was pawing madly at the door, almost taking it off the hinges. He was shaking as he crawled under my bed.

It was too quiet to be one of the Agnews' war wagons, I told myself. But was it? After a couple of minutes, I coaxed Roscoe out from under the bed and rubbed my hand over his fur, but he didn't seem to be bleeding. We huddled in the middle of the floor. Cassie started to say something, but I told her to stay quiet. We sat there that way for about five minutes before I got up and turned on the light. Roscoe was still shaking but he wasn't injured.

"Did somebody shoot at Roscoe, Dad? Why would they do that?" I wasn't ready to answer that question.

"People drive around out here and shoot off their guns, just for the hell of it. They like to shoot at signs and stuff like that."

She was startled when she saw the pistol lying on the floor next to us. Her eyes told me she didn't believe me. But it could have been the truth.

It didn't necessarily have anything to do with me. And they might not have been shooting at Roscoe.

"Then how did you get that gun so fast? I never even saw you get it."

"It was dark and the gun was right where I always keep it."

"Oh, God, I was so scared something had happened to Roscoe," she said.

"Me too. But he's all right. And we're all right. That's the main thing." I tousled her hair. "Right?"

"Right," she said, without much conviction.

"Try to get some sleep. Everything is fine now. It's been a long day."

And she tried, but her eyes followed me as I did the dishes and picked up around the cabin, the gun not far from my hand. Following a big yawn, she asked, "Dad, did you guys make the bust on those dealers?"

"I didn't, but yeah, we got them."

"But how did they do it without you?"

"Maybe I wasn't as important as I thought."

"You and Roscoe are that important to me," she said.

Bending over, I gave her a kiss on her forehead.

"Same here," I said, swallowing hard, tears coming to my eyes. I turned away and fooled with the dishes.

She yawned again and a few seconds later she was snoring softly. I turned off the lights and slipped outside to look around. There was nothing to see. But the gunshots still rang in my head. I couldn't stop thinking about the little furrow that creased the thick hair on Roscoe's neck—or how scary it was to care so much for another human being.

CHAPTER 15

As the new-morning sun first peeked over the mountain, the phone rang. Night chill was still settled in the cabin. On the second or third ring, I blinked open my eyes and saw small cumulus clouds skittering across the sky to the east. My head was still a little fuzzy as I kicked free of the blankets, stumbled across the room and grabbed the phone. Cassie mumbled but didn't awaken.

"Yeah?" I said, not too gently, knowing it could only be more bad news.

"Aaron? This is Harlan. Sorry to call ya' so early, but somebody broke into your office last night." A chill ran up my spine.

"Well, that proves your theory about the stepped up patrols. What was taken, can you tell?"

"Not really. Abigail is out of town and so is Terri. All of the computers are still there, all the stuff that someone would steal to sell for money. Things were pretty messed up, though. I was wondering maybe you could come in to take a look."

"Yeah, but it'll be a couple of hours. Is that soon enough?"

"Sure. If we figure out something is missing, I'll call Ray to print the place. It's probably a waste of time, but we'll do it if we need to."

"How did you find out the office had been broken into?"

"Billy Estill again, gettin' ready to open the feed store. He noticed the door was open and looked inside."

"Harlan? Somebody took a shot at Roscoe last night." He whistled a soft, descending note. "He's not hurt, though."

"Goddamn, I don't like it, not one little bit."

"It might not mean anything," I said, unconvinced.

"Yeah, maybe not," he said.

"Anyway, I'll see you in a couple of hours. Tell Tresha that she and Cassie can go up to the high school and shoot around when we get there."

"That'd be fine. It surely would," Harlan said. "Tresha hasn't stopped talking about that daughter of yours since she got home yesterday afternoon."

Roscoe was lying in the tall grass not far from the back door. He appeared to have recovered from the night before. I sat on the steps as the sun's rays dappled the meadow around the cabin.

The carpet of white, spring wildflowers had been swallowed up by lush mountain grasses dotted with blue spikes of penstemon and lupine. Honey bees, bumble bees and hummingbirds plied wildflower blooms for nectar. Birds with sharp wings carved the air.

A crow, sounding its raucous alarm, twisted and dove like an aerobat through the sky, harassed by a tiny bird. A towering anvil of cumulus clouds was already forming in the west.

The air was so sweet and clean it exploded in my lungs—a life-giving substance instead of life-robbing city air. The sun had chased away the chill and began to dry the tiny prisms of dew on the grasses.

Large ponderosas stood like sentinels scattered around the edge of the meadow, lending an air of serenity and security to my cabin, my land. But the security was an illusion. There was danger out there somewhere. I didn't know who or why or what. But it was unmistakable. Menace floated like the odor of an old carcass.

While Cassie stayed snuggled in her sleeping bag, I ran through the list of what had happened in the last week. It was like a lifetime of highs and lows all crunched into five days.

A few minutes later, Cassie got up, went outside and walked off toward the outhouse, another reminder of how different her life had become in the last week.

When she returned, she was hungry. "Dad? Could we have huevos rancheros for breakfast?"

Having no beans, eggs, or tortillas in the larder, I suggested shredded wheat. She shrugged and said sure. Roscoe was stretched out, sleeping in the grass, so I thought we'd have a little fun.

"Hey, you want to see something funny?"

She looked unsure but said, "Yeah, I guess so."

I got a blue metal bowl and spoon and walked to the back door. "Watch Roscoe's ears." I ran the spoon lightly across the bowl. Roscoe was dead to the world, but on the third or fourth time, his ear trembled. I waited a few seconds and did it again. This time his miserable excuse for an ear became erect for a few seconds, before it lay back against his head.

I pinged the bowl with the spoon. Both ears shot up and he lifted his head off the ground. Cassie was chuckling, trying not to give the trick away. She whispered, "Dad, that's mean. You shouldn't tease him."

Unable to determine if he had heard anything, Roscoe relaxed once more. But his ears stayed up. Then I sat the bowl on the floor with a thud and the spoon rattled against the metal.

Somehow, Roscoe had turned over and was up and running for the door. He bounded up the steps, stopped in the doorway and looked around. A string of drool hung from his mouth.

"Oh, yuk, that's so gross," Cassie said, erupting into giggles. "Why does he do that?"

"He likes to clean my cereal bowl. When I'm about done with it, he hears the spoon and knows it's time to come in."

Cassie looked like she might be ill. "You let him lick your dishes?"

"Well, yeah, but I boil the water when I wash them so it kills all the germs." One eyebrow hiked a fraction of a millimeter and she looked around like 'What have I got myself into here?'

"You boil the water, huh?"

"Yep."

"And that kills the germs?"

"Sure does."

"Well," she said, examining her bowl closely, letting the light reflect off the inside, before nodding.

If Roscoe was disappointed at being tricked, he didn't let on. After all, he realized it would be only a few minutes till he got his treat. And today it would be a double.

As I was cleaning up from breakfast, the phone rang again. Two calls in one morning. In other circumstances, I might have pulled a Hunter Thompson and blasted the goddamn thing to smithereens. But now there would be a teenager living in the house. Wood heat—no problem. An outhouse—no problem. No telephone—forget it.

Grabbing it off the wall, I growled, "What now?"

"Good morning to you too, Aaron. What are you doing today?" It was Earl.

"You mean besides trying to figure out what was stolen from the newspaper office last night?"

He didn't say anything for a few seconds. Ah, he didn't know about the break in. Cops take it as a personal affront when you know something about a crime they don't.

"I hadn't heard about that. We're pulling up the names, as best we can, on people in the anti-mine group and will be checking them over the weekend against criminal and military records. The ATF is giving us a little help in this endeavor. Speaking of which, the initial investigation seems to point toward C-4 explosives planted under the floor and remote detonation. It's military grade, the good stuff, and common as hell, unfortunately. Unless we get a break, this will be a tough one to crack, which, by the way, is about our only clue. Somebody who knew what they were doing sent that trailer to the great mobile home park in the sky."

"Just about what you figured."

"Yeah, for all the good it does us. Anyway, I'm going to be in that wacky little town of yours this morning. You ready to go fool a few trout?"

"Meet me at the Miner about noon. If we're done at the office, we could shoot over to South Creek."

"Sounds good. There's a big meeting at the town hall. The governor is sending some people from the Colorado Bureau of Investigation up. He's serious with this shit about sending the National Guard to keep an eye on things. But County Commissioner Davenport and the Sheriff Webb are going to try to keep them out of it. Their point is that it would just aggravate the situation, not to mention get national news coverage. They figure that possibility would cool the guv out. The last thing he wants is that kind of publicity. Of course, now that Gottlieb's trailer was bombed, Bartholomew, Brill and Fontaine are screaming bloody murder. I hope we can keep the guard out," he said and paused. "And I hope it's the right decision."

"Is Webb putting any pressure on you?"

"No, he's protecting me from it, for now," Earl said. "But it's there. All this crap about martial law—never mind. I'll see you at the Miner."

Earl McCormick was a tough guy to get to, but I could see it was happening. "By the way, there was somebody up here last night. They took a shot at my dog. It could just be a coincidence. This place is pretty secluded."

"You know what I think about coincidences," Earl said.

Cassie was in the meadow trying to get Roscoe to chase a stick, but he wasn't interested. She came inside and asked, "What were those phone calls about?"

Telling her might make her worry but not telling her could make it seem even more sinister than it probably was.

"Somebody broke into the office."

She turned her head and scrutinized me. "Does it have something to do with the murder?"

The question surprised me because we hadn't discussed Stephanie's murder, but Cassie had been in the office the day before with copies of the last two editions of the newspaper spread across every desk, even tacked to the wall. Of course she knew.

"I doubt it, but I don't know. It's possible nothing was taken."

"Maybe just some juvenile delinquents?"

"Yeah."

"You think it had anything to do with the gunshot last night?"

"It's possible, but it doesn't seem like it." I didn't want to tell her about the fight with the Agnews.

In case we made it to the creek, I wore khaki hiking shorts, a faded green polo pullover and some old running shoes for wading and stuck some jeans, a couple of clean shirts and a good pair of shorts in my athletic bag. Cassie put on purple bib overalls, a yellow tank top and multi-colored Converse sneakers

"I'm going to drop you off at the high school. You and Tresha can shoot around while I check out the office. After that, a friend and I are going fishing for a couple of hours. You can come along if you want."

"Can I decide later?" she asked.

"Sure."

I got down my fly rod and vest, slipped my pistol into the front pocket and headed down the hill. Roscoe was standing at attention, waiting for a signal. I nodded my head toward the car and he took off like a bat out of hell—a furry mass of quivering happiness.

Tresha was bouncing her basketball in the parking lot when I dropped Cassie off. They picked up like old friends and started chatting in conspiratorial tones, even though there was nobody for a hundred yards to overhear, as they disappeared inside the gym.

It was spooky how quiet the town had become. The stores and shops were all open, but there were very few people on the street. Cars would drive right through town. It was clear the news coverage, playing up he possibility of more violence, was having an effect.

Harlan and Earl were waiting for me. Earl was a big guy, taller and heavier than Harlan or me. He was clean shaven and had thinning black hair that he combed straight back. And he was incongruously decked out in a color coordinated fly-fishing outfit and a crushed felt hat that came off the shelf looking battered. Colorful flies were placed strategically around the hat band.

"Afternoon, Earl. Did you go to the meeting dressed in that spiffy outfit?"

"Yeah, I wore it to the meeting, figuring it would defuse some of the tension. We convinced them to back off for now, so it must have worked," he said.

"Maybe so. But you'll be lucky if the trout stop laughing long enough to swallow one of those flies," I taunted.

"This is the outfit of a serious trout fisherman, something I'm sure you wouldn't know anything about," casting an askew glance at my khaki shorts, scruffy shirt and old running shoes.

"We'll see how serious you are by the end of the day," I told him.

"Yeah, we'll see for sure," he said, tightly.

"Harlan," I nodded.

"You want to step inside and look around. See what's missing. Then you can get to giving those minnows a toothache."

Harlan was a bait fisherman. He'd never understood the attraction of fly fishing, and catch and release was something akin to the Red Menace to him. He liked to eat trout—especially big trout. He couldn't figure out why they were getting so hard to find.

"Sure," I said, following him inside.

There didn't seem to be any damage to the door frame. Who knew if the door was even locked last night, with everybody in such a big hurry to haul out of town?

Earl followed along, trying to be an innocent bystander but unable to suppress his curiosity. Things weren't as much of a mess as I thought they'd be. But papers were scattered around. It took about thirty seconds to realize what was missing—the court papers on the lawsuits against Canaus Minerals and Robert Gottlieb. My heart sank.

"Goddamn it," I said, slamming my fist on the desk. "They took the legal papers I got last week about Gottlieb's Canadian mines."

"Well, I'll be damned," said Harlan, shaking his head. "So it wasn't just kids. This is a horse of a different feather. Were they worth stealing?"

"Somebody must have thought so."

Earl was looking the room over, searching for something we had missed. But the only thing missing were the court papers.

"I practically told Gottlieb I had them and then left them on the desk. How stupid can one person be?"

Earl face was blank, which said everything it needed to.

"Oh, hell. Let's go fishing," I said.

CHAPTER 16

Earl smirked as we loaded my paltry collection of fishing gear into his new Ford Bronco. He looked less pleased when I opened the rear door and let Roscoe jump into the cargo space.

Not used to such utilitarian quarters, Roscoe lay down with a resigned sigh.

"I got to go see the girls. You mind if they come with us?"

Looking into the rear view mirror and seeing Roscoe's head peering over the seat back, Earl said, with a hint of resignation, "What the hell. The more the merrier."

Tresha and Cassie were just coming out of the gym doors as we pulled into the high school parking lot, heads together and laughing about something. They saw us and waved. Earl pulled up to them.

"You guys want to go fishing with us?"

"Will you take us by my house so we can get my gear?" Tresha asked, in a mild flirt.

"Sure," Earl said, smiling, his gruffness gone.

"Let's roll, Starsky," she said, giving Cassie a high five.

We picked up Tresha's gear and made the short drive south to Rowland, turning west on Tolland Road. We drove about two miles and parked at the first railroad crossing

The route is the main east-west rail corridor across Colorado and used by dozens of trains daily, which are ferried under the Continental

Divide by the Moffett Tunnel, emerging at the other end near Winter Park. Laid above the creek bed for the first twenty miles, the tracks then drop into the foothills and snake their way into west Denver.

It was a popular area and tended to be over-fished. The trick was to find an area that was farther from the road than the average redneck would carry a beer cooler.

We headed for a stretch about a mile up, where the stream veers away from the tracks and cuts through a narrow canyon. Roscoe followed, running down to the creek to give it a smell or to take a drink.

When we got there, Tresha wandered out into a wide spot in the stream well after it came out of the canyon. The banks were low and brush free. Cassie sat down on the stream bank and watched as Tresha began casting. Roscoe was hidden in the grass, watching the girls and waiting for a propitious moment to pull some of his hijinks.

I dropped down right at the mouth of the canyon and started working a seam that had been cut into the bedrock granite. Earl hiked up into the narrows of the small canyon, where the bigger fish lurked.

Sunlight danced across the crystalline, riffly water and illuminated pink stone and moss-covered pebbles in the stream bottom along slower stretches. An occasional gold aspen leaf floated by like a Lilliputian skiff.

The sun was high, warming the stream. A few caddis flies flitted above the surface, mimicking helicopter landings and takeoffs, so I tied on the old standby, a number eighteen elk-hair caddis and side cast up and across, letting the crumpled-looking fly drift down, stripping line to position it over the seam. As it passed, I let the line out so it floated freely in the current and hooked back toward me about twenty feet. Nothin' shaking on the first pass.

Following the fly downstream, I could see Cassie in the stream with her pants legs rolled up. Tresha stood behind her, guiding her as she false-cast and stretched out the line. Overhead, puffy white clouds floated lazily in the cobalt-blue sky.

If I'd been more interested in catching some big fish, I would have climbed up in the canyon with Earl, but staying close to Cassie was more important, to absorb as much of my daughter as possible, trying to make up for the years we had lost, not knowing when she'd be gone again.

In the tall grass, Roscoe was standing, alert for his chance.

I cast again upstream. As the fly drifted even with my spot, a flash of rainbow colors emerged from the shadows. Something wasn't quite right so it returned to its hideaway.

The little tan fly floated past and, just as it was making its sweep across, a hard tug jolted the line. At first the fish ran toward me, then to the opposite bank. As I started reeling in, the fish jumped and threw the fly. Ten inches or so. I lifted my line, false cast a couple of times to dry the fly and threw the line upstream once again.

A shriek from downstream caused my heart to freeze for a second until I saw the reason. Cassie had hooked a fish and Roscoe was barreling into the stream like a freight train, rooster tails of water erupting behind his feet. The girls were startled; neither had seen Roscoe in action before.

Cassie still had the fish on the line. But both girls were preoccupied with trying to dodge as Roscoe jumped and slashed and bit at the water in a hydrophobic frenzy . Cassie shrieked again from the shock of icy water as she slipped on the slick rocks and sat on her butt in the creek. Tresha had grabbed the rod, but both were laughing hysterically. Then the line went slack—a blessing under the circumstances. Roscoe walked regally out of the stream, shook the water out of his coat and curled up in the sun—his work done.

Holding the rod up, Tresha pulled Cassie to her feet and they walked to the bank, giggling and holding on to one another the way girls can still do.

In the canyon, Earl whooped and his rod bent double as a large fish fought the hated line. He worked the fish well, bringing it at last to his net, which he held high for me to see. I knew he was smiling.

By the end of the afternoon, Earl had hooked three more big fish. I had caught and released about a dozen medium-sized fish. The girls had given up fishing and sat in a sunny spot on the bank talking.

Everybody was dog tired when we were ready to head back. And speaking of dogs, Roscoe was damp and smelled like a dead fish.

"Oh, yuck," the girls said in unison.

The windows were down as we drove, allowing a breeze to carry some of the odor away. I caught Earl grumbling and sneaking looks into the mirror like he was trying to catch Roscoe further defiling the upholstery in his new Bronco. Fortunately, Roscoe, a highly intuitive animal, stayed out of sight.

As we pulled into town, Cassie asked me if she could spend the night with Tresha. The question made me wonder if I had done something wrong. But I was also relieved because there was no denying she could be in danger hanging around me.

"If Harlan and Hattie don't mind," I said.

"They won't," Tresha said, leaving me with the distinct impression this had all been worked out in advance.

When we stopped to let them out, I asked Cassie to hang around for a second.

"Did you have a good time today?" I asked, leaning against the fender while Earl tried to suppress yawns in the front seat.

"Dad, this was the best day of my life." She paused. "It's only been two days and this already feels like home. Can I stay? Please?"

She continued. "It's not about Mom. She's just…Mom. It was mostly my fault we didn't get along. But being here with you is, like, where I always should have been, you know?"

I wanted so much to share her certainty. It's easy when you're fifteen. Worse, it was out of my hands. I had been putting off the call because I was afraid to push things, afraid of the outcome.

"We'll call your mother and talk things over. You have to remember that if she wants you back, there isn't much I can do about it."

"I know," she said, sounding wise beyond her years.

Tresha called from the house, "Is everything all right?"

I waved and nodded, "Yeah, everything is fine." To Cassie, "Go ahead, I'll call you in the morning." She hugged me and went, almost skipping, up the walk.

Back in his Bronco, Earl and I went over the investigation, the burglary, and the bombing. We talked about the shots fired near my cabin the night before.

"For what it's worth, I agree with you. There's something off-kilter about this whole deal," he said. "But I can't put my finger on it. With most crimes, there's a logic, even if only to the perpetrator. On the face of it, there seem to be easy explanations for this stuff. But that's part of the problem. They are too easy. But then again, maybe I'm missing something."

I swallowed guiltily and looked out the window, thinking of Steph's travel plans.

"What's missing is the motive," I said. "That's the big gap in all of this. She just wasn't that much of a threat to the mine and neither is her group. But the bombing makes perfect sense if someone believes she was killed to stop her opposition to the mine."

"You still like Wiley for the murder, Sherlock?" he asked.

"It's not out of the question that somebody who isn't too bright took Al's line of bullshit about this "War on the West" seriously. You can't argue that Wiley fits that bill. You heard what he said about me ending up 'like your Jew-bitch friend?'"

"I heard. Right now that makes as much sense as anything else, I guess. We'll start Monday and interview everyone again," he said. "We missed a few people the first time, but we'll call them in, lean a little harder. I'm getting real tired of having to pussyfoot around the political sensitivities in this town."

Earl paused. "By the way, we got a hit on the background checks of Stephanie's group. A guy called Lazarus, an explosives expert and a tunnel rat in Vietnam, who lives in a ravine right off the canyon where the tailings pond would be built. He's also on the DEA's watch list but, as far as anyone can tell, he's been out of the business for a while. He may have had a grow operation up there a few years ago. Now he's got four young kids and keeps to himself. Our information is he helped finance the group with a little seed money, but he's never been to a meeting or a demonstration. Strictly low profile."

"Have you talked to him?"

"Yeah, he's coming in Monday for a chat."

"You're being kind of casual about it."

"If he's agreed to come in, I'm not going to go up and try to grab him out of the hills. Most of those people are armed to the teeth and don't like being hassled. Our patrol officers do not like taking down suspects in these remote areas. Way to many places for people to hide, and shoot if they're so inclined. Just mentioning we might have to make an arrest in the mountains gets their sphincters all twitchy."

Earl chuckled and said, "Let me give you an example but you got to keep this to yourself. We're talking death penalty here, if it gets around. Agreed?"

"Agreed." This was going to be good.

"A couple of our officers were investigating a break-in at an empty house over in Coal Creek one night. Some transient had been squatting in the place. It looked like he was long gone, but they found an empty .38 caliber cartridge box in the stuff he left behind."

A big smile split Earl's face.

"So they're walking to the car, hear a couple of gunshots and figure he's out there shooting at them. They call in that they are under fire, meanwhile they've hit the dirt, rolling around trying to figure out where the shots were coming from.

"So we set up a road block, and send in the SWAT team, and these guys are shittin' kittens too—they can't see a goddamn thing because we forgot the night-vision goggles. Anyway, nobody's shooting when they got there, and no sign anybody had been—no bullet holes, no cartridges, nothing.

"When we got them out of there, they had dried pine needles, twigs, leaves, in their hair, down their necks, between their teeth, places you wouldn't think possible. We're taking down the roadblock when this old fart in a beat-up truck drives up and asks what all the ruckus is about. It turned out he lives in a shack up the mountain from where our officers were 'pinned down.'"

Earl had a merry gleam in his eye, his body shook with silent laughter. He placed his hand on his forehead, massaged his temples, then shook it off and continued.

"So we ask him if he heard any shooting. He says, 'Well, I fired a couple of .22 rounds off into the ground trying to keep that gol darn raccoon out of the chicken coop. But that's all.'"

"'About what time did you do this, sir?' we asked him. And he said, 'Oh, a couple of hours ago, I reckon.' And that right there is why we don't go after people up here without a good reason. If those guys last in the job, that story'll be on 'em like the mark of Cain. Course, you'd know that," he said with a wicked smile.

"Go fuck yourself, Earl."

He ignored me. "Besides, if Lazarus skips, then we've got a suspect."

"What do you think?"

"On paper, sure, he looks good for the explosion at the trailer," Earl said.

"But?"

"He's too obvious. Besides, he's had the place up for sale for a couple of years because of the kids. And the Realtor said it isn't worth much now, even without the mine going in. And Aaron—"

"Yeah, yeah, I know. It's all off the record."

CHAPTER 17

With two hours of daylight left, it was too early to go home, and a hot shower was waiting for me at the gym. Roscoe's fish-stink had diminished to a bearable level. He was sacked out in the car so I parked in some shade, left the windows down and headed for the club. Toby Echoheart was just going inside when I got there.

Since I smelled of fish and sweat, I decided to take a shower before working out. Reveling in the hot water, I debated whether the technological revolution reached its apex with the creation of the hot shower or the whiskey still. And I couldn't decide. My grandfather thought it was when they put stickum on cigarette papers. There was a large streak of the philosopher running through my family tree.

I dried off, dressed in shorts, a T-shirt and clean running shoes and headed for a *Stairmaster*. The action in the gym was about normal; it would obviously take more than a threat of war in the streets to scare off the endorphin junkies.

The prime spots in the workout room were the Stairmasters in the back row. From there you could check out any women in the gym, especially the ones on Stairmasters in the front row. It made the workouts go a lot easier and took my mind away from the tedium and pain.

Toby was already on one and the machine next to him was vacant. Just as I climbed on, a gaggle of Lycra-clad, leggy young women rushed the room. Toby and I looked at each other and considered high fiving.

But that would have been too obvious. Cool was the thing in the work-out room. Toby flexed his well-cut muscles, covered only by a sleeveless wide-mesh shirt, a time or two for their benefit, and a couple rewarded him with demure smiles. If I would have flexed my muscles, nobody would have seen them under the layer of fat. So who said life is fair?

About three minutes in to level five on the Blast Off program, a stone fox came in. Something about the way she moved caught my eye before I had even really looked at her. Our eyes met briefly, and then we looked away. But I continued to watch her on the sly. She seemed familiar.

She was wearing a baggy gray T-shirt, cut off high enough to show a nice tight belly and quick glimpses of a lacy black jog bra when she leaned forward, and loose gray running shorts. Her hair was black, streaked with gray, and twisted into a fat braid that fell almost half way down her back.

She had that coltish look of a young girl whose body stretches out before it has a chance to fill in, but she was no filly. Her complexion was ruddy with too much sun over too many years, but it was more of a healthy glow than weathered. And the tan was uneven, darker on her face and arms and stomach, less on her legs. Her hands were thin, fingers long and slender but not quite delicate. Her eyes were deep brown.

I watched her, mesmerized by the unselfconscious way she carried herself, all grace and poise, like someone comfortable using her body—such a difference from Terri. This woman wasn't worried about surprises. Bring 'em on, her body said. Using an old weight-room trick, I watched her in the mirrors. But she was so absorbed in her workout, I was sure she never caught me at it. Sweat was streaming down my chin as the Stairmaster hit the top level near the end of the 30-minute workout.

She gathered her bags, put a towel around her neck and stepped toward the doorway leading out of the weight room. Just then, the Stairmaster hit cool down, the pedal resistance stiffened, and I almost

vaulted over the front of the machine before grabbing the handrail. As I
flailed for balance, she turned her head over her shoulder and looked
right at me, as if she just discovered my presence in the universe.

The hint of a smile worked the corner of her mouth, she tossed her
head to get a thick strand of hair out of her eyes and walked out. Her
move hit me like a stun gun.

Toby whispered, leaning closer. "Earth to A-Ron, Earth to A-Ron.
Come in A-Ron."

"Huh?"

"Man, you better come back down. You were out there for awhile."

"Uh, yeah. Who was that woman who just walked out? "

"You mean that older babe you were drooling over for the last thirty
minutes?"

"I wasn't drooling." My hand took a reflexive swipe at my chin, anyway.

"Ha!" he said.

"Come on, Tobe. Who the hell is she?"

"That's Gary Fontaine's big sister," he said, laughing.

"You got to be shitting me."

"No, I'm not shitting you, man. She's a widow. Got a ranch up near
Jade River, Wyoming, as I understand it. Down here visiting her little
brother. Life must be tough up there if visiting that little weasel is a
vacation."

Oh, great, smitten with the sister of the human being I despised
most. It never occurred to me that any of his family walked upright
instead of slithered around under rocks and got run over while warming themselves on the highway.

As we toweled off, Toby asked, "You hear what happened to your
buddy Gary today?"

"No, why don't you tell me," I said, relishing any misfortune visited
upon the self-important town manager.

"He was driving down the canyon trimming nose hairs in the mirror
when somebody tagged him from behind. Drove those little scissors

right through his nose. He had them removed at the hospital emergency room," he chuckled.

Perfect, just perfect, I thought and resigned myself to another lost cause. As if reading my mood, Toby's expression became serious.

"Say, Aaron, what you asked me about that dream?" He leaned toward me so he could speak without being overheard. His voice had lost its lightness.

"Yeah," I said, taken aback by the change in his demeanor. Toby appeared to be choosing his words carefully.

"This is just something I remember hearing as a child," he said. "Don't know how much you should pay attention to it. I'm just passing this on. You understand?"

"Sure. Tobe. Sure," I said, but my heartbeat was speeding up.

"The old people on the Res say an animal coming to you in a dream can mean something. It doesn't have to but it can. You dig?"

"I guess."

"It can be good, or it can be bad," he said, gazing in my eyes for a hint of comprehension. "Or it can be both."

In the craziness of the past week, the whole deal with the mountain lion had become a vague memory. Now it was back. "But, I don't—"

He raised a palm. "Look, I told you, okay?"

"Thanks, Tobe." There seemed to be more to it, but I shrugged and put it out of my mind.

Taking another shower to wash off the sweat, I pondered lost opportunities and realized my life story was full of them. Yet, when I walked out she was leaning against the wall. Her hair was damp and her face was scrubbed to a dusky glow, She wore tight jeans, a denim shirt with the tails tied up in front, revealing her belly button, and beaded moccasins. Should I say something? Could I, with my heart crawling up my throat? She saved me the trouble.

"You don't look nearly so dangerous without all that blood on your shirt," she said, smiling. Her voice was low and rough, like it had been damaged by bad whiskey and cheap tobacco, or maybe trail dust. Then it hit me; she was the mysterious cowgirl in the Jackass Inn. For some reason, that gave me courage.

"I don't know about dangerous. Thinking back on it, I must have looked pretty dumb."

"Well then, dangerous and dumb. It sounds like a bad combination," she said.

"So I'm finding out."

"You want to go someplace for a beer or three?"

This was not happening—not to me. But a baby rattlesnake had crawled into the area below my belt and buzzed like it was lying on a hot rock. A twinge of guilt was slithering around somewhere in the back of my mind. But Terri was off camping with Bob or Bill the insurance agent, doing God knows what.

I squished it like a slug on the sidewalk. Then another thought intruded.

"You're Gary's sister?"

"So I've been told."

"Gary and I aren't the best of friends, to put it mildly. I wouldn't want to cause you any trouble."

"He's my half brother, but I can't help thinking he must have been adopted. So don't worry about it."

The rattlesnake was crawling up my spine on the way to my brain. That solved, there was only one way I could answer.

"Sure. Let's get a beer."

"By the way," she said, holding out her hand, eyes twinkling, "My name's Emma, Emma Sodenberg."

"I'm Aaron Hemingway. Nice to meet you." We shook hands.

Roscoe was still asleep in the car. Since it was only a short way to the Jack Ass, we decided to walk. Evening was coming on and it was still warm. We made small talk about working out and I had to stop myself from grabbing her hand like some elementary school kid as we walked.

It was early, so the bar was still quiet. We sat in the booth nearest the back—the same booth she had sat in while she watched me get shit-faced five days earlier.

Seeing us together, Alvie actually came to the table to take our order. Normally he'd just lean across the bar and shout, "What'll it be, Pilgrim?"

"Evenin' Emma," he said and nodded to me, "Scribe."

"Lone Star, no glass," Emma said. The Jack Ass was one of the few local places that stocked Lone Star beer. I had never tried it, but this was no time to be cautious. "The same."

"Two locos, coming up," he said and lumbered back to the bar.

"Did he say 'locos?'"

"Lone Star has an unsettling effect on some folks," she explained.

Aha. Unsettling. I'd let that pony ride for a spell, sitting across from this beautiful woman.

She got an amused look in her eye. "So, Scribe, you got a girlfriend?" My composure fled. "No…not really," I stammered. "No, definitely not."

"Well, do ya' or don't ya'?" Her dark eyes were laughing.

Finally, joining in the joke, I said, "Only in my mind. Not in hers."

"Sort of a lusting-in-your-heart kinda thing?"

"Lust is too strong a word. It's more of a little mind game to occupy some idle moments."

"I see," she said, nodding but not taking her eyes away from mine.

"Are you always so…right to the point?"

"I like to know what's what," as if that should explain it.

"OK, my turn. How about you?"

Her eyes got a little cloudy while she considered. "Nope, no husband, no boyfriends, no lovers, just a lot of suitors. Can't tell if it's me they want or the ranch," she said in a way that made it seem it didn't much matter which.

After what appeared to be a very sultry start to the evening, we talked about our kids, her ranch, her husband's death, my job. She seemed to need someone to talk to. She could have picked anyone, but she picked me.

Thoughts of Terri kept worming their way into my brain, but it was kind of ridiculous. Since our initial affair, our relationship had changed very little. And there were no indications it would in the near future. Talking to Emma made me realize a romantic interest in Terri was a way of keeping that part of my life alive. I did care about Terri. But without some encouragement, it seemed pointless beyond giving me an excuse not to get involved with anyone else.

Not that I needed one. After my marriage fell apart, I didn't have the guts to try it again. But here I was, right in the thick of it. And it felt pretty damn nice.

After about an hour, the Jackass Inn was getting crowded, and as hard as I tried, I couldn't suppress a yawn. Some scruffy-looking guys started hauling musical equipment past our booth. Stenciled on the drum case was "Levi Strange and the DeRanged." We looked across the table at each other and knew it was time to go.

She leaned over the table, grabbed my hands, and said, "Listen, Aaron, let's call it an evening, shall we? I'm pretty tired, too. Maybe we could get together tomorrow night."

"I'd like that." We went outside and stood together on the wooden sidewalk in front of the bar. As she was turning to leave, she hesitated. Our bodies came together and we kissed, not a passionate kiss or a polite kiss, but something in between; a kiss of promise. I stood there and watched her walk up the street, get into a big pickup truck, roar the engine and drive away.

Roscoe was still passed out in the back seat of my car. A hard day rescuing damsels in distress will do that to you. I stopped at the liquor store, bought a quart of Evan Williams to celebrate and drove home.

Another drink or three sent me tumbling into a troubled dream about Emma. She had blazing green eyes like the mountain lion. I tried to kiss her, only to find it was her brother in my arms. I awoke in a cold sweat, then, and realized that although Emma had suggested getting together tomorrow, we hadn't talked about how that was going to happen.

CHAPTER 18

Sunlight suffused the weak haze that clung to the ground the next morning, giving the world a soft glow. Despite the previous night's drinks, I didn't feel too bad. The nightmare of almost kissing Gary Fontaine had likely scared all the alcohol out of my system. In fact, my body hummed with a strange energy.

In deference to potential hangover, going for a hike sounded better than a run. I got my shorts and a sweatshirt on, laced up my hiking boots and trudged up Forsaken Rock—one of the towers behind the cabin. Roscoe followed but lagged behind, ambushed by the cornucopia of lingering scents on the mountain. Even hiking, my legs were burning and my lungs were burning, but then the endorphins cleared the lingering haze from my brain, and I caught my second wind. Near the top, I looked down and saw Roscoe burst through a clump of quivering young aspens. A six-point buck thundered out the other side.

Roscoe was no match for the buck's speed and lost interest as soon as the deer was out of sight. Those chow legs aren't much good for anything more than a short burst of speed. It was just a game; make the big animal run away. He scurried around with his nose to the ground. As I reached the base of the uplifted slab, the haze had thinned and the sun was shining through like a burnished gold coin.

Skirting the base of the rock, I looked down on a flat area bordered by berry bushes and mountain maple. A pile of trash had accumulated on the ground, and a narrow gap had been torn in the foliage.

A jolt of adrenaline hit me. I climbed down and kicked around at the trash—cigarette butts, junk-food wrappers and a Pepsi can. Someone had spent some time up here. From the gap in the brush, my cabin was in plain view.

Transients often set up camp in the mountains and go into Boulder or even Jack Springs to panhandle during the day. But this was too far from the town for that explanation and too isolated for someone to have just stumbled on it.

The cigarette butts were stale, the can was dry. A line of tiny red ants was carrying off the sugar bounty. How long the trash had been there was anybody's guess.

Roscoe came up, panting hard. He stopped, sniffed and started growling. That was good enough for me. Maybe I was being paranoid, but my gut instinct told me I had stumbled onto what could very easily be a sniper's nest. Grabbing the can in a cellophane tuna sandwich wrapper, I headed down the hill.

"Come on, Roscoe," I said, slapping my leg. We got to the house in record time. I took a large drink of water, brought the gun down from its hiding place and sat it on the counter. Then I filled a large bowl with shredded wheat, poured milk on it and ate it. I made a cup of black tea with milk and lots of sugar and sat down to read James Crumley's novel, "The Last Good Kiss."

C.W. Sughrue was drinking beer with an alcoholic bulldog named Fireball Roberts, who served double duty as the bar mascot and bouncer. My mind wandered to the rendezvous with Emma. The thought of talking to Gary Fontaine soured me on calling his house looking for her. I didn't want to talk to him, to be reminded he was related to Emma. And I didn't want him to know of my interest in his sister.

So, as was often the case, I did nothing.

About 10:30, the phone rang. On quiet mornings, the phone's ring came as a shock. Lately, it was beginning to sound like a fire alarm. It was Earl, and I could tell from his voice it was more bad news.

"Somebody tried to run Terri and her kids off the road in Boulder Canyon last night," he said. Before the full impact sunk in, he added, "She's all right but it was a close one. Somebody hit her from behind right below the narrows. Lucky they all had their seat belts on and she managed to steer into a pull-off that ran right down to the creek. Another fifty feet and there would have been a twenty-foot drop into the creek."

I let out a heavy groan and slammed my fist into the wall. This whole fucking thing had gotten too personal. People I cared about were in danger and that sparked a bad instinct in me. It was called kill first and ask questions later. But who to kill?

"Did she get a look at the vehicle?" I asked.

"No, not really. She said it was big. It came up behind her with the lights off. But from the damage to her car, it appears it was a pickup with some kind of protection over the front end, like those brush catchers they're putting on the fancy four-wheel drives, or an old work truck with a heavy bumper and a grill protector."

Like a miner's pickup truck, Earl didn't have to add.

"Say, Earl, there's something you ought to know," I said, realizing my fears had almost come true.

"You mean about Stephanie Goldman's plan to go to Mazatlan? Terri already told me. And I got to tell you, Aaron, it pisses me off that you withheld potential evidence in a murder investigation. That just might have gotten Terri and her kids killed."

He was right, and I tried to explain the thinking that had gone into the decision but he wasn't buying it.

"The bottom line is that you had no business doing it and, well, you know the rest," Earl said. I judiciously declined to point out that if the cops had been doing their job, Terri would never have found that travel brochure, though it was tempting.

"Anything else I should know about?"

"No, nothing I can think of. Terri finding that travel brochure was the only thing we hadn't reported. And I still don't know if anything in those papers was enough to provoke any retaliation. Now I probably never will," I said, cursing my stupidity. "You know, if we're wrong and the answer to all these crimes are just the obvious ones, things could get real hot before it's over."

"Yeah, well, one thing at a time," Earl said. I started to dial Terri's number when the phone rang again.

"Aaron, this is Terri," she said, her voice brittle like the crust covering a volcanic cauldron. Before I could ask if she was all right, she said, "I've got Gottlieb's court file. I made a copy and took it with me to Grand Lake."

"Good. One of us was thinking, anyway."

"Yes, well—"

"Did you tell Earl you had them?"

"No, I didn't."

"Why not?"

"Because I'm fucking angry that somebody tried to kill me and the kids. It could have something to do with the story on Stephanie's murder, or the mine, or something. If it does, I'll be goddamned if I'm going to let them chase me off the story," she said.

Whew, in the two years I'd known her, she had never said anything more vulgar than golly gee or gosh darn it! This was a new side of Terri Smith. It made me wonder how much we ever know about someone else. So much is tied to circumstance. But still, it worried me.

"I don't mean to be—"

"Patronizing?" she chimed in.

"Well, maybe, but have you considered the possibility that you could still be in danger?"

"Yes, I've considered it. The kids are going to stay with mom and dad for a while," she said, "and I'll have some personal protection."

An image of mild-mannered reporter Terri Smith packing an Uzi flashed through my brain, giving me a chill and making me want to laugh at the same time. "Terri, what the hell are you talking about, personal protection?"

"You'll see tomorrow," she said and hung up.

Since I was already holding the phone, I called Harlan at home.

"Hello?" It was Hattie.

"Hattie, this is Aaron. Is Harlan around?"

"He and the girls are out in the driveway shooting baskets," she said.

"Would you tell Cassie to meet me at the Miner in a couple of hours."

"All right, Aaron, I'll tell her. You're welcome to come over for dinner if you'd like."

"Let me see what's going on at the paper first. I'll call you from there, if that's okay."

"That would be fine, Aaron."

There wasn't much to do at the Miner, but I wanted to get away from the cabin. Somehow, the place felt violated by whomever had shot at Roscoe and whomever was sitting up on the hill watching—if that's what they were doing. I would have liked to believe that they were just coincidences but, like Earl, that explanation didn't do much for me. If it was Wiley, and if he had killed Steph, why would he be after Terri? I hoped something would break in the next couple of days to provide some answers.

In the meantime, I decided to take Roscoe to town, worried the next bullet would be better aimed. It was still hazy but the haze was like a worn sheet now. It was warming up so I put on some Levis, a work shirt and cowboy boots for Sunday dinner and slipped my gun into a work-out bag before heading down to the car.

Roscoe wasn't around so I went into town alone, unable to shake the cold hand of dread squeezing its icy fingers around my heart.

Trying to break the mood, I turned on the radio in time to hear Garth Brooks sing the haunting first verse to "*The Dance.*"

The song, one of the most beautiful, bitter-sweet ballads ever recorded, always put a big lump in my throat because it reminded me of a cop who had died in a shootout with a man who was going to kill his girlfriend. With her dying breath, she had put a 9mm slug into his chest, and he died crawling to her door with the gun in his hand.

Her cop-fiancee asked that "The Dance" be played at the funeral. From the third line on, there wasn't a dry eye behind the two-thousand pairs of sunglasses in the place. By the second verse, many were openly weeping, including a lot of big, tough cops.

And that's what the song is about—heart-shattering loss.

I turned off the radio.

Late Sunday morning isn't a good time to go to Bob's Bakery if you want to grab a quick donut and coffee or to casually read the newspapers because all the churchgoers drop in on their way home.

But it had become my ritual too. The tables, as expected, were all filled, but George Gunther had one to himself and he invited me to join him. Gunther never inspired strong feelings in me—one way or the other. He carried himself with a military bearing, which made more sense after learning he had been the town marshal at one time, but not a lot more after all this time. Maybe Gunther was just one of those people who carried himself like he had a broomstick up his ass from the cradle. But he opposed the Dark Angel mine, a tough call for a politician in Jack Springs, and earned my respect, so I sat down.

His thick black hair was turning gray; dark circles under his eyes and a day-old beard gave his face an ashen, haggard look. His hand trembled as he lifted his coffee cup.

"How's it going?" I asked

He looked like he was going to come back with "Fine," but his eyes took on a shade of bitterness and he said, "Things aren't good on the home front."

Flashing back to my past home-front problems, I must have looked sympathetic, so he continued. "Julie Ann has gone to stay with her parents for a while. We'd argued quite a bit before she left because she thought I was losing my drive to get elected county commissioner. She's pretty ambitious—for me I mean."

Julie Ann was George's young wife, about half his age. They had been married a year. The talk around town had her a gold digger, but the only gold George was going to come up with was political gold, so I suspected he was right. I wasn't going to say any of this, but George, his face darkening, was obviously ready to get something off his chest.

"My business has been hurt by my lack of support for the mine, and the start-up campaign expenses are high. But the enviros have been coughing up some bucks. If I can win this primary election, maybe she'll come back."

This was tough to listen to. My own problems were as much as I could handle. And it must have showed because George gave a quick shake of his head as if he were flinging away the troubling thoughts and suddenly pulled back into himself.

"I'm sure it'll work out," I said. The silence was tense. "So Harlan tells me you've been around here for quite a while."

"About 30 years, give or take a year," he said, caution steeling his voice.

"What do you think about Wiley? Would he try anything to get back at me after the fight we had?"

George grimaced and sucked air through his clinched teeth. "I don't know what to tell you about Wiley. I was around here when his daddy died in that awful accident. And even if those boys never released the brake on that 'dozer, there's no way in hell they didn't hear him screaming. It's enough to frost your balls, thinking they could be that cold blooded. He must of abused those boys something awful to make them hate him that much. There must of been something else rotten in that family, but I'll be goddamned if I could tell you what it was. They were a closed bunch before the old man was killed, and they've stayed that way since."

"What about this militia stuff? Do you think he could be involved in that?"

"He would be a prime candidate for that bunch. Whether he's in or not, I don't know," he said. "I used to rent the old man equipment, but I haven't been up there or had hardly any contact with them since he died. I just hear the same rumors everybody else does."

"What rumors?"

"Nothing you haven't heard, I'm sure," he said, looking at his pocket watch. "Got to go to work. Can't afford a day off with a campaign to run."

Before he could escape, I grabbed his arm and pulled him down a little so I could whisper the next question. "Can you think of any reason he would have killed Stephanie Goldman?"

"I don't think Wiley would need a reason, at least what we think of reason," he said. At the door, he stopped, turned and stepped back to the table.

"That stuff about Julie Ann and me, that's just between us. I had no business talking about it." Pain had returned to his eyes and tremors shook his hand.

"Just between you and me, George."

He nodded and left, the screen door slamming in his wake.

At the Miner office, there was a note tacked to the door with my name on it.

"Aaron, something came up at the ranch and I had to get back. Sorry. I'll be in touch. Emma." She'll be in touch. Yeah, right. I wadded the note up and started to throw it into the yard. Rather than litter, I decided to

throw it in a trash can inside. Instead, I opened it up, folded it in a neat square and put it in my top drawer.

I sorted and stacked papers that had been thrown around in the burglary, glancing at the Sunday papers but not reading much. Mostly I looked out the window at the mountains. I felt violated, cheated.

The depression lifted when Cassie walked up the street with…well…an alien life form badly disguised as a teenage boy. I went outside to meet them and got the first inkling of the father of a teenage daughter's worst nightmare—a boyfriend who looks like an extra in the cast of *Blade Runner*.

This guy had the hair shaved off one side of his head, but stubble had grown in. The hair on the other side was purple and woven—if that's the right word—into dreadlocks, a ring through his nose and another through his lip with a corroded copper chain connecting them. But no earrings; earrings were passe, I guessed. His skin was pale, his face dimpled by acne. Baggy green shorts revealed the crack in his ass and hung to below his knees. His shins were scraped. He had a pink and brown T-shirt with the sleeves cut out almost down to his waist. The shirt said, "Butt Trumpet World Tour." He was carrying a skateboard that was nicked and cracked and covered with scrawled writing in Day-Glo colors.

Cassie was smiling. "Hi, Dad. This is Moonstone. He's from California." Well, that was a relief; he wasn't from the Andromeda galaxy, come to spread a plague on the planet.

Buck up, I told myself. Be tolerant. He's just another kid. Yeah, sure. He stuck out his hand, and I inspected it for open sores and vermin. There were none obvious so I shook it, but not before noticing his fingernails were chewed down to the quick.

"Nice to meet you, sir?" he said, unfailingly polite but making it sound like a question. Cassie looked chagrined.

"So, where did you two meet?" I asked Moonstone.

"In the supermarket parking lot?" he answered, causing my jaw to clinch and my teeth to grind.

"Huh?"

Cassie turned away and began studying the front door.

"So, when did you two meet?"

"Just now?" Moonstone replied.

"That's what I want to know. When?"

"Huh?" he said, frowning at the confusion of it all.

Cassie turned back and said, "It was nice meeting you, Moon. But I've got to talk to my Dad about something. I'll see you around." Moon? Already using his nickname. Not a good sign.

He took the hint, fortunately, because I was getting ready to break his scrawny, dirty neck right there on the porch—maybe even twist his head off like a chicken headed for the Sunday stew pot. No offense to chicken.

"Bye?" he said, and sulked away with his mangled skateboard under his arm, joining the faceless ranks of rejected suitors down through time.

Cassie said, with a hint of mischief in her eye, "Dad, can I, like, have the money to go to basketball camp at the university with Tresha? It starts tomorrow and costs two-hundred dollars." She looked all serious.

I started laughing and laughed until tears were running down my face and I had to sit down on the steps. Finally, Cassie joined me.

"I guess that would be, like, a good idea?" Up the street. Moon had slouched almost out of sight.

"I guess it, like, would?" she said, and we laughed some more.

I felt pretty good about the way things had worked out and wondered if she had set me up or she had just capitalized on the situation? It didn't make much difference. Anything that made me laugh these days was worth some money. And money wasn't a problem. That's one of the advantages of living simply. Low overhead. And it served plan B very well; get Cassie out of harm's way.

My mood had improved enough so that dinner at Harlan and Hattie's sounded good.

CHAPTER 19

Despite haranguing Harlan about his diet, Hattie had fixed an all-American Sunday dinner. There was pot roast surrounded by potatoes, carrots and onions, a big green salad, home-made bread and the smell of an apple pie baking in the oven. Maybe Sunday was Harlan's reward for watching his diet.

Hattie was still a lean woman and she stayed that way by walking several miles a day, usually early in the morning when traffic was light. She also did a little gardening in the short mountain growing season. Their white clapboard house, sporting a new covering of white, never-needs-painting vinyl siding, was surrounded by flowers. There were also flower boxes on the porch and around the kitchen windows. A big poplar tree shaded the front yard. Visiting the Silbaugh home was like stepping through the looking glass into a Norman Rockwell painting.

The girls were on the couch, playing some kind of computer game in which a karate guy demolished villains right and left with his kicks. When he connected, the villains disappeared in a puff of smoke. And when things got too hairy, the good guy would somersault about fifteen feet in the air and come down out of harm's way—for a few seconds anyway. The guy would have been one hell of a rebounder.

My mood brightened considerably at the normalcy of sitting down to a Sunday dinner with good friends. The food was good and the conversation was relaxed, at least until Hattie made the off-hand observation that I was getting a little scruffy looking. Her remark made me think back to Wiley calling me a hippie, and my face must have registered some sign of discomfort because Hattie quickly added, "I just mean the hair, Aaron. A little trim would do you up fine."

Harlan became absorbed in dicing up a thick slice of roast into tiny pieces, but the girls looked at each and giggled.

"Oh, dear," Hattie said, blushing, her fingers loosely across her mouth.

The situation was getting out of hand. "You're, right, Hattie. Someone even called me a hippie a few days ago. I've been too busy to get into the barbershop in Boulder."

Somewhat mollified by my agreeing with her, she said, "Lila June is keeping her shop open on Sunday afternoons. I'll bet she'd be glad to do it. I know she needs the business, what with her becoming a foster Mom, and all."

"That sounds like a good idea. Maybe I'll get a buzz cut or even have my head shaved."

Tresha and Cassie both snapped their eyes to me, mild alarm on their faces. Hattie looked horrified, but Harlan, who knew me best, just smiled.

"Just kidding," I said. "But who knows, maybe I'd look good with a shaved head." From the way Cassie and Tresha rolled their eyes, it was apparent they didn't believe it for a second.

I left Cassie at Harlan's so they could get an early start to basketball camp and drove to Lila June's Salon, which was just inside the town limit on the highway down to Boulder. It was in a complex of metal buildings also housing a body shop and a towing service. Her sign was so large, upon quick inspection it looked like she owned the two automotive businesses as well.

Lila June's blue Chevy Citation was parked in front and the neon sign was on. I pulled up, parked and went inside. She was sitting in a barber's chair reading a magazine and looked delighted at either the idea of company or business, or maybe both. Lila June was a big-boned blond from Mississippi, but she had been around Colorado so long there was little more than a trace of her southern accent. If the mood struck, however, she could revert to pure hillbilly.

Her hair was piled high on her head, glitter-framed reading glasses were perched on her nose as she watched me come in. "'Bout time you got your butt in here, fishboy. You're gettin' a mite shaggy, unless of course that's just camouflage so as you kin sneak up on those poor little fishies." Seeing me, the mood had apparently struck her.

Not long after she came to Jack Springs, Lila June had talked me into giving her some fly-fishing lessons. I agreed, only to learn it really was fishing lessons that she wanted. Lila June had given up after a couple of months, though. She told me, "These damn fish around here are too smart for a country gal like me. In Mississippi, them dumb ol' fish were so easy to catch you had to hide behind the bushes just to bait your hook."

As I sat in the chair, she swung the plastic bib around me, put some tissue around my neck, and cinched the bib string up tight. "So, fishboy, what are we going to do to that mess of yours?"

"How about taking a little off the sides and putting it on the top, Lila June?"

She guffawed and slugged me on the arm. "You're such a kidder, fishboy!"

"Okay, then, how about cleaning me up some, hair and beard. These damn gray hairs keep popping out all over the place making me look like a wild man."

She slugged me again. "Well, fishboy, you are a wild man. You think I don't hear the stories?" Fearing my shoulder was going to end up dislocated if I kept kidding around with her, I asked her about her kids as she snipped away.

"Well, June Bug is still cuter than a tick's ear and sweeter than pecan pie. Billy Bob is getting the first flush of testosterone, so he thinks talking real loud and strutting around makes the girls notice him. My new one…well, the jury's still out on her. Lean your head forward."

While she combed down my hair and worked her way around cutting about an inch off the ends, I recalled her kids. June Bug was seven or eight years old now—a leggy heartbreaker already, with honey-blond curls and big blue eyes. Billy Bob was a few years older than June Bug, a gawky pre-adolescent with a bad attitude and spikey hair.

"So what made you take in a foster kid, Lila June? Too much time on your hands?"

"Not hardly. She was in a summer camp with my kids. They became attached to her and I found out her grandparents, who weren't going to be able to take care of her any more, were going to put her into a group home, so I took her in." Lila June was doing a masterful job cleaning up my wild mane without taking off too much hair and, broaching a serious subject, she spoke like the college graduate she was.

"So, what's the problem?"

"Tilt your chin up. Let's get that beard off your neck. You'll have to shave to get it clean, unless you want me to use the straight razor on it."

Gulping at the thought, I said, "No, I'll do it myself." Sure thing.

"Well, Brianne's got what's called reactive attachment disorder. Kids get that when they're neglected by their mothers from birth. Brianne's mother was a drug addict and disappeared a few years ago. The problem is these kids can be real charming most of the time. You'll never see it until something sets them off—usually when they perceive they're losing control of their situation. They can fly into a terrible rage, hurt people and even kill them."

"You mean they get that way from being neglected?" I asked, skeptical.

"There's different levels of being neglected, fishboy," Lila June said patiently. "In Brianne's case, or with most of these kids, they had no physical or emotional contact with their mothers from the day they were born. It's the emotional equivalent of being thrown in a cage at birth."

She was running the trimmer through my beard and tiny hairs were getting into my nose, eyes and ears. "Has that happened with, what's her name, Brianna?"

"Brianne. Yeah, she's fought me, ripped stuff out of the wall, broken things, like that. I'm kinda worried about June Bug bein' around her, but June Bug just loves her. Billy Bob hasn't quite figured out what to do around Brianne, now that she's around all the time. I think them hormones have got him all befuddled."

Lila June got out some tiny scissors and snipped at gray hairs bristling out from my beard.

"You know, they say that a lot of the serial killers and mass murderers were kids with reactive attachment disorder." She vacuumed the hairs of my face and neck.

"Is this disorder something that was just discovered?" I asked. "Why have I never heard of it?"

"Its been around as long as there have been mothers and babies," Lila June said. "But it's kind of controversial because it's…well…there's one school of thought that says conventional treatment methods don't work. That school supports a rebirthing experience as a way to get these kids connected with other human beings. The other school calls that mumbo jumbo and says conventional methods do work, but they can't back it up with any data. It's my opinion, anyway, that the treatment community doesn't want to acknowledge something they can't cure." Sadness overtook her face.

"So what are you going to do?"

"Quit talking about it, for now anyway. I don't know, fishboy, I just don't know."

Roscoe was waiting for me in the driveway and stood still, as if he didn't quite recognize me at first. Already feeling like a newly-shorn sheep, it fed my paranoia. But in truth, Lila Jean hadn't taken much off either my hair or beard. Then I realized he was probably looking for Cassie.

I slapped my leg and said, "Wanna go for a hike?" As soon as Roscoe heard the word 'go,' he started to rumba. With my gun in my pocket, we hiked the long way, going half way around Forsaken Rock, before climbing. Nothing had changed at the spot I had found that morning. I have to admit that made me feel a little better.

Back at the cabin, the whiskey bottle stayed under the sink. I read some more of the *Last Good Kiss* by James Crumley. The guy that Sonny Sughrue had been hired to find had just been shot in the ass in a bar fight. It sounded like something that could happen in the Jackass Inn.

It was an uneventful evening, and I got a good night's sleep. My brain was too tired to even dream.

Moving on silent feet through the dark meadow, the young cat was taken by surprise when the big truck glided around the corner. The bright headlights froze her momentarily as she tried to comprehend this strange thing bearing down on her out of the night.

The truck crunched to a stop in the gravel.

"Gimme the damn gun before he gets spooked," said the husky voice. Without understanding the words, the cat sensed the tension and, even at that distance, could smell the strong scents of hate and fear. The spell of the headlights was broken and she crouched, moving close to the ground to get into the thick trees surrounding the meadow.

As she moved, an explosion rocked the stillness and sent a whistle of air over her back.

She broke into a run for the trees, extending her claws for a better grip, and had just reached the cover of the forest when another shot rang out and splattered a tree limb just over her head.

"Goddamn, the sonofabitch got away," said the man with the gun. "And I had 'im dead in the sights on that first shot. It was like the bullet passed right through him, or somethin'."

"Yeah, sure it did, old man," said the driver. "And Vanna White is waiting naked for you at home."

"I'm tellin' you, I put the bullet right behind his shoulder. It was like he disappeared off the scope. A spooky damn thing is what it is."

"Whatever, we better get out of here before somebody comes to see what all the commotion is about."

The man set the rifle in the window rack and shook his head. "Ah, hell, I jist missed him, that's all."

"That's right," said the driver. "You just missed him."

CHAPTER 20

Monday morning, the sun rose with a vengeance into a blue-clear sky, and I puttered aimlessly around the cabin trying to shake the bad feeling that had crept back into my guts. Questions and errant thoughts bombarded my brain.

Would Earl come up with something on one of these crimes? How to deal with Terri? Would we learn anything about Stephanie's trip to Mexico? If we did, would it change the focus of the case?

Cassie was on her way to basketball camp, so that was one less complication for a few days. And what in hell was this protection Terri had mentioned?

That night, the Forest Service was going to have a meeting in town to take the final round of testimony on the Dark Angel mine. It was going to be a real wing-ding and had the potential to bring tensions over the mine to a head. Word had it that Gottlieb was going to be there. Nobody knew how the bombing would affect attendance. But the Forest Service, in deference to bureaucratic sensibilities, had declined to postpone it, over the objections of the District Ranger who would be right in the middle of it if it all went boom. They agreed to let ATF bomb-sniffing dogs go over the place before the meeting and to call in extra security.

On the way down Magnolia Road, a dust cloud hung magically over the road, as if the laws of gravity were suspended.

Surprisingly, the town was humming with activity. Tourists were out full force in anticipation of the warm weather. Dust and fumes hung over the town, and it wasn't even nine a.m. yet. No bombings in five days and everyone figured the danger was over. And it didn't even take a declaration of martial law. I stopped by Annie's when I saw Harlan's Jeep. He was presiding over a mug of coffee and a cinnamon roll.

"Morning, Harlan. How were the girls last night?"

"Them two are like nitro and glycerin, I swear. Put 'em together and something is going to go bang."

I waited for him to say, "No pun intended." When he didn't, I asked, "Was there some trouble?"

"Naw, nothin' like that," Harlan said. "They just got so much energy, it's hard to keep up with 'em. I never seen Tresha take to somebody like that. She's always been kind of shy."

"Except on the basketball court," I reminded him.

He smiled at the thought. "Except then."

Fathers and daughters. Who would ever understand the mystery of that bond? Oh, there were probably all kinds of psychological theories. But I bet none of them comes close to unraveling the mystery. And maybe that was the thing—girls or women will always remain a mystery to a man. With sons, the father usually knows what the boy is thinking, like it or not. With girls you get mystery.

Harlan swept the crumbs into a napkin, balled it up and swished it in the can next to the door. "That was pretty good luck that Terri made a copy of those papers," he said. "She seems to be having a run of good luck, these days."

"Yeah, she does," I admitted.

"What's the deal with you two? You used ta get this strange look in your eyes when I mentioned her. Now, you're like that kid in the funny papers with a little black cloud hanging over your head."

"She took off with some neighbor to go camping this weekend. He sells insurance, for Christ's sake." I didn't dare mention Emma.

"Well, I don't know if that's anything to get into a snit about."

"It's probably not," I agreed. "Hell, I'm just some homicidal maniac she works with."

"Think what you want," he said, "but I think you're wrong there. In a couple of days it'll be like whiskey under the bridge." He sighed and gathered his thoughts for answers to the questions I was sure to ask. "Anyway, Merle and Davey are coming in today. But it seems as Wiley up and disappeared. At least that's what they say. Some of the truck owners on our list are coming in again, too. Same with that guy Lazarus. I know Earl doesn't think he's much of a suspect, but I've run into him before and there's a few cards missin' from his deck. I don't believe he'd think twice about doing something like blowing up Gottlieb's trailer."

"Well, being a tunnel rat in Nam could do that to you."

"That's just my point," Harlan said. "By the way, did you bring that stuff in you picked up behind your place?"

"Yeah, I'll get it when we leave."

"Maybe we can find some prints on it."

We walked outside. He wiped sweat off his forehead with the back of his hand and grabbed a pinch of Copenhagen out of the can, pulled his lip back with two fingers and packed it in. It was invisible except for a slight bulge in his cheek.

"It's gonna be hotter than hell's half-acre today," he said, squinting at the sun. I agreed and got the Pepsi can out of my car and handed it to him.

"Hell's half-acre?"

"Yep."

"That sounds pretty hot."

"That's the idea," he said. "Say, I thought you were going to get a haircut."

Still feeling stripped naked, I brushed my hand along the back of my neck wondering how the hell anybody couldn't see the difference.

Just as I was ready to pipe up, Harlan pointed his finger like a gun and pulled the trigger. "Just kidding," he said as he got in his Jeep and drove away.

A big pickup was parked in front of the Miner. It looked like a ranch vehicle, with a stock rack on the bed, an empty gun rack in the back window, dual wheels, and lots of chrome. Inside the Miner, a very large cowboy was sitting next to the door in a chair that looked like it might collapse under his weight. On his lap was a shapeless athletic bag that had something long and not too thick in it. My eyes widened and I glanced at Terri. As she looked at me, her face scrunched up as if she was looking for the last piece in a jig-saw puzzle that was nowhere to be found.

"Did you…wash your hair or something?"

"I got a haircut, Terri."

"Really," she said. "Anyway, this is my cousin Buck. He's agreed to look out for me for a few days. Buck, this is Aaron, my co-worker."

Buck was the perfect name for this guy. He was six-four, two hundred and fifty pounds, at least. And there didn't appear to be an ounce of fat anywhere on him. He placed the bag carefully on the seat as he got up, walked over and stuck out a hand the size of a baseball mitt.

"Pleased to meet y'all," he said and shook my hand as gently as he could. "My cousin there pulled my lil' behind out of the crick when I was just a young'un. I reckon to be sure that purty hide of hers stays in one piece." He returned lightly to his seat. So this was Terri's personal protection. Good choice.

"Buck is a veterinarian in Odessa, Texas," Terri said. Buck dipped his big black cowboy hat like 'aw shucks, Terri,' but he remained silent. Abigail looked at her watch when she saw me, shook her head and resumed talking on the telephone. She must have forgotten I was working late that night.

Terri began to type. "I'm glad you and the kids are okay," I said.

"I appreciate that," she said with a studied indifference.

"Let me know when you want to talk about Gottlieb's court papers," I said. She stopped typing and looked at me with an unreadable expression.

"I'll be done here in a few minutes," she said. "Then we can talk."

"Fine." She resumed typing, a bright pink blush like a new sunburn creeping up the back of her neck. A good sign. It might have been hate, anger or consternation, but it wasn't indifference. Nothing is worse than being treated with indifference. Even Emma left a note.

I looked through my mail and made some notes about the hearing that night.

At last, Terri's keyboard was silent.

"Ready?"

"Sure, let's go into the conference room," she said. She was dressed in a black T-shirt that said Clint Black on Tour on it, baggy tan slacks and Nike running shoes. Her hair was pulled tight into a bushy pony tail, which was pushed through the back of a Raiders football cap. Wisps of hair were sticking out around her face, ears and the back of her neck. Buck started to get up.

"Buck, we'll be all right in there," Terri said. "If you want to run out to get something to eat, go ahead."

"Nope, I'll just stay right here."

He grasped the bundle carefully and sat back down. Buck reminded me of a big loyal dog who doesn't seem dangerous until his teeth have sunk into your neck.

Abigail looked up and scratched her head with a pencil again as we walked past her office. Her face was flushed. I think Buck's linebacker shoulders, narrow waist and big ol' cowboy hat might have been a mite unsettling for Abigail.

Terri set everything down. On top of the pile was a yellow pad filled with notes.

"Before we get started, I want to talk about this weekend," she said, her green eyes steely hard. "I don't owe you an explanation." She stared down any thought I might have had about interrupting. "But I want to give you one anyway." After a pause, she resumed, "Bill's been a good friend for a long time. He was there when I was having trouble with Ed, my husband. He's never been married or even seemed interested in marriage as far as I can tell. He does have girlfriends and I'm not one of them. I told him the kids were getting a little restless, so he offered to take us to Grand Lake.

"I used the weekend to read the court papers while Bill took the kids fishing and boating. He slept—"

I started to interrupt, then looked at her eyes and thought better of it. She pressed on.

"As I was saying, he slept in his tent and we slept in ours." She paused, gathering herself. "I was planning on explaining all this to you, but I never got the chance until right before we left. And when I tried, you just walked away, showing me how little you trust yourself or anybody else. I realize this past week has been hard on you. But just when I begin to think we could have something between us again, you pull some stunt like that fight with the Agnews. And when we get past that, you freak out over something like my going camping with a neighbor. Maybe I should have said something earlier in the day, but I didn't really think it was that big of a deal. And it got swept aside by everything else that was going on. I do care about you. But too often you remind me of my ex-husband. And I'll never put up with that situation again."

She looked me straight in the eyes to be sure the point was driven home. Then, letting me off the hook before I could screw things up, she said, "Let's get to work. We've got a story to write—a couple of stories as a matter of fact." She paused, "I found the clinic. Stephanie was scheduled for treatment this week. It costs $40,000 and she made a $10,000 deposit. The rest was due when she arrived."

After about ten minutes of running down both stories as she understood them, Terri set the pad down. As expected, she hadn't missed a thing in the court documents and had discovered some important details.

"So the bottom line is that for at least two of the mines Canaus Minerals has developed, the engineers cut corners to save money," I summed up. "In both cases, Gottlieb had taken the investments and profits, and when things started to fall apart, he declared bankruptcy and ran with the money. His investors sued him and lost both times. He somehow obtained court orders to keep the information sealed."

Terri nodded. "And now he wants to build the Dark Angel Mine above our town. Let's run this by Abigail."

So we told Abigail about Stephanie's plan to get treatment at the clinic and about Gottlieb's shenanigans in Canada. Her eyes kept flitting in Buck's direction, but when we got to the end, she said, "Holy shit, Martha!" That was enough. It meant we had a big story on our hands.

"The final hearing on the EIS is tonight," I said. "My sources say it's all but a done deal. Gottlieb's satisfied, on paper at least, all the concerns that were brought up throughout the process. But he's coming tonight to testify anyway, kind of a good-will gesture. I'd call it gloating, myself. If we wait until Friday to publish the story, the permit might be approved before the story comes out and it'll probably be too late to derail it. Is there any way we can publish something tomorrow, another short sheet?"

There was fire in Abigail's eyes. She wanted these stories. But there was something else there too.

"I better tell you," she said. "I've accepted a job with the Vail Valley News. I'm leaving Friday. Escamilla is in South America tending his flower business, and nobody is sure when he'll be back so he doesn't know. If we put this story out tomorrow without authorization, I could be fired. But now that's not a problem. I'll take responsibility, but there's no guarantee that he won't fire both of you, too."

That sobered us up a bit. Neither could afford to be out of work, but this was the chance of a lifetime. Terri could have one hell of a story on

Stephanie's murder, a story that could blow the case wide open. And I, for one, couldn't pass up the opportunity to take those corporate rape-and-run bastards down a couple of notches. Sorry was for later. I could tell that Terri was torn, however, between writing the stories and taking a chance on losing her job.

We looked at each other, and I could see the resoluteness I heard in her voice the day before. The excitement was there—like standing under a tall tree during a lightning storm and having the hair on your arms and neck stand up.

"Let's do it," Terri said. I wanted to hug her. Hell, I wanted to hug Abigail. But neither seemed a good idea at the moment.

Then Abigail cleared her throat, straightened her outfit and said, "Let's get to work. Knock out the story the best you can. Aaron, if Gottlieb's at the meeting tonight, I want you to ask him for a response. But don't use too much detail. Nobody else gets this story until we print it. Whatever he says, we'll use it. I doubt that he'll feel like going into details, in any case. As soon as you get him on the record, call me. We'll plug it in and send the copy to the printer under armed guard." I was thinking that Abigail might ask Buck to come back and do it, indeed, that it might be the reason she agreed to the deal in the first place.

She thought for a moment then continued.

"Terri, you're going to have to call Earl McCormick now and run this past him for a comment. See if he's picked up any more information. If they didn't find any money, we'll just leave it hang there for people to draw their own conclusions. Or maybe we'll frame it as a question. It's going to piss a few people off, but that's the way it goes."

Just as she was walking out the door, Abigail turned, smiled and said, "I can't resist giving this lunatic asylum of a town a kick in the ass on my way out the door." Then she wheeled around and went into her office. Once seated, she said, "Buck, could you come in here a sec, please?" Buck got all wide-eyed, glanced over at Terri and said, "Yes 'm." He sat his black bag down, shuffled in and took a seat. I'd have given anything to see what was in that bag, but on the other hand, I wasn't sure I wanted to know.

Terri was moving back to her desk when I asked, "By the way, how did you get the clinic to confirm Steph was scheduled for treatment?"

"Just what you suggested," she said. "How do you figure out stuff like that?"

"Being a cop for ten years, you hear every lie, justification, sleazy scheme and con in the book. After that, it just becomes second nature." She wrinkled her brow, wondering, no doubt, if there weren't something more to it.

The day flew by after that, and both stories were finished by five o'clock. They were good—no doubt about it. Terri turned up a solid lead in a murder investigation that appeared to be going nowhere. Earl admitted he had gotten zilch, so far, from the Federales in Mexico. And he said there was no evidence—bank account or anything—of Stephanie Goldman having any money. He planned to call her few surviving relatives and ask if they knew anything about it, as well as Western Union and the area banks to see if she had already sent it south to be picked up when she arrived.

On the other side of the coin, Gottlieb's plans for the Dark Angel could take a hit. Fiduciary responsibility—the intention and financial ability to pull off a mining project and to stand behind the agreement—was essential to gaining approval.

Gottlieb had wheedled, lied, threatened and made promises for two years to get the Dark Angel Mine approved without this information ever coming to light. He used the same tactics to get local support for the mine that had torn apart other communities in the West, pitting brother against brother, father against son and neighbor against neighbor. Only this time his schemes very likely left behind a dead body. And we were going to pull the plug on his big row boat. Maybe he'd be tarred and feathered and run out of town on a rail when the story came out. If only justice were that simple these days.

Just after five, Earl called to report on the day's interrogations.

"We got Merle and Davey in today and leaned on them hard, but we drew a blank. They gave each other alibis. And we can't prove them wrong," Earl said. "They said they don't know where Wiley was that night and I believe them. He's been hanging out with those guys up in Central City. And he's been gone since right after the ass-kicking you gave him last week."

That's real comforting, I thought, but kept my mouth shut for once. "What about Lazarus? By the way, is that his real name?"

"Yeah, Jimmy Lazarus. He changed it legally after he'd made it out of a VC tunnel that collapsed on him. He blew the tunnel himself because he ran out of bullets and Charlie was getting ready to make him into hamburger. I think we can eliminate him as a suspect. His leg is in a full cast and he needs crutches to walk. He's got a compound fracture from an accident up at his place a couple of months ago. I believe the sono-fabitch came in just so he could see the look on our faces.

"And Aaron, the prints on that can were a bust. They were smeared. There wasn't enough to get any kind of match," Earl said. "I'm sorry. I know that doesn't help much—one way or the other."

Hearing the news about Wiley compounded my paranoia, and made me glad Cassie was away for a few days. Where the hell was he and how could I watch for him with all this other stuff going on?

"You still there?" Earl wanted to know.

"Yeah, yeah, I'm here. I was just digesting what you told me. Tell me there's something you can do about this shit, Earl."

"You know we can't arrest him," he said wearily. "But we can look for him. And if we find him, well, there are ways to dissuade him. Not strong arm stuff. Just a lecture, so to speak."

"That's very comforting," I told him.

"Goddamnit, we don't even know if he's been near your house so save the sarcasm. You know how it works. This isn't Los Angeles. This is Boulder County, Colorado, the capital of civil rights and sensitive, community-based law-fucking-enforcement and neither one of us would have it any other way."

"Don't kid yourself," I said. "Right now, I'd throw the Bill of Rights right out the window and stomp it into the mud if you could get Wiley behind bars."

Earl stayed quiet. "It's just frustrating with my daughter here," I said. "I can take care of myself. But I can't protect her without locking her up. And I don't believe that would go over very well."

"She's at basketball camp, isn't she?"

"Yeah, she'll be staying at the university for a couple more days."

"That's good. When's she due back?"

"Wednesday."

"We should have gotten in touch with Wiley by then. Don't worry for a few days."

"Sure thing," I said, trying not to sound sardonic.

CHAPTER 21

The paper was laid out with the lead story on Gottlieb's Canadian mine boondoggles and the second story on Stehpanie Goldman's missing money and her scheduled trip to a cancer clinic in Mazatlan, with a headline that danced around a very sensitive subject—"Did activist sell out her cause?" The drop head said, "Cops baffled by missing money." Another story reported no leads in the bombing.

It was still hot, but the humidity was low and unless you were standing in direct sunlight, it was bearable.

I got my pistol out of the car, slipped it into a fanny pack then walked over to Fat Jack's deli for a turkey sandwich on rye. The tourists were gathered in the shade on the porch, taking up all the tables while they were eating frozen yogurt and watching the explosive-sniffing dogs check out the building, cars and surrounding area. Forest Service Special Agents, armed to the teeth, were watching everything closely. I'd never met anybody with the Forest Service who didn't look like a bureaucrat, but these guys were scary.

A shapely young girl with a tan, bare belly and honey-blond hair swept high looked very bored in the company of her mother and father, who were both overweight and wearing souvenir Colorado Rockies T-shirts and hats. She was rolling her eyes as her mother explained their plans for the next day.

She was interested, it seemed, in Zak, a local cowboy who sat back against a rail in front of the restaurant. With his scuffed boots, big black hat and Boston Blackie mustache, he managed to look cool and detached. The more she looked, the cooler he tried to become. It appeared to be an effective technique.

Since the Town Hall was next door, I sat on the bench to eat my sandwich and watched as the people began to arrive. From the turnout, it seemed the bombing was going to have no effect on attendance, or in some way might have even increased it. Despite Gottlieb's trailer being blown into anti-radar chaff, the pro-mine people were animated, much to the annoyance of grim-faced mine opponents.

Dark Angel supporters smelled victory, and it smelled like money— big money.

Right on time, a *Lincoln Towne Car* limo pulled up with Gottlieb and his entourage. Toadies exited and scurried around like disoriented lemmings, locating the important people so their boss wouldn't have to rub shoulders with the unwashed. Tourist cars were clogging the street while the limo refused to give ground.

Just then, some people broke out anti-mine signs and lined the sidewalk into the Town Hall. Two weeks ago, Stephanie would have been at the front of the group, waving the biggest sign, just short of whacking Gottlieb on the head. It was a favorite tactic of hers. Toby, Ray and Harlan all stepped outside the marshal's office next door. Sheriff's department vehicles were parked at the far side of the street, the deputies spread out, looking nervous.

As if on cue, Gottlieb stepped out and the crowd fell silent. He was dressed in a dark Italian suit, with his hair greased back over his head and his eyes covered with green-tinted sunglasses.

Talk about cultural sensitivity, Gottlieb looked as out of place as a rattlesnake in a prairie dog village. It was a tactical mistake, but he was arrogant now and had little need to placate the locals. The big paychecks were closer than ever. That was all the support he thought he needed and he was probably right.

Bartholomew, Fontaine and Brillo stepped to the curb to greet their sugar daddy. Like a man of the people, Bartholomew was dressed in a light flannel shirt, jeans with high cuffs and work boots. Brillo wore a yellow golf shirt, lime-green slacks and sandals with black socks. He'd obviously tried to brush down his wiry hair but that had only made it look like a blown-down lodgepole pine forest.

But Fontaine outdid himself, in a purple polo shirt, white deck pants and white patent-leather loafers with no socks. And a big white bandage covering his nose.

As much as I disliked Brill and Bartholomew, it was Fontaine who pushed my buttons. Speaking over the din of voices that started after the shock of Gottlieb's appearance wore off, I said, "Gary, what the heck happened to your nose?" Before he could react, I snapped my fingers and said, "Hey, I got it! You were practicing for when the big fella showed up and Al farted."

A few people laughed. Gary took a couple of quick blasts on his breath spray, shot me a mortified glance, then swiveled away to glad-hand Gottlieb. They bowed their heads together, looked over at me, smirking.

I should have just ignored them but couldn't. "Get your laughs in early tonight gentlemen, it could get rough in there."

Most of the crowd ignored my reply. But not Gottlieb, Bartholomew or Gottlieb's head toady, Christine McDermott. I had their attention. Gottlieb spoke to one of the bone-breakers who was with him, and the man stationed himself between us and grinned, as if daring me to approach.

Harlan walked though the crowd, looking for a polite place to spit. After unleashing a brown torrent into the street, sending a few white-legged tourists scurrying, he came over to me.

"Aaron, what the hell are you up to? There better not be any trouble tonight. I'm not kidding around on this. You start trouble, you'll be staying in the town's guest room for the night, I swear."

"It won't be like that, Harlan, " I said, trying to act indignant at the suggestion. "I just have a question to ask Gottlieb about those mines in Canada he ran out on. That's all."

"Holy shit," he said, almost the same response Abigail had earlier in the day. "Do you have to do that at this meeting?"

"I need to get his real reaction to the story in front of everybody—not some manufactured bullshit by his press office. That son-of-a-bitch is a crook and he's willing to tear this town apart, if he has to, to get his fortune from that valley. He's going to leave this town holding a very nasty bag, and I want everyone to see what a skunk they are dealing with."

"Lordy, Lordy," he said, shaking his head and walking away to confer with Ray and Toby. Soon, they too were shaking their heads, but Toby looked over with a slight grin. Just as everyone began to file in, Merle and Davey Agnew drove past and caused a ripple of comment.

Christine McDermott sidled up to me, leaned over and spoke out of the side of her mouth—an indication, I was sure, that she was going to say something true for a change.

"I don't know what you're up to, Aaron. But you should know that if you intend to cause us any more trouble, we've got some very interesting information about you when you worked for the Denver Police Department. We're not afraid to use it."

I should have been expecting this. "Ah, Christine. Are we slipping off the white silk gloves? Is this hardball we're playing now? You know what they say about yesterday's news, don't you?"

Appearing surprised at my indifference, she said, "Just be forewarned."

That did it. I grabbed her arm, held it tight. She tried to pull away but didn't want to make a scene and offend the happy-faced god of public relations. I held on, pinching her tricep a little and said in her ear, "Forewarned? Oh, I'm forewarned all right. Stephanie Goldman was murdered and dropped on our front door. Somebody broke in and stole the court papers and my colleague was run off the road two nights ago by a hit-and-run driver with no lights on. I've been threatened with several lawsuits. A maniac might have been staking out my home. I'm fucking forewarned, don't worry about that.

"But I gotta tell you, Chrissy baby, you're not dealing with a rational person here. If somebody fucks with me, or my daughter or my friends, or my dog, or for that matter my dog's friends, they won't end up in court. They'll end up dead. You can tell Gottlieb that. And I won't stop with the flunkies, I'll get the man that pays the bills. By the way, that's all off the record." I smiled and winked.

She "eeeked" like a mouse, wobbling on high heels across the rough lawn, and disappeared inside the Town Hall. I think it was the wink that got her.

Playing by the rules was never this much fun, I reminded myself and followed her in.

CHAPTER 22

Bob Alexander, the Boulder District Ranger, called the meeting to order. He was a decent guy and tried to run his little corner of the national forest more in tune with the community than many would have. But he had earlier explained that his hands were tied on the Dark Angel Mine because the Mining Act of 1872 all but guaranteed that anybody who's willing to invest the money and go through the process was going to be approved. And he was right.

The U.S. government was going to give Canaus Minerals a half-billion dollars worth of gold for about two grand, then pray that nothing went wrong and millions of gallons of toxic mine run off would be successfully treated and discharged into Boulder Creek for about a thousand years. That assumed that seven years of gold production would pay for a millennium of expensive treatment. If anything did go wrong, that poisonous soup would flow downstream like a death-dealing flood into the town, the reservoir, the city of Boulder and points east.

But when there's money to be made, why sweat the small stuff? Well, tomorrow the town was going to learn about some big stuff; Gottlieb liked to cut a few corners here and there; maybe put a thinner liner in the tailings pond than required and save a few hundred thousand; fudge a few test results and save a few thousand more; get the money and run back to Vancouver.

Alexander, rapping a gavel sharply to quiet the crowd, explained that smoking was not permitted in the building during a federal government hearing. Following a collective groan and some snide comments, a number of men broke out pouches and cans of chewing tobacco. He then explained, as per government procedure, that everyone would have three minutes to comment on the Environmental Impact Statement, which was several hundred pages long and piled on tables in the back of the room.

Merle and Davey Agnew had slipped inside, standing at the back of the crowd. They didn't look so tough without Wiley around. They looked so skittish, in fact, that a chicken fart could have blown them to the Kansas border, as Harlan would say.

Where the hell was Wiley?

About a hundred and fifty people had squeezed in to the room and thirty were scheduled to speak. Harlan, Toby and Ray, as well as a half-dozen federal agents had stationed themselves around the room.

Calling in a couple of favors with Alexander, I was scheduled to speak fourth, after Bartholomew, a small gold-mine operator named Mac McKendrickson, and somebody whose name I didn't recognize.

Alexander called Bartholomew's name. The crowd quieted and he stepped to the microphone. Our freelance photographer, a young guy who was trying to make a name for himself, squatted in the aisle in front of the podium.

"I've got two things to say," Al said, his blotchy face twitching. Having his meal ticket in the room seemed to be more pressure than he was used to. He looked over at Gottlieb.

"First, I want to condemn the mindless violence by some faction in this issue that lead to the bombing of Mr. Gottlieb's headquarters."

"What about Steph's murder, Al," said somebody in an angry voice, sending a bolt of tension through the room, but nobody moved, sensing that this was where it could all come apart.

Alexander pounded the gavel and drew the attention back to himself.

"We all abhor the violence, Mr. Bartholomew. But for purposes of this hearing, please limit your comments to issues dealing with the mine." Al colored slightly, as if he realized trying to earn brownie points with Gottlieb had backfired.

"Sorry. I just wanted to say that I've read the EIS and it looks to me like Mr. Gottlieb has done his homework. That mine is going to be an environmental masterpiece—"

"Bullshit, Al," or "You're so full of shit your eyes are brown," shouted some in the audience. Another said, "How the hell would you know, Al? Your's was a disaster." The crowd erupted. Men stood facing each other and shouting but stayed near their seats. The Forest Service agents started down the aisles as Alexander pounded the gavel furiously.

"Order! Order!" he shouted. "I'll cancel the hearing if you don't quiet down." As the noise subsided, one of the miners in the room added, "Come on, Al. You can't even read the directions on a package of dick rubbers." Then everyone was laughing—everyone except Bartholomew—whose face had turned heart-attack red. Even Gottlieb had covered his mouth and turned away. Bartholomew was so pitiable I almost felt sorry for him.

"Not that he's ever needed to," chimed in someone else, drawing more laughter and diffusing some of the tension.

Alexander was not amused, however. The decorum of an official U.S. government hearing was in disrepair. "I mean it," he shouted. "If the crowd doesn't stay in control, I will cancel the hearing. If you want your say tonight, you'd better stay quiet. Mr. Bartholomew, you may continue."

He pulled at the collar of his shirt, swallowed, and turned his head from side to side. "Well, I guess that's about all I have to say, your

Honor," he added, mistakenly. The crowd tittered as he walked back to his seat near Gottlieb.

"Well, praise the Lord for small favors, your Honor," somebody said under his breath. Some snickered but did not laugh as Alexander raised his gavel. He lowered it without striking.

"Mr. McKendrickson, you're next," Alexander read from his list.

McKendrickson, the owner and operator of the Holy Chalice Mine near Caribou, raised his stocky frame from the folding chair and walked to the microphone. He was well liked in the community, ran a solid operation, never had any serious environmental violations and employed about twelve people in his mine. From the boisterous crowd there was nary a peep.

"Mr. Alexander, I too have read the EIS," he said, paying Bartholomew a back-handed vote of support. "And I agree that on paper the Park Angel Mine is a model of environmental responsibility. But I'm still troubled. The mine's opponents are saying that something always goes wrong with these operations."

The crowd was deathly still, realizing that something serious was coming up, not wanting to miss it. I glanced at Gottlieb, and although he appeared calm, a thin sheen of perspiration shone on his face.

"Well, it's true, Mr. Alexander. Things do go wrong. They go wrong at the Holy Chalice Mine. But we're a small operation and we've planned for these breakdowns and have contingencies when they do. Still, it takes a lot of money and work to do this.

"The proposed Park Angel Mine is bigger than anything that was ever even imagined in this area when we restarted our mine. There will be more people to make mistakes, more equipment to break down, and more danger when it happens. As near as I can tell, the Park Angel Mine hasn't budgeted, percentage-wise, as much of its operating costs to environmental protections as we do at the Holy Chalice. I don't think it's enough to avert an eventual disaster, even before the ore is played out."

Voices rose in surprise and dismay, but nobody was shouting at McKendrickson. Alexander pounded the gavel two times and the crowd came to order. Gottlieb looked like he was going to be sick.

"I know I've used my time but I would like to continue, if that's possible," he said. A matronly woman in the crowd said, "He can have my time, sir. I'm Susan Stratherton."

Alexander nodded and checked his list. "Go ahead, Mr. McKendrickson."

"I and some other small mine owners have stayed quiet on this up 'til now because we all operate in a political climate. That climate has been anti-mining for some time, but the responsible mine owners hereabouts have been accorded a measure of respect for our efforts. But I've come to believe that if there is a problem at the Park Angel Mine, it will mean the end of mines like the Holy Chalice. It'll be like nothing we've ever seen, to this point."

Gottlieb was squirming, his hands clasped as if trying to strangle each other. The green-tinted sunglasses were finally off. His face, already pale, was deathly white. Brillo, ever the politician, sensed that things were going sour and started to slide away from Gottlieb, Fontaine and Bartholomew.

"But just as important, I don't like what has happened to this town since the Park Angel Mine has been proposed. I don't like what Al Bartholomew has done trying to rally support for the mine. This us-against-them stance is just wrong and it certainly may be responsible for the rash of violence, including the murder of Stehanie Goldman, that has struck our town." A chorus of muted assent swelled in the room. Alexander never moved a muscle.

McKendrikson turned to look at Gottlieb and Bartholomew, leaning on his large forearms along the sides of the lectern. Gottlieb was sweating like a politician on judgment day, no mistake about it.

"For the reasons I've just given, I categorically oppose the Park Angel Mine. I wish I had earlier. I realize that now it's probably too late. Thank you." He turned and walked back to his chair as the camera flashed.

At first the crowd was silent, each person stunned for different reasons. Some started to applaud, then more and more, swelling to about three fourths of those in the room, who stood as if calling for an encore.

McKendrickson sat impassively, but I detected a slight nod of thanks toward the crowd.

Again, Alexander banged the gavel until the crowd settled.

He called the name of Nathan Greenhouse. The man, with an over-stuffed accordion file eight-inches thick under his arm, rose and walked with an air of gravity to the microphone. With long black hair to his shoulders and a full beard streaked with gray, Greenhouse looked like a prosperous old hippie, but the fires of obsession burned in those dark eyes.

Once there, he raised three fingers and ticked them off as he spoke, "*McDonald's, Wendy's, Burger King* and the acidic processed crap they sell as food are the real culprits. It has made us soft-minded, turned our brains to mush—"

"Turned your brain to mush, you mean," somebody yelled from the audience. "Bring back Al," yelled another. The crowd tittered.

Alexander was pounding the gavel, "Order! Order! Let the man finish!" When the crowd quieted, he asked, "Mr. Greenhouse, could you tell us what this has to do with the proposed mine?"

"It's all part of the conspiracy by multinational corporations to enslave the American people," he said fervently. "First, they get us hooked on this junk food. Then they rip off our resources. I've researched this for twenty years and got the documents right here. I can prove it. Trust me. It's part of the Tri-Lateral Commission's plot to institute a one-world government and rob us of our national identities. " He was yelling and waving his free arm spasmodically.

"All because of junk food?" Alexander asked, incredulous.

"Yes, yes, that's it! That's it!"

"Your time is up, Mr. Greenhouse. Thank you for your comments," Alexander said, looking relieved.

Greenhouse wandered back to his seat, still muttering. Gottlieb smiled and shook his head dismissively, looking around at his followers to collect their nodded assents.

"Mr. Hemingway, it's your turn. This has something to do with the mine?" Alexander asked, making a little joke most of the audience missed because they were still laughing.

"I assure you it's about Mr. Gottlieb's proposed mine."

"But aren't you violating some kind of reporter's ethic by testifying about an issue you've reported on?" Alexander asked.

The crowd was rumbling again as I walked to the microphone. Someone said, "Reporter's ethics, that's a good one, ha, ha, ha."

I put my hand behind my back and flipped them the bird, eliciting more snickers. "Well, Mr. Alexander, I'm not going to make a statement. I'm just going to pose a question to Mr. Gottlieb. If that's all right."

"Mr. Gottlieb, is that all right with you?" Alexander asked.

He could hardly say no, but there was little doubt he wanted to.

"That's fine, Mr. Alexander. What's your question?" he said softly. A fancy monogrammed handkerchief dabbed the sweat from his temples.

"I've read the EIS and there isn't anything in there about what happened at the Ruby and Takeetna mines in British Columbia? Don't you think we should know about what happened up there?"

Gottlieb exploded almost before I could finish. He stood up and screamed, "Those are lies and slander! If you write anything about that, I'll see to it you will never even write graffiti on a bathroom wall, let alone for that rag you call a newspaper here."

Alexander was pounding again, but I continued.

"Sorry, Bob. I've got the documents," I said, grabbing a pile of papers that had fallen from Nathan Greenhouse's cache. "The court records are right here." I held them up and waved them at him, just to rub it in. "And by tomorrow, the whole town will know what happened."

Gottlieb's veins were pulsing in his face as he turned and grabbed Bartholomew around the neck. His face frozen in contempt, his eyes bulging, he began strangling his main supporter in the town. Gottlieb's body guards and Forest Service security agents started moving towards them.

"You incompetent piece of shit. I thought you said—" Gottlieb screamed as our photographer materialized two feet away, got a close up of the scene and ducked through the arms of Gottlieb's bodyguards.

Unable to chase him through the pressing crowd, they grabbed their boss and started hustling him out the door before he could say any more. Christine McDermott picked up Gottlieb's briefcase and followed quickly. Once again the crowd was stunned, but soon the shouting began. People stood and screamed at each other. Alexander struck his gavel so hard it sounded like a gunshot. The head finally popped off and sailed about twelve feet into the air.

"Mr. Hemingway, can you tell us what that was about?" he yelled over the noise. Harlan had reached Bartholomew and was talking to him, helping him to his feet.

"Sorry, Mr. Alexander. You'll just have to read about it in the Miner tomorrow morning," I shouted back and made for the door. The Agnews were already gone. Alexander screamed over the chaos in the room.

"This hearing is canceled! This hearing is canceled!"

My mouth was dry and an icy bottle of Dos Equis called out my name as I walked past the Jackass Inn, but I kept going.

Abigail was sitting at her computer. "How'd it go?" she asked.

"He denied everything, called them slanderous lies and threatened to make sure I'd never even get a job writing graffiti on bathroom walls if we printed the story."

"Is that all?" she asked, delighted at his outburst.

"Yeah, except for when he reached across the table and started strangling Al."

Abigail's mouth dropped open, showing what must have been a good twenty grand worth of orthodontics. "You're shitting me," she said when she regained her composure.

"And our photographer got a close up of the action."

"Great," she said. "We're going to have to rewrite the story, plugging in Gottlieb's antics and the cancellation of the hearing. We'll have to cut a little to make up for the additional copy. Either that or I'll have to call in some help and change the layout." She looked at me quizzically, wondering what my reaction would be. She knew how hard we worked on the story.

"Get out the knife, " I said.

"OK, give me three hundred words," she said. "I'll start cutting."

We worked quickly, trying to put the story to bed once and for all. I saved my story to a disk, got up and was walking toward her office when a thunderclap shook the building. Except it wasn't thunder. The skies were clear.

By the time I got to the porch to see what the hell was going on, a second explosion shot a fireball into the sky above the shopping center parking lot. Abigail almost knocked me down coming out of the door. When she disentangled herself, she held her hands to her cheeks and said, "Holy Mother of God!"

For the first time since this whole thing began, I was stunned beyond words. I realized that things had indeed gotten very, very bad.

And the bottom was falling out of my world because I knew that Cassie would have to go back to her mother. The danger was now omnipresent and indiscriminate.

By the time we arrived at the parking lot, Al Bartholomew's old pickup truck was mangled, nearly blown in half and burning. Through the smoke and flames, we could see glimpses of someone in the driver's seat. There were pieces of the truck scattered around the lot. The fire department arrived within three minutes but there was nothing to be done besides put out the fire.

Windows in the shopping center were shattered, but the truck was far enough away from the buildings that there was no chance the fire would spread.

It was near chaos as people started arriving on foot and in cars. Since some of the Forest Service cops were still around, they helped Harlan control the crowd, pushing people back in the event there would be another explosion.

Abigail managed to snap several photographs before they pushed her away, too. Still shaken by what had happened, we walked silently back up the hill to the Miner.

Up in the Dark Angel valley, a chorus of coyotes wailed like crazed banshees over the sounds of the flames.

We pulled three people in to redo the paper and agreed we needed to try to verify it was Al in the truck, although it seemed to be a foregone conclusion. Harlan was in his office and was willing to fill me in. He said he had talked to Al after the meeting broke up and that Al had left about five minutes before the explosion. And he was not at home.

Al was pretty upset at being manhandled by Gottlieb, Harlan told me, and had admitted to stealing the court papers from the office. Al said that Gottlieb had told him he better do something about the papers but that Gottlieb never told him to steal them.

I'd already began filtering the information, trying to figure what had to be in the story and what could be left out. Harlan helped with this decision.

"Look, Aaron, for now let's keep this stuff quiet," he said. "Besides, that's not the half of it. And I don't want to be in the same county with Earl if this hits the papers before we have a chance to verify it." He paused, took a deep breath and let it out.

"Al said Gottlieb had given Stephanie fifty thousand dollars to end her opposition to the mine. She approached Gottlieb through Al, without giving any explanation."

My temples had started to throb, trying to assimilate the information even though we weren't going to use it in tomorrow's newspaper.

"Anyway, Al said Gottlieb's lawyers had Stephanie sign an agreement, and the cash money was delivered about a week before she was killed."

As much as I hated to admit it, the story made sense in light of what we knew about the cancer clinic in Mexico. I hated to admit it because it seemed to let Gottlieb off the hook, but also because it didn't shed any light about Stephanie's murder except to suggest the oldest motive of all—money.

But who else would have known about the money and where was it now? How did this affect my scenario of Wiley as the murderer? Or could the crimes still be separate; two motives and two perpetrators? Shit, my head was pounding like a steel drum.

"Al said Gottlieb was furious when he heard Steph was murdered," Harlan said. "The money was down the drain and he knew he was screwed if the deal came out and screwed if it didn't because he knew the mine's supporters would be blamed."

Harlan sounded exhausted, his voice little more than a whisper. And any more information would have short-circuited my brain.

"Thanks, Harlan. We'll just go with the story saying positive identification hadn't been made by press time but Al couldn't be located."

"Keep me out of it," he said.

"Of course."

Somehow, Buck had slipped into the office while I was on the phone and was with Abigail in her office. She saw me put the phone down and looked like she was going to come out, but I started typing and she stayed in there with Buck. Ten minutes later the story of Al's apparent demise was done.

In the layout, the bombing had knocked our lead story down a notch, but it didn't matter. The thing we couldn't believe, that somebody was trying to pay back big time for Stephanie Goldman's murder, seemed to have come true. If so, they were wrong but wouldn't likely know it for several days. But this time they were willing to risk killing innocent people to do it. The whole thing had descended to a level of insanity in which there might not be any explanation until we found out who was responsible for the murder, the bombings or both. Until then, there would be no peace and no safety in Jack Springs.

Crawling into bed about 3:00 a.m., I felt like a shell of a human, with all the guts sucked out of me. No amount of whiskey was going to keep the demons at bay and help me get to sleep, but I took a couple of big drinks anyway.

I put the gun in the boot next to my bed, took another pull on the bottle of Evan Williams then tossed and turned until the sun came up.

CHAPTER 23

A Dreamsicle slash of cirrus clouds greeted me as I opened my grit-filled eyes. To the west, the sky was clear; not even a cumulus cloud floated over the mountains. Still woozy from the lack of sleep and the booze, a feeling of dread had invaded my being.

It didn't have anything to do with the newspaper, which was the best we'd ever put out or ever would. The problem was pretending to normalcy when the world was coming apart at the seams.

The only thing that motivated me enough to get up was wondering if anyone had been watching the cabin from the spot up on the mountain where I found the trash. I dressed and drank some coffee. Then Roscoe and I hiked up the mountain. We approached quietly, but there was no evidence anyone had been there. So we hiked over the hills until the sun was well up.

The sweet mountain air cleared some of the cobwebs from my mind. And I realized there was nothing to be gained by sitting on my butt and stewing in depression all day. We went down and I got ready to go to work. Knowing I might need some diversion besides work from what was on my mind, I pulled my fly rod down from the wall, put my pistol in the front pocket of my fishing vest and carried them down the hill to the Subaru. Roscoe was nowhere to be seen. I started the car and drove slowly down Magnolia Road into Jack Springs.

Terri and Abigail were looking at the paper when I walked in. Terri was subdued but Abigail, appearing to have recovered from the shock of the night before, looked pleased but tired.

"The governor is having a press conference about the situation here," Abigail said. "He's expected to make an announcement at 11 a.m."

That was all we needed, for the 'situation' to become politicized. "So the National Guard will be coming to keep order in Jack Springs. Why am I not comforted?" I said, a question which required no answer.

Abigail said, "I've been trying to get Earl and the Sheriff on the phone. It sounds like they are meeting with the governor."

"Maybe there's hope," I said.

"Well, what happens now?" I asked, seeking anything that would delay the inevitable phone call to Madeline.

"We wait for the governor's announcement and we start on the follow up stories," Abigail said. "Get some reaction from the locals. Try to contact Gottlieb. Keep in touch with the Forest Service and the U.S. Attorney's office. Who knows? Maybe they'll solve one of these crimes and we'll have another real news story."

Despite my problems with her, the thought that Abigail was leaving in three days hit me hard, and then I realized that it might be over for Terri and me as well. There was nothing to do but keep working. If we could be fired for doing our jobs well…what the hell. Keep on keeping on, as we used to say in Vietnam. Abigail went into her office and Terri and I to our desks.

It was hard to believe, but Terri hadn't heard about the recent bombing until she got to town. Prepared to celebrate our big scoop, her clothes were a little on the flamboyant side—a filmy, sleeveless purple blouse with tiny pink and blue flowers embroidered thickly across the more interesting areas, boot-cut Wranglers, and expensive purple cowboy boots with hand-tooled silver scroll work peeking out below her cuff. And that was fine with me. Anything that brought light and color into the gloom and doom was more than welcome.

She saw me looking and blushed.

"They're left over from my rodeo days. I hadn't worn them in years. Today seemed like a good day," she said, thinking it was the boots that had caught my eye. I played along. "Until I found out about Al, that is. It doesn't seem like we should be celebrating anything."

I disagreed with her and said that we had put out a dynamite newspaper. But my voice didn't convey the sentiment very well.

"Let's split up the work," she said, trying to get things back on track, "You get the governor's announcement and the cops, and I'll talk to people here for reaction. You keep up with the Forest Service and the federal attorney. Should we flip a coin for Gottlieb?"

"Why don't you give it a try?" I said. "He probably won't talk to us at all, but there's no way he would talk to me after the hearing last night."

There was a leaden quality to our actions, despite our effort at pretending the work was still important.

"By the way, where's your bodyguard this morning?" I asked Terri. "Don't tell me. He's all tuckered out from delivering the paper to the printers."

"He'll be coming in later to give me a ride home," she said, sounding a little peeved, whether with me or Buck was hard to tell. "He had a late night." It was a situation ripe for comment, but I didn't have the energy. And a troubling thought, brought on by Buck's absence, came to me; nothing that happened explained who had run Terri off the road Saturday night.

I went back to my desk and started making phone calls.

About 11:30, Harlan called. "Earl and the Sheriff prevailed upon the governor and got the National Guard idea killed for now. But they've agreed to a task force with the feds, including the FBI, the Bureau of Alcohol, Tobacco and Firearms, the CBI, and a couple other of them agencies I've never heard of, and they're meeting Thursday morning," he said. "I think Earl is resigned to the situation after what happened to Al. But he doesn't like it."

"Goddamn it, something has to be done," I said with rising anger.

"That doesn't sound like you, Aaron," he said.

"It doesn't feel like me," I said. "But I'm going to have to send my daughter home. You know, the one who showed up on the steps after four years, the one who your daughter likes so much. And goddamn it, Harlan, it's breaking my heart."

Harlan ignored my diatribe. "Maybe I ought to send Tresha some-place for a while. At least they're at basketball camp until tomorrow."

"Yeah, at least they are."

I looked out the window and saw Joshua standing in the street, as if trying to get his bearings.

"Thanks for leaving what Al told me out of the paper," Harlan said. "I'm going to talk to Earl about it later."

I was barely listening, focused instead on Joshua's apparent dilemma. That guy always seems to be around. Hell, it was a long shot but—.

"Harlan, has anyone questioned Joshua about the night Stephanie was killed? He might have seen something. He seems to be hanging around this part of town a lot."

"Well, no we haven't," Harlan said. "But now that you mention it, that might be a good idea."

"He's standing in the street out front. You better get him before he disappears."

"I'm on my way," he said and hung up the phone. Within minutes, Harlan was leading him out of the bushes along the creek bottom. Joshua was animated, holding his hands about eighteen inches apart in the classic fisherman pose for a Big One.

There seemed to be a space where nothing was happening, so I picked up the phone and dialed Madeline at work.

She didn't seem surprised to hear from me. "We heard about what happened on the news," she said. "I was just about to call you."

"Madeline, it's worse than you've heard," I said. "Somebody took a shot at my dog Friday night. And there's a place up on the mountain side where it looks like someone has been watching the place."

"I'm not sure I understand," she said.

"Before Cassie arrived, I got into a scrape with a guy who might be a suspect in the murder. He seems to have disappeared. This guy is bad news, even if he didn't commit the murder."

"It seems under the circumstances, you might have called sooner," she said, her voice dripping with disdain.

"Madeline, she's been at basketball camp at the university since Sunday night," I said, trying to restrain my anger. "Except for the shot at Roscoe, which could be unrelated, all this stuff has happened while she was gone. I was thinking about calling you anyway, and after the bombing last night, well, it seems this guy is no longer worried about innocent bystanders."

"Oh," she said. "When does she get out of camp?"

"Tomorrow afternoon."

"I'm tied up in an important case right now, but I should be free by Friday," she said. "Tell me what you think, Aaron. Is she really in danger?"

"I don't know. There's a lot of ways at looking at what has happened," I said. "I'm just trying to be careful."

"I appreciate that," she said. "If she wasn't scared to death of flying, you could send her back. But—"

"Let's see what happens tomorrow and play it by ear," I told her.

"All right. But if anything comes up, call. Otherwise I'll be there Friday night."

"Fine," I said, thinking at least I'd have a couple more days with my daughter. Madeline's calmness made me feel like I was blowing the whole thing out of proportion. Maybe she was right.

Terri had slipped out during the conversation, and after an hour of staring at the papers on my desk, trying to focus through the slight mist that kept pooling in the corners of my eyes, the phone rang. It was

Harlan again. "Well, pardner, your suggestion to talk to Joshua pro-
duced something interesting but not about Stephanie's murder. He
swears, though, that he saw a man murdered up near the Dark Angel
Mine about 20 years ago. He said the body is in a mine shaft and he can
take us up there. Earl is coming up. We're going to take a look. Want to
come along?"

If I ever needed something to distract me, it was right fucking then.

Twenty minutes later, we were headed into the Dark Angel valley.

CHAPTER 24

Harlan and Earl were in the front seat. Joshua was in the back seat with me. All the windows were down. As hot as it was, he still had his parka on, and he emanated the odor of beef stew gone bad. Toby and Ray followed in another Jeep with some climbing equipment.

The way Joshua described it was an old mine shaft "way up there," pointing to the valley where Gottlieb wanted to mine. The road to it passed Stephanie's empty house. As we got up in the labyrinth of old mine claims, Joshua had a hard time concentrating, and several times we missed turns we needed to make.

"I d-don't use the roads much," he said, explaining he had a network of foot trails he used to avoid running into people in the mountains "because sometimes they hassle me." But he seemed to know where he was going, if not exactly how to get there by vehicle. We drove a little farther, stopped where Joshua told us to and got out.

"It's u-up t-there," he said, shivering and wrapping his arms around his sides. We started walking. The mine scrag still covered the ground but some yellowing grasses grew in thin pockets of soil. The few trees that grew were stunted and skinny and many were blighted by tumorous-looking growths. It looked like a forest of death.

"W-watch it," Joshua said. We stopped short just as a large mine shaft was visible over the top of a pile of decaying granite. It was wide and nearly straight down.

"You're sure this is it?" Earl asked, still skeptical of the story. "You saw somebody murdered here?"

"Y-yes, I d-did," Joshua said, turning away from the hole. "I was c-camped over there and heard a car. People didn't come up here much in those days. I got nervous and wanted to see w-what was going on. There was a man standing and talking and another on his knees like he was praying. All of a sudden, he came up and knocked the other m-man over. Then he grabbed something that was on the ground and started running up the hill. There were some loud p-p-pops, and the man fell into the hole. The other man walked up and looked into the hole. Then he left. I got scared and went back and moved my camp away."

"You said before you didn't see either man clearly, you didn't see their faces," Earl pointed out.

"T-that's right. But I heard his voice. I'll never f-forget that v-v-voice," Joshua said, his frail body shaking like he was having a mild seizure.

"Lordy, lordy," Harlan said, shaking his head. The realization sunk in that somebody was going down into that hellish hole.

"I'd go down," Toby said, "but it's against my religion. We believe evil spirits live in mine shafts."

"Bullshit," Ray said. "You're just chicken."

"No, seriously, man," Toby said, his dark face becoming a shade paler.

"Whatever," Ray said.

He strapped on a climbing harness and ran the rope two times around a nearby tree. "Just far enough to check it out. Who's got the flashlight?"

We hoped the old hermit was wrong but had to take him seriously. Ray went over the edge. We lowered him a few feet at a time. After a pause he said "lower." Finally, about the fifth time we let him down, he said, "Hold it! I see something. A little more. Okay, I'm down!" A couple of seconds later "Aw, shit!" came out of the hole and we knew Joshua had been right.

"Okay, get me the fuck out of here," he yelled.

We hauled him up. After he got some of the gear off, he dusted himself. Joshua was sitting off to the side, his hands over his ears, rocking back and forth.

The rest of us waited for Ray. "There's a body down there, all right. A skeleton, anyway." But there was something else showing in Ray's face.

"There are some cuffs on that dude's wrists," he said, breathing hard.

"Say what?" Earl asked.

"Handcuffs," Ray said, sweat beading on his shaved head. "Like those on your belt, Earl."

"Aw, shit," Earl agreed.

"There were a bunch of rocks in the hole, too," Ray said. "Part of the body was covered by them. Up near the top here, there's a place where the rocks appear to be scorched like somebody might have tried to blow the hole closed. I wouldn't have noticed but the rock there looks less oxidized and is the same color as the rocks on the body."

We walked over and looked. He was right about the color of the rock. Rather than dwell on what we had discovered, Earl said, "Let's get the hell out of here. I'll call for somebody to park up here tonight, just in case. We'll try to get a removal team and evidence technicians up here tomorrow. He isn't going anywhere." He shook his head as if trying to clear a bad dream. "Jesus, what next?" No one had an answer.

We headed into town. It was a quiet ride, for a lot of reasons.

After Harlan dropped everyone off, he and I went next door to the deli, where he ordered a triple scoop of frozen yogurt. The guy's appetite was not affected by anything. "It's non-fat, ya know," he said. "It's not the calories that kill you. It's the fat."

I wasn't in the mood for our usual back and forth about his eating habits, so I told him about the conversation with Madeline.

Anything he said about the situation with Cassie would have come off as banter, so he became absorbed in eating his frozen yogurt.

He was almost finished when I asked, "What's on tap for tomorrow?"

"We'll let the S.O. retrieve the body," Harlan said, pausing to crunch what remained of his cone. "George Gunther is scheduled to come in because he has a pickup truck like the one we were looking for. We don't really need to talk to him now that we know it was Al's pickup everybody saw at Steph's, but I haven't been able to get a hold of him. The people at the rental yard said he went to see his wife. By the way, I told Earl what Al said, and he agrees with me that it seems to clear both Al and Gottlieb from suspicion."

Hearing that rankled me but, hell, it seemed like the truth. "Thanks for taking me along this afternoon. I needed a break."

Harlan nodded and walked across the lawn to his ramshackle office. There were no messages at the Miner, no people either. Everyone took off early. That was fine with me. I didn't want to talk to anyone anyway. But neither did I want to go home and sit around for hours waiting for Cassie to call.

Some river time would be just the thing to soothe my jangled soul.

Heading south on the Peak-to-Peak highway, I was tempted to go on down to Blackhawk and play poker for a couple of hours. Almost tempted, anyway.

When gambling was approved, the casinos were for the most part old bars and funky mom-and-pop operations, and I'd spent a few entertaining evenings playing stud poker. Since then, the big money operations had come in and torn down the historic brick buildings and Victorian gingerbread homes and built towering steel and glass casinos, trying to outdo each other to get gamblers at their tables.

When they ran out of room, they shaved off more of the mountain sides that rose above the old town and kept expanding. Some even knocked down three-year-old casinos and built more elaborate structures, some five and six stories high. With unstable rock from the new cuts looming over the multimillion dollar casinos, they hired contractors to polish and plaster the canyon walls.

Now, if you squinted your eyes pulling into town so that things were slightly out of focus, Blackhawk resembled nothing so much as a jewel-encrusted butt crack, and that, coupled with the odor from the overtaxed sewage treatment plant, driving through town made me nauseous.

So fishing it was.

Instead of turning west at Rowland to my regular fishing spot, I turned east and parked behind the Stage Coach Inn. There was a 'honey hole' downstream—a flat stretch where the railroad track grade squeezed the stream into a deep, slow channel.

A couple of years ago, I had hooked an eighteen-inch rainbow in that hole. And I had seen him since but never got him to take a fly. He was a cagey old coot and getting up in years.

The sun was starting to slide behind the peaks as I hiked downstream. Growing fingers of shadow from the fir trees along the bank fell onto the creek. I tied on a size-ten stimulator, figuring a big fish like that would be more tempted to come out of his hole by something that looked big and tasty, waded into the stream below the hole and cast upstream, stripping line as the fly came back toward me, over and over. There was not a ripple of interest from below. Sometimes just being out here is enough. Today it wasn't. I wanted some action.

Stepping out of the water, the sun warmed my stiff legs as I headed downstream. Ahead, the tracks veered away from the stream, which cut into the granite like a knife, leaving a clean, cool riverbed. With my back to the tracks, the stream itself seemed untouched by human hand.

Spellbound by the beauty before me, I was startled when the ground beneath my feet began to rumble. Within moments, a freight train rounded the bend from the west and let a long blast with its powerful air horn. Four diesel locomotives belched black smoke as the train lumbered past, the noise and the vibration so intense my body seemed in danger of coming apart.

The locomotives rounded the next curve, leaving the cool whine of the coal-car wheels as they glided along the steel ribbons.

So much for the illusion of unsullied nature. But losing that illusion didn't sully my desire to catch a fish or two.

Following the creek, I crossed a gravel bar where the stream cut a deep channel against the rocks. The water flowed smooth for twenty feet or so then slid over a small waterfall into another glassy stretch.

I stood on the bank, letting warm sunlight bask my legs, and dropped the fly up current about twenty feet and then let it drift back toward me. Nothing seemed interested, but I was getting into the hypnotic rhythm of the stream and the arcing casts.

Feeding out some line, I let the fly drift into the shoot that fed the next pool. As it was swallowed by the froth, a silvery fish with a vermilion stripe shot two feet above the water. It zigzagged to the opposite bank before running back to me. At the release of the line pressure, it jumped again and hit the line with its tail.

It threw the fly, but I had slipped the wearying bonds of civilization and left my cares behind. It was time to go home.

A menacing pastiche of black, white and gray thunderclouds had piled over the divide all afternoon and were racing eastward as I got to my car. A cold, gusty wind blew a wall of icy raindrops and dust down the street.

I had just climbed inside the car when it hit full force, throwing rain and hail down onto the land like a gray shroud. Within seconds the roads were covered with white slush. The hail pounded my car like a thousand snare drummers. Lightning cracked the sky—a white/orange fissure burned into my brain like a flashbulb. I shifted into four-wheel drive and slogged up the hill.

Before I turned onto Magnolia Road, the storm clouds had moved east and little patches of blue were showing through the high haze. Grasses and wildflowers on the Reynolds' place were vibrant and green between islands of hail. Raindrops dimpled the pond in the meadow. Faint appreciation for what I was seeing tugged at my brain.

A few minutes after the scene receded in my rear-view mirror, I pulled into my driveway where Roscoe was waiting, soaked and muddy. He seemed disappointed that no one was with me.

Sorry, dog, I miss her too. I shrugged and walked to the cabin. The sky never cleared completely and the air was cool so I built a fire in the woodstove and read. Roscoe was on the floor about six inches away and the warmth spread wet-dog odor throughout the cabin. I opened the door to the deck and threw more wood on the fire.

It was too early for a drink, but that didn't stop me from wanting one. What I really wanted, however, was for these crimes to be solved in the next day and for Madeline to call and say Cassie could stay with me.

As darkness fell, Cassie called and said she and Tresha had been named to the camp all-star team and would play a game against the counselors the next day.

"Could you come and watch?" she wanted to know.

"Wild horses couldn't keep me away," I said, looking out the window as sheet lightning flashed crazily through a towering thunderhead looming over Dragonback Ridge.

CHAPTER 25

A shadow streaked across the meadow as I gazed, and I bobbled the phone while trying to hang it on the wall. It fell, dangling by the coiled cord, to the floor.

As I bent over to grab it, the window imploded, sending hundreds of needle-sharp shards of glass across the room. I hit the floor and rolled toward the power cord that connected the cabin's lamps. More shots rang out from the mountain side. A spray of bullets thudded against the side of the cabin, forcing me back to the floor, as the shooter gave up on accuracy in favor of saturation. Frantic, I raised my face up off the broken glass and jerked the plug, throwing the cabin into darkness.

Roscoe, who had been snoozing inside the walk-in and protected from the glass, was freaked, too, crashing around, whimpering, looking for a place to hide. I rolled across the glass-strewn floor to the kitchen stove, which afforded more protection than the thin cabin walls, feeling tiny of pricks of pain through my thin shirt. Roscoe lurched past and I wrestled him into the stove's protection, but another shot came through and ricocheted with an impersonal, deadly whine off the wood stove and splattered the wall right over our heads.

Fuck this, I thought. He could keep shooting until something connects. My fishing vest, with the gun in the pocket, was across the room on the bed. When there was a pause in the gunshots, I lunged across the room to the bed and pulled the vest to the floor. After struggling with the zipper, I got the gun free, crawled to the deck door and kicked it open.

"Roscoe! Come on!"

He ran for the door and we dropped into the darkness beneath the deck. "Car! Go to the car!" I yelled at him. He bolted down the trail. More shots rang out and splattered the ground around the cabin. In mid stride, the ground exploded beneath him and rolled him over. He came up yelping and continued his dash for the car. It was impossible to tell if he were injured.

After the burst knocked Roscoe over, the shooting stopped. Maddened by adrenaline and anger, I sprinted as hard as I could up the mountain, aiming for a spot above the sniper's nest.

My legs and lungs were on fire, my throat choking on the taste of chemicals flooding my body as I pumped upward into the tree line.

Desire for resolution and retribution was not hampered by a sense of survival. What I was going to do if I found the shooter never crossed my mind.

But all doubt was gone; somebody wanted me dead and they were within reach. Clearing the meadow and moving into the trees, limbs whipped my face and tore at my clothes. Loose rocks gave way beneath my feet and I fell to my knees and sprawled on my face. But I protected the gun and came up running.

Sweat poured into my eyes and nearly blinded me. About a hundred feet above the saddle, I crouched down, listening and watching. It was as still as an old cemetery. My eyes adjusted to the dark. Beneath me, no one moved. But up the mountain, some rocks broke free and came crashing down. If somebody was going over the ridge, they were probably headed for the road that ran behind Dragonback Ridge, so I took a parallel route and ran for the top. Just as I reached the crest, the rumble of a big engine came to life not far below.

Lights were coming on along the road and a truck perched high on oversized rims sprayed gravel as it headed out.

I took some heaving breaths and watched. It was one of the Agnews' war wagons, no doubt about it. There weren't many trucks that looked and sounded like that.

"Motherfucker," I said, over and over and slammed my fist into the ground in frustration. My legs were shaking hard as I walked back down the mountain to my car and found Roscoe wedged beneath it. I got a flashlight out and shined it on him. There wasn't any blood but his eyes were wild with fear. After trying a little longer to get him out, I walked up the hill to the cabin, turned on the lights and surveyed the damage.

Glass was everywhere, and at least a two-dozen holes splintered the cheap paneling on the walls. A bright spot of metal glowered from the wood stove where a bullet had struck. The phone was dangling and making funny noises. It still worked, so I called Harlan at home and spent some bad minutes until he arrived.

Harlan stayed with me in the cabin while Ray, Toby, Earl and some deputies searched the hillside and talked to the people who lived along Dragonback Road. Toby said they found 60 rounds of spent .223 cartridges scattered around the saddle. Wiley had burned two full M-16 clips trying to kill me.

"I don't think that ol' boy cares for you, Aaron," Harlan said. I couldn't even smile at his effort to lighten up the situation.

As soon as he heard about the shooting, Earl called a friend on the CU police force and had a guard stationed outside the hall where Cassie and Tresha were staying. I just sat on the bed with my head in my hands.

At long last, Earl came in, looking tired and concerned.

"So he missed, huh?" he asked with the shake of his head and a tight smile.

"Either you're real lucky or he's a bad shot. Or both."

I nodded, feeling stupid doing so.

"It was Wiley," he said. "Some of the people who live down there recognized him. We've broadcast a be-on-the-lookout, armed and dangerous, with a request to hold him for questioning. I'll get a warrant first thing in the morning. Then we can get with the Gilpin County Sheriff's people and search the Agnew's compound. I'd be surprised if he's there. We called and talked to Merle. He said he and Davey are there, but they still haven't seen Wiley. I didn't tell them why we wanted to know, but they must have figured out something happened."

"Let's try to keep this quiet until I figure out what to do with Cassie," I said.

"She can stay with us," Harlan said. "So can you."

"Not me. I'll stay right here."

Harlan looked alarmed. "Now, Aaron, I don't like what I'm thinking. You better leave this to us."

Earl nodded.

"I'm not going to do anything," I said, my voice rising. "But that motherfucker will not drive me from my home!"

"Sure. That's fine. Whatever you say," Harlan said. They were getting up to leave when Earl's PAC set came alive. He stepped outside for better reception, then came back in.

"Wiley just passed through Central City. They lost him on some mining roads but he appears to be headed west into the mountains."

"Where the hell can he go from there?" I asked. "That's a dead end up in those peaks."

"Not for his truck, it ain't," Harlan said. "There's old four-wheel drive tracks all over those mountains and he knows ever one of 'em."

"Well, we'll try to make sure he doesn't come back this way," Earl said. As they filed out, I said, "Why? Why does he want to kill me?"

"Let's just try to keep it from happening, for now," Earl said. "We can figure out why later."

After they left, I spent an hour picking up the worst of the glass and another half hour vacuuming the rest. It was an obsessive act, as if by removing the evidence of the attack, I could destroy the reality of what had happened.

It was still dark when I finished, but morning was only about two hours away. I took a big drink of whiskey. The warmth hit the back of my neck first and spread down my spine to my legs, finally wrapping my body in a big warm towel. After several more drinks, I stretched on the bed and descended into the purgatory of tormented half-sleep.

Deep in the night, a noise on the steps brought me wide awake. Even before my eyes were open, my pistol was pointed at the doorway, my arm stiff. I was squeezing the trigger as Roscoe poked his head through the cabin door. I raised the gun, relaxed the trigger and let the hammer fall back on the empty chamber.

As I tried to go back to sleep, one question keep haunting me; what in hell was that shadow running across the meadow?

CHAPTER 26

Morning broke cool and clear. In the light, chips of glass I had missed the night before sparkled like sequins in the carpet. I broke out the spikes that remained in the window frame and stretched plastic across it. Photographs of wolves, bears and mountain lions torn from the pages of magazines covered some of the worst damage to the walls.

I dressed in a dark denim western shirt with pearl buttons, Carhartt jeans, cowboy boots and my faithful old wool sport jacket and put the gun and a full box of cartridges in my pocket. Roscoe stayed home, still scared shitless from the previous night.

I drove into town and found Harlan at his office. He nodded like he was expecting me.

"Howdy, Aaron," he said. "We got more news. The Winter Park police tried to stop Wiley, just outside of town. He fired a couple of shots at 'em and took off again. He wrecked his truck, hit a boulder or something and tore out the drive train or some such and took a hit from a shotgun. So he's wounded, but not bad enough to stop him. Anyway, he's on foot. They're organizing a search party, helicopter and all. That's about forty miles on foot, so it would appear he's out of our hair for a while."

Wiley could hide in the thick timber for quite a while, but unless he hijacked another truck, he couldn't get back across the divide on foot without exposing himself.

"Well, that's something I guess." I said, feeling relieved—at last.

"How are you doing this morning?" Harlan asked.

"I'm okay," I said, wondering what that meant.

"I hear tell you're going to get to watch the girls play. I'm glad, because I can't go. Do you mind giving Tresha a ride home?"

"Sure, Harlan, I'd be glad to do that," I said. "What are you up to today?"

"Not that much," Harlan said. "We've sorta put everything on hold until the task force gets together. Since we know where Wiley is, Earl isn't going to worry about a search warrant, and he can't get his boys up to the mine shaft until this afternoon. Gunther was supposed to come in about four and we still haven't gotten a hold of him. And we've got Joshua in the holding cell. He had a bad night and got a little crazy. If he's quieted down by this evening, I'll let him out. If not, I'll probably have to take him to the hospital for a mental-health hold. I hate to do it. It'll just make him nuttier. But I can't have him walking around town screaming that crazy shit. Scares the tourists to death."

"Can't have that," I said.

He didn't like my sarcasm. "No, we can't."

"Has anybody heard about last night?"

"Not yet," he said. "But you know how it is."

"I know. Anyway, I've got to get to work."

I pulled around the corner and parked in front of the Miner. Abigail was in her office, door closed as usual, talking on the telephone. Terri wasn't in.

Abigail opened the door and said, "Terri's kids are sick today. She's staying home with them." She paused and raised a well-plucked eyebrow. "Say, Aaron, I've been getting calls from people about some shooting up in your neck of the woods. You wouldn't know anything about that, would you?"

"Not me," I said. "Try Earl."

"Yeah, right." She closed the door and went back to the telephone.

It wasn't easy working after last night, but it was either get busy or sit around and dwell on it. The thought was tickling my mind that finding Wiley might unravel some information about Stephanie's murder, but I dismissed it as wishful thinking. And there was no way Wiley was responsible for killing Al Bartholomew.

I tried calling District Ranger Alexander. His secretary said he would get back to me. Yeah, sure. Same with the U.S. Attorney. Ditto the mayor. There was no point in calling Fontaine.

I hung up the phone in frustration and then decided to call Terri, hoping that she would somehow console me.

It rang three times.

"Hello."

"Terri, this is Aaron."

"Oh...Hi," she said, sounding surprised.

"If this is a bad time, tell me. I just wanted to see how your kids are doing."

"That's nice of you. Both of them have some kind of flu. They're not real sick, but I couldn't find anyone to take care of them."

"I'm glad to hear that. I'm just sitting here going crazy. Nobody seems to want to talk to me. So I figured to keep calling until a real live person answered. You came to mind."

"Speaking of phone calls, Gottlieb talked to me," Terri said. "He insisted on taking the call himself. And he told me he is confident that the permit will be approved."

"It wouldn't surprise me at this point," I said. "Anyway, I just wanted to see if everything is okay," I said, prepared to hang up.

"How are things going with Cassie?"

"You heard me talking to her mom. She's going to come and get her on Friday. Today Cassie and Tresha are playing in all star game against the camp counselors."

"You must be proud of her," she said. "Are you going to watch?"

"Yeah."

"That's nice," she said. "Tell her good luck, for me."

With my eyes flicking to the mirror, I drove down Boulder Canyon and even pulled over at Boulder Falls for a few seconds. Call me paranoid, but knowing that Wiley was on foot and forty miles across the Continental Divide just wasn't as reassuring as it should have been. I got into Boulder early and went to the library to see if any new mysteries were on the shelves. The stacks were pretty depleted so, instead, I went to sit in the Peace Garden by the creek. Brightly clothed runners, cyclists and in-line skaters sped by on the sidewalk. A five-year-old riding a *Hot Wheels* terrorized senior citizens. Youngsters waded in the buff, shrieking when cold water slapped their little behinds.

And a lithe, blonde goddess-mother in *Dayglo* spandex tights skated behind a double baby carriage that probably cost more than my car was worth, oozing good health and prosperity.

Across the creek, a sallow-complexioned youth dressed in black sat staring morosely into the passing stream. Every so often he took a deep drag off a long, thin cigarette and sighed, like the weight of the world was on his shoulders.

As if to punctuate the unreality of the scene, two transients were screaming at each other on the creek bank. They wrestled, and one slid down the steep bank and fell into the rushing water. When he tried to stand, he slipped on the slick rocks. The current went over his head.

"Help me! Help me! I'm drowning!" he beseeched bystanders, over and over as he tumbled down the eighteen-inch-deep stream. Nobody did and he got to his feet, cursing, and climbed out.

Any emotions or even amusement I might have felt at the high and low drama had been burned away.

Enough was enough. I drove to the campus.

Inside the CU Events Center, the campers were demonstrating ball handling skills. There were about a hundred people in the audience. The all-star game was next and then awards would be given. Tresha saw me in the stands, smiled and waved. I waved back. Then she nudged Cassie, and she waved too. But she looked nervous. She was probably one of the youngest players on the team—a pretty good reason to be nervous. Well, I'll get to see how she responds to the pressure. See how the season that might have been could have turned out.

Neither Cassie nor Tresha played the first quarter. The campers were down 18-8 at the end of the quarter. It was a respectable score, considering the counselors were either current or former college ball players.

Cassie and Tresha went in together, with Cassie at point guard and Tresha at post. This could be interesting, I thought. Not much happened on either end during the first couple of possessions—too many outside shots.

Then Cassie brought the ball down the left side, cleared out the forward and pounded a bounce pass into Tresha, who was posting up on the low block.

Tresha turned and shot-faked, which brought her defender off the ground, took a hard dribble to the middle. Another defender picked her up there, she faked another shot and as the defender came down, stepped around her for a layup. She made the shot and was fouled. She made the free throw and turned to point to me in the stands before sprinting to get back on defense. I gave her a pumped fist in acknowledgment.

"All right," drawled out a kid in the stands. The crowd applauded. One of the counselors threw the ball to half court before the campers could get back and a short, quick counselor went all the way for an easy lay-in. The kid booed.

The next time down, Cassie went right, cleared out everybody except Tresha and fired her another bounce pass. This time, the counselors double-teamed Tresha, who passed it right back. Cassie pulled up behind the three-point line with a backwards dribble and iced a three-point shot.

The kid and a friend sitting nearby high-tenned, laughed and fell over nearby seats. This time the crowd got into it and cheered the campers. Tresha had tapped the ball after it went through the net, keeping the counselors from getting it for a quick inbound pass and the campers got back this time.

The counselors' coach was yelling at the referees because the tap was illegal. They just shrugged and looked puzzled. But I was proud. I'd taught her that little trick. The counselors worked the ball around once and a short girl drove to the basket. Tresha stepped in and slapped the shot to another player as Cassie was breaking down court. The girl passed to Cassie, who bobbled the ball a little but drove to the right baseline. Two of the quicker counselors got back and one picked Cassie up as she drove to the basket. Seeing the defense, Cassie reversed herself and dribbled towards the corner. When the counselor stepped away to find the player she was supposed to be guarding, Cassie spun again and drove for an easy lay-in. The crowd went crazy, as did the bench. The counselor's coach threw her clipboard to the floor with a clatter and called time out.

The score was now 20-16, and the campers' coach substituted five new players. The crowd booed. Cassie and Tresha got high tens from everybody on the bench. The new group kept the score close until half time.

Tresha went in at the beginning of the second half. Without Cassie to pass her the ball, she didn't get it very much. Once at the high post, she drove in for a nice, short jump shot.

The counselors got another easy fast-break lay-in off the long inbound pass. From then on, they started to run away with the game.

After sitting on the bench while their team got behind, Cassie and Tresha were sent in again at the beginning of the fourth quarter. Cassie got a steal on the side, and she and Tresha ran a two-on-one fast break. Right at the basket, she passed behind her back to Tresha, who laid it in the basket. The bench went crazy, as did the crowd and one proud father and coach in the stands. I got a lump in my throat, my heart swelled up like a balloon. I thought of the championship slipping away.

Tresha was taken out of the game and Cassie played a few minutes longer. She didn't do much, and it became obvious that she and Tresha brought out the best in each other on the basketball court. Seeing their friendship blossom, I wondered how Cassie would take it when she found out she had to go back with her mom. I wasn't going to tell her until tomorrow, now that I had some breathing room.

After the campers got reorganized into their teams, the awards were handed out. Cassie got rookie-of-the-year award as the best young player. Tresha got the coaches' award for best work ethic, coachability and all around skills.

Both girls were flying high after the camp and chattered non-stop on the ride home about things that had happened in the game and the people they had met.

It went something like: "And then I go…And she was all, like…And they do…"

I dropped them off at Harlan's house to shower. My mind was elsewhere. I had to go by the Miner to check on phone messages. It was getting to be crunch time for follow-up stories on the mine, but my hunger for the task was gone. There were no messages at all.

After reading the Post and News, I walked up the hill to Bob's for a cup of coffee. When I got back to the Miner, the phone was ringing. Harlan was shouting. "Thank God you're there," he said, just short of hysteria. "Get on up here as quick as you can."

"What's wrong, Harlan?"

"Just get up here right now, goddamn it. Do it!" he shouted and slammed the phone down. It didn't take much imagination to realize something was terribly wrong. Harlan had never gotten that excited about anything in the four years I had known him. Had Wiley somehow made it back over the mountain?

CHAPTER 27

With my mind crackling like a downed powerline at the potential horror that awaited, I ran out the door and sprinted the five blocks to the Town Hall. Harlan was sitting in his office, his face showing the lackluster deadness of a witness to a terrible crime. The place looked like a twister had swept through; furniture askew, phone wires cut, the radio destroyed. Joshua lay quietly on a bunk, moaning, his eyes staring as if they had seen a specter.

Harlan stood and motioned me to the chair he had been using. "Aaron, for God's sake, sit down and listen," he pleaded. I didn't sit down.

"Don't fuck around, Harlan. Just tell me."

Harlan took a deep breath, gathering strength for the task. "Cassie has been kidnapped. It was Gunther. He might be the one responsible for all this."

George Gunther? The name echoed in my head. Harlan didn't have to worry about me doing anything stupid at that moment. I was trying to ask him 'responsible for what?'" A fuzzy picture was forming in my brain when my world collapsed. My mind raced down a dark tunnel, choking my vision into a smaller and fainter light until it was little more than the weak beam of a flashlight. My legs went out from under me.

Harlan lifted me and sat me in the chair. Just before the light went out completely, I grabbed the chair's arms, squeezed as hard as I could, and screamed like a wounded, cornered bear. I rose but Harlan was ready and shoved me back as hard as he could. With the jolt of the hard chair, I came to my senses. I focused on Cassie's face. The light came back up.

"Harlan, what the hell happened?" I whispered, wondering if the question was just in my mind.

With his hands still holding my arms, Harlan told me. "George came in. Joshua was still in the cell back there and had calmed down a lot. I was getting ready to let him out. I noticed he was listening very carefully to George as he talked. Out of nowhere, Joshua started shaking the bars and screaming, 'Murderer! Murderer!'

"When he went off like that, George pulled a gun and held it on me. He was scared, real scared, his head jerking right and left like he was having a fit. I thought he was going to kill me sure. Instead, he hand-cuffed me to the bars of the cell, cut the telephone lines and smashed the radio.

"He said, 'I'm sorry, Harlan, I had to stop the mine. Too much was at stake.'"

Pieces of the puzzle began to fall into place as Harlan went on, "Right then, Cassie came in the door looking for you. There wasn't any more handcuffs in the office and George didn't want to open the jail cell with Joshua carryin' on, so he took her with him. Just grabbed her arm, showed her the gun and took her. Aaron, there wasn't nothin' I could do. There just wasn't."

My mind was working again. "So it wasn't Wiley," I whispered to nobody in particular. Gunther sounded like he was on the edge but not over it, or he would have killed them all. He was running scared now. But at least it wasn't Wiley. How's that for a choice of evils?

"How long ago did this happen?"

"About a half hour," Harlan said, still shaken. "I started kicking the furniture and screaming. Somebody heard it and told Fat Jack next door, and he came over and got the keys from the desk drawer and let me go. I already called in a "be-on-the-lookout" for George and his truck from Fat Jack's office before I called you. Earl's on his way up. Ray's outside taking radio messages."

"Have you heard anything yet?" I asked.

"Maybe. But it ain't good. A Gilpin County Sheriff's deputy called and said he thought he saw George's truck just before the BOLO went out. If it was George, he's headed for the Agnews' place. But he wasn't sure it was him. And he didn't recall seeing anybody with him. But then again, he wasn't lookin'."

"George must have lost it and just headed for the first place he could think of," I said. "You've got to go up there and search that place."

"We can't just go up there, Aaron. First of all, it's in Gilpin County. Second, we'd have to get a warrant, and Earl isn't sure we can get one based on a possible sighting."

"So what do we do, just sit and wait, while a killer decides what to do about my daughter?"

"Let's just wait for Earl," Harlan said. "He'll be here soon." For some reason, that comforted me, but I couldn't see what Earl could do, either.

"What's the story with Wiley? Have they caught him yet?"

"No, they're still lookin, is the last thing I heard. But they've got him sealed up in there. There's no way he could get out. There's about forty men out searching for him. All the roads are blocked."

Just then, Earl walked in. Harlan and I both jumped up and started to speak at the same time. Earl raised his palm to silence us.

"Hold on a second," he said. "I've got a plan."

CHAPTER 28

"We recovered the skeleton up in that mine shaft and found a .38 service revolver next to the body. Fortunately for us, it was nickel plated so we raised the serial number right away. It was registered to Gunther. There was also a missing person report from about the time he quit, in August 1971, of a transient that George was having a lot of trouble with. So I think we've made him for that murder," Earl said, getting through the information rapid fire. "And then he must have murdered Stephanie Goldman, apparently to stir up more trouble about the mine.

"I guess he didn't want anybody going into those shafts and finding the body. Not when he had so much to lose, with his Barbie Doll new wife and a run for the county commission planned. And Ray was right about that section of rock in the mine shaft. It had been blown and fairly recently, within the past year or so. The trace evidence indicates it was military grade C-4. And it was C-4 with a motion-sensitive trigger that blew Al's truck."

"Dear Lord," Harlan said, shaking his head. "It was Gunther behind all of that."

"Here's my plan," Earl said. "What we need is a reliable informant to confirm that Gunther is at the Agnew place, if in fact he is. That's you, Aaron. You've got to get in there. I'll have the Boulder and Gilpin County SWAT teams get ready and deployed. And we'll get the sheriff over there to draw up an arrest warrant and find a judge, have him ready to sign. You get in there, confirm over the radio that Gunther is there and give us everybody's location. Then we'll get the warrant signed and come in. Think you can do it?"

It was the perfect plan, I thought to myself, but not necessarily for the reasons Earl laid out. Whether he knew it or not, he was allowing me to do exactly what I wanted to do—go in myself. If George had Cassie in the Agnews' compound, there was no way in hell I was going to let a SWAT team go in there with guns blazing. This was a one-man job. If he knew what I was thinking, and I suspect he did, he wasn't letting on. Harlan must have realized it too. But he was playing along, as well.

"You're goddamn right I can do it," I said. "But isn't that old mine like a fortress or something? Does your plan include a way in, or am I supposed to walk up to the gate and ring a bell."

Earl smiled and said, "Would you like to see an aerial photograph of the place?"

"That would work."

"The lady from the Jewish Defense League sent me one," Earl said, handing it to me. "You take a look at the compound. I'm going to get the operation started." He went out to his car and got on the phone.

We decided that I would be dropped off a mile down the road from the Agnews' gate and follow a marshy stream bed to the north side of the compound, cut the fence and go in through some ancient, rusting mining equipment. The trailers were side by side, across a clearing from the equipment and sitting right beside the mine shaft. The place didn't look much like a fortified compound—just a big mining claim surrounded by a pretty good fence.

It seemed doubtful the Agnews had any kind of electronic security equipment, but I'd just have to take a chance. There were dogs, three or four dog houses anyway, so Ray had bought a pound of sausage and picked up some knockout pills from the local veterinarian.

The plan was to get to the fence just about dark, knock out the dogs and wait until dark to go in. Most busts are set just before sunrise, when the suspects should be in deep sleep. But this situation ruled that out–every minute was critical. Harlan gave me an old-fashioned flak jacket with a lot of pockets. I'd also have a radio, wirecutters, flashlight and the knockout bait.

"There's one thing I've got to do first."

"What's that?" Earl asked.

"Get my dog."

They both looked at me like I was crazy.

"Trust me on this." But there was something else at home I needed.

Harlan shook his head, but said, "Whatever. You better get going. We've got about three hours of daylight. We should leave here by 6:30."

It was 5:09. I left and drove home. "Cassidy Ann, what the hell have I gotten you into?" I asked aloud.

I had to believe she was there and still safe in order to function. Otherwise, there was no point. But a little worm of doubt twisting in my stomach reminded me to be ready for the worst.

CHAPTER 29

For the first couple of miles, my legs shook so hard it was almost impossible to drive. But there was also the realization of what an incredible clusterfuck had come down. In any case, the only real question left was how to get Cassie back. The was no other scenario to consider. I would do whatever it takes, with no qualms about any other outcome. But the worm was turning. What felt like resolution in my heart and head felt like water in my guts. That watery feeling turned into a wave of nausea, and I pulled to the side of the road and vomited.

With that purging, I was able to clear my mind. The future depended on saving Cassie. If I failed, there was no future.

And for that I needed my dog. It was a well-kept secret that Roscoe was a K-9 corps washout. He would have graduated top of his class, but he never got over his fear at the sound of gunfire.

I supplemented his training with love—pure and simple. And his good nature became his dominant trait. But beneath that lovable exterior, he was still an attack dog.

Tonight, we'd see if he was up to snuff. True to character, he was waiting for me when I pulled up to park, as if he knew something was wrong.

I opened the back door. He looked up and rumbled a patented "Whuf."

"They got Cassie, Roscoe. We're going to go get her back."

"Whuf," he answered and climbed slowly into the back seat. I ran up to the cabin and took the 10-guage double barrel shotgun out of its hiding place in the closet, sawed the barrel down to twelve inches and the stock off just behind the grip. Trimmed down like that, it was what the Sicilians called Il Lupo—The Wolf. It only had one use. I put a slug in one barrel and a regular shot shell in the other and two of each in my pockets. And then I taped it to my back, under the flak jacket. It was uncomfortable as hell but well concealed.

Roscoe was sitting up in the back seat when I returned. I patted his curly, massive head.

"You ready?"

"Whuf."

Harlan, Earl, Toby and Ray were waiting for me in the office.

"Let's go," Earl said. "We can go over a few things on the way." They were all dressed in camo gear, vests, and carrying M-16s. A crowd had gathered and watched us leave. They knew about George. Fat Jack had, without a doubt, spilled the beans. But they didn't know where we were going—we hoped—because the Agnews had friends in town.

"We'll have men in position in an hour. There are already some watching the road to be sure Gunther or nobody else gets out. And another deputy is watching the place from the hillside across the valley. They said it's quiet as hell," Earl said. "The last thing we'll do is put two vehicles on the road almost at the gate. The first one will ram the gate. It all begins with your signal. Go. That's the signal. Go. Got it?"

"I got it. Let's just get one thing straight. Nobody moves until I signal. Nobody."

"That's the way it will be. And I have to advise you not to take unilateral action," Earl said, with a noticeable lack of conviction. "You're a civilian, Aaron. You can be charged if you hurt or kill anybody. You are not authorized to use force." He looked at Harlan, who nodded. It was ass-covering time. Fine. I would do the same thing in his position.

But one thing nobody knew was that Earl and I owed each other. He had been my supervisor when I shot the rip-off artist in Denver, and he had helped me get rid of the body. Earl's motivation had been two-fold; he didn't want the operation to fold up before the bust came down, and he took care of his people.

For my part, I had never talked about it to anyone, even to Earl. It was buried. There was an unspoken, unshakable bond between us. But we still had to play the game for the rest of the world.

"I agree to all of the above stipulations. All I want is to get my daughter out safely. That's it. Nothing else matters."

"I understand," Earl said. "If that was my boy in there, I'd want to be in exactly the position you are in. By the way, are you carrying?"

"Just my rapier wit."

"Humph," Earl snorted. Hell, he had to ask and I had to lie. By policy, he should have searched me as well. But I knew he wouldn't.

The five of us were in a big, unmarked Chevy Suburban. We had turned off the Peak-to-Peak Highway at Rowland and went west on the Tunnel Road, right past my regular fishing hole. We made it across just before a long coal train thundered past, heading east.

Earl checked in on the radio, the "blue" channel that supposedly couldn't be monitored by the public. There was no movement at the mine, according to the deputies who were watching. No one had left. There were a couple of pickups in sheds. They couldn't tell the color or license plate.

Earl filled me in on Gunther as we drove. He'd taken the marshal's job after returning from Vietnam as a Marine Sergeant in 1969. That was his only qualification, but the town wouldn't pay enough to hire trained officers so the marshal and his deputies were more like hired guns.

George was one of the roughest, Earl said, and there were complaints from the citizens as well as the transients. He resigned one day without explanation and, after his wife died, bought the rental business with the life insurance money. Nobody knew what happened to the hippie at that time. It was commonly assumed that he just got tired of the heat and split for one of the coasts. After two years, his family, well-heeled Long Islanders, filed a missing person report. But nothing ever came of it. Most everybody was just glad that he was gone.

We were quiet after that, but Toby, who was sitting by himself in the rear seat, seemed to be chanting softly. Across his knees, he cradled a wicked-looking electronic-scoped M-16A1. It was eerie but also comforting for some reason I couldn't explain.

Ray, sitting next to me, was relaxed, as though surviving ten years on the streets of Baltimore made this little more than a walk in the park.

After about five miles of rough dirt road, we turned left and climbed out of the valley. The Agnews' mine was situated just beneath the tree line, on a little feeder stream for South Creek. Except for the claim itself, the area was heavily forested and the creek bottom was overgrown and tangled with brush and scraggly stunted trees. The mine road ran parallel to and above the stream on the south side.

Finally, Earl pulled over in a wide spot. It was a relief to get out of the Suburban because the shotgun was killing me. I filled my pockets with equipment and laced up my hiking boots. The radio was snapped on my right shoulder. My .22 magnum was already in the vest. Two guns, 14 bullets. More than enough. This wasn't going to be a shooting war. If it took more than one or two shots to do the job, well—

Roscoe was sitting quietly beside me, his head cocked as if he were listening to our conversation. Ray and Toby were standing back, locked in quiet discussion. Toby was back in the here-and-now, but his dark eyes were flat and cold like a viper's.

Harlan's vest was tight over his belly. He didn't look comfortable. There was no reason for him to be here except one—he was my friend.

Earl and Harlan faced me. They both shook my hand and said good luck. Toby and Ray nodded. Harlan held my hand a little longer and looked me right in the eye.

"Go get the girl, Aaron."

"I will. Roscoe," he perked his ears, "Search." Roscoe dropped silently into the brush.

"I'll be goddamned," Harlan said.

Within the first fifty feet, thick mud swallowed my feet and icy water seeped into my boots. Willow and salt cedar branches slapped at my face and tore at my clothes. It was a pain in the ass, but it was perfect cover. Nobody could see me in this mess. Roscoe stayed a little ahead, sticking his nose in interesting spots. The water was slow and didn't drown out the sounds from above.

I had turned the receive volume completely down, so incoming calls wouldn't give me away. As I slogged through the muck, it occurred to me that what I was doing at that moment was the perfect illustration of my life; tramping through the wilderness with a dog that was a failed military experiment and two guns that were about as worthless in this situation as tits on a boar hog.

Throughout my life, I had always given myself plenty of excuses to fail and used them regularly. Only this time, the stakes had changed.

These thoughts played through my mind like a skipping record.

The fence was at the top of a steep grade of decaying mine rock, with the brush and trees cut back about ten feet. I sat at the bottom of the hill and listened. Dead silence from the compound.

I hit the send button and said, "I'm at the fence." That was it. But I had to play along, or the cavalry would come riding in. I took six sausage balls with knockout pills in them and threw them over the fence so they were spread out. That way one dog wouldn't eat most of them and leave the other dogs awake. Then I whistled and ran back into the trees. In seconds, three dogs were walking the fence line and growling. There was a brief fight, but nobody yelled at them. Roscoe was looking at me, smacking his lips.

"You don't want these doggie treats," I told him. He looked back like he wasn't sure he believed me.

Fifteen minutes, the vet had told Ray. The dogs would be out for about two hours. I hoped he was right. I waited twenty minutes, took off the vest and unwrapped the tape that held the shotgun. My hand touched the pistol, left it in the vest pocket because the shotgun was a two-handed operation. Shooting it with one hand would probably fracture my wrist. We climbed the hill to the fence, waited and listened. There was still no sound from anyone within the compound. It was deathly silent. No, I caught myself—just real quiet.

The sun was well beyond the mountains, but it was not yet dark. The shadows were growing long. The sunset breathed a wildfire in the west sky. Little stars were twinkling in the east already. I cut the fence and we climbed through the hole.

Once inside the fence, Roscoe sniffed the sleeping pooches, all mutts of indistinguishable breeds but big and mean looking, and proceeded to urinate on each one. Scent marking, they call it. Or counting doggie coup.

I held the shotgun out, pointing in front of me as I ran between rusting hulks of mining glory. The first trigger was a slug, the second was shot I kept reminding myself. The first could blow a car off the road. The second would mow down a small forest—a chance I couldn't take until I knew where Cassie was. At every machine, we stopped and listened. Five minutes at least. Just as night got a choke hold on the light, we made it to the machines nearest the trailers—a crumpled up conveyor system that looked like it had been in a nuclear strike and the remnants of an old, rusted crane. Scrap iron was everywhere. I could still see the three double-wide trailers fairly well. The entrance to the main shaft was right next to a deserted cabin.

A broken-down crusher plant was to the right of the mine shaft. Everything was rusted. Piles of yellow, decaying mine waste dotted the compound like mountains on the moon. But there hadn't been any mining going on here for a long time.

As it grew darker, I could see weak light coming from the farthest trailer.

"I'm inside the fence," whispered into microphone. There was about a hundred yards of open ground between our location and the nearest trailer. Waiting became unbearable because any time now an irrevocable decision could be made. Yet time dribbled away like a melting glacier; each minute seemed like an eternity. Roscoe was next to me, whining in frustration.

"Easy boy," I said. "We're almost there." At last, full darkness was upon the compound. The light in the trailer was bright, but everything was still quiet. Too quiet. Somebody was in there. But they weren't moving around or talking.

We ran across the hundred-yard space in a crouch and arrived at the nearest trailer. Then we slipped to the back and started down the line.

My heart thundered in my head. My leg muscles were quivering. There was a flicker of movement in one of the darkened windows of the middle trailer. But the window was open. It might have been a breeze fluttering a curtain. Another curtain in another window moved. A shape appeared in the trees ahead. I jerked the shotgun around. But the image faded. There was no one there. It was a stress hallucination. Tiny green lights flitted like fireflies around the periphery of my vision.

I crept up behind the trailer with the light, peeked in a dark window at the rear, saw nothing and moved to the next. Again nothing. The light was coming from what I assumed was the living room. And finally I was next to it. My back was flat against the wall. I took a quick look in the window, ducked back.

Merle and Davey were sitting on the couch. George Gunther was facing them with a semi-automatic pistol in his hand. They were quiet, appeared to be waiting for something. Cassie was not in the room.

Stepping out away from the light, I took another, longer look.

Where in hell was she? I couldn't see the whole room, but all attention was focused between the Agnews and Gunther. If there were somebody else in the room, they were being ignored. Sometimes Merle would nod his head towards the back of the trailer. George would react, raising his gun. They all seemed to be getting agitated.

I took aim through the window and thought about shooting Gunther. It was tempting. I could very easily have justified killing him right then to save my daughter. But what if I missed and set him off? The SWAT team would engage. Or what if the slug somehow injured Cassie? At that moment, she was either safe or she was dead. I had to assume she was safe. And I didn't want my daughter to look at me as a cold-blooded killer if she survived. Neither did I want to think about what I'd do if she were dead.

So I whispered into the radio that I had Gunther in the first trailer and crept back up to it. Roscoe walked beside me, ears up. I knocked on the door and ducked down almost to the ground.

"George, this is Aaron Hemingway. I want you to let my daughter go. We'll walk away, and then you're on your own." There was a sound like furniture being knocked over and two bullets ripped through the door. I rolled towards the rear of the trailer. At the gunshots, Roscoe bolted back across the compound for the fence.

"Dad, I'm in here!" Cassie screamed.

"Shut up!" Gunther yelled.

Strange noises came from the radio.

"Damn it to hell, George! That was real dumb! We could have talked for a while. Worked things out. Now the SWAT teams are going to come charging in here in two or three minutes." I inched towards the front again.

"I need time to think!" Gunther yelled back. "I need time."

"You're out of time George, they're coming. Is Cassie hurt?"

Silence. "George, answer me! Is she hurt?"

"She's not been harmed," he said.

"Please don't hurt her. I lost her for awhile and just got her back. Don't punish us, we didn't do anything to you. George?"

The lights were getting closer. There was movement on the hillside above the trailers.

"You're right, Aaron. Come on in. I won't shoot."

"Throw the gun out the window first, George. Throw it out!"

"No, I don't think so," George said, his voice faltering. "It's all over now anyway." A measure of strength returned, "It's all lost." And then a gunshot went off inside. I flinched but grabbed for the door handle.

"He's done killed hisself!" Davey screamed. "He just blew his fuckin' head off."

It sounded true, but I couldn't be sure. I jerked the door open and rolled into the trailer, shotgun extended, with my finger on the shot trigger. Davey and Merle were standing there stunned, mouths agape, looking at George. He looked like he was having a nightmare, a painful grimace frozen on his face, except there was a mass of blood, bone and tissue where the top of his head should have been. Drops of blood and pinkish-gray brain matter were already dripping off the ceiling.

I pointed the shotgun at Merle and Davey. "Sit the fuck down, now!" They sat quickly back on the couch. "Cassie, are you okay?"

A door in the rear of the trailer squeaked open. "Daddy, I'm all right. Dad?" Those were the sweetest words I had ever heard. As much as I wanted to shout for joy, I wasn't ready to try and sort this out. For now, everybody here was an enemy.

"Come out here, Cassie. Keep against the wall and look straight ahead."

"Don't do anything stupid, Aaron," Merle said.

A hum of static erupted from the radio, but the volume was too low to understand anything. I wanted both hands on the shotgun until I got us out.

As Cassie came into the room, against my will I started to relax. It was time to call off the full-scale assault that was coming and I reached up to make the call. As I did, Davey's eyes darted to the door. Cassie put her hands to her mouth and screamed.

I swung around, and an apparition from the deepest recesses of Hieronymous Bosch's twisted soul stood there holding a black pistol with a barrel so big a bear could hibernate in it. He was covered with soot and grime, which was mottled over what looked like dried blood along his right side. He stunk like death, but Wiley was alive—barely it seemed. His breath rattled in his chest, and he was having trouble standing.

The soot looked like coal dust. The goddamned tunnel. He came through the mountain on a coal train. And he was aiming the pistol right at my stomach.

All of this had barely registered in my consciousness when he said, "You're going to pay now, you sonofabitch," slurring his words so they were almost unrecognizable, but his meaning was clear enough. He staggered and the pistol wavered. That was all I needed and brought the shotgun around and pulled the trigger—the wrong trigger. The slug went past him and blew the door clear off the trailer. Merle was up and moving towards me when Wiley fired. The bullet hit my shotgun, wrenched it from my hand and ricocheted into Merle's side. The impact knocked Merle into Cassie, and they slammed back into the hallway.

I tried to pull my revolver from the flak jacket, but the hammer got hung up on a fold in the pocket. Wiley's knees buckled but he didn't fall. Then, as he swung the gun back towards me and struggled to pull it up to eye level, an unearthly growl came from the darkness beyond the door. There was little doubt what was coming next, and the sound seemed to penetrate Wiley's toxified brain. He turned and pointed the gun out the door. I launched myself toward him, but just before I could bring my forearm down onto the gun arm, Wiley's head lurched , a red mist blowing out the back of his throat. He face was frozen in surprise, as though a terrible revelation had passed before his eyes. Then he pitched forward and fell towards the door. His legs twitched and his jaw worked soundlessly as nerve impulses were derailed by the damage to his brain stem. But he was already dead.

Davey was getting to his feet behind me when my pistol ripped free and I swung the stubby barrel towards him. "You're a dead mother-fucker if you take another step." There was no mistaking the resolve in my voice, and he sat back down. A rusty scream protested the invasion as vehicles crashed through the gate.

Mashing the transmit button on the radio, I yelled, "We got 'em, We got 'em. No shooting!" and turned the receive up. In the confusion, the only thing clear was shouting in the background. Roscoe stepped in the door, still growling, and stood over Wiley's body.

Keeping the gun on Davey, I moved over to where Merle's body covered Cassie, fear stabbing my heart. I pulled Merle's body away, and Cassie raised up on her hands and looked at me. There was blood all over her, but I couldn't tell if it was hers. She never made it to her feet, though. She just sat there looking at the blood on her hands and cried.

I moved to her, put one arm around her and pulled her to me. At first, she resisted. But then she crumpled against me like a rag doll. I rocked her gently in my arms, wanting to make it all go away.

"I'm so sorry, baby. I'm so sorry." And I cried with her.

Just then, Earl came through the door with his gun out. He snapped it towards Davey when he saw us.

"Aaron, are you guys all right?" he asked.

"No, we're not all right," I said. "But the shooting's over."

"Well, that's a start, I guess," he said as he walked in.

As I held Cassie, tears of relief streaming down my face, I asked, "Who shot Wiley?"

Before he could answer, I heard someone run up behind Earl. He stood to the side, and Toby Echoheart, face painted black and still carrying the sniper rifle, stepped into the light. He nodded to me.

"You didn't think I'd let you go in without any backup, did you?" Earl asked, his face creased in a grin. "Hell, if you got injured and had to be sedated, there's no telling what kind of nonsense might come out of your mouth."

Toby looked down at Wiley, kneeled and put two fingers in the pool of blood beneath his body and wiped red slashes across his blackened cheeks. Then he stepped into the darkness.

CHAPTER 30

An ambulance pulled up to the trailer and we hustled Cassie into it, trying to block her view of any more carnage than she had already seen. I rode with her while the paramedics checked her out. She was quiet on the trip to the hospital in Boulder. She hadn't been physically injured. But she seemed to be in mild shock, which was no surprise and confirmed by the emergency room physician. He wanted to keep her in the hospital overnight, but she was having none of that. She wanted to go home.

Harlan, Hattie, Ray and Tresha were all at the hospital with us. Harlan had stopped and picked up some clean clothes for her, but he and Ray left as soon as it was apparent Cassie was going to be released. The nurses scrubbed most of the blood off her while we waited. The emergency room physician asked Cassie if she wanted something to help her sleep. She looked at me and said "no." I was proud of my tough kid.

On the way home, she talked about her hours with George. "He was so quiet I didn't know what he was going to do," she said, in a faraway voice. She had her arm between the seats, running her fingers through Roscoe's hair, and he groaned contentedly. She didn't seem to remember what had happened in the trailer. And I hoped she never would. Three people had died violently in the space of a few heartbeats—so quickly that even my memory had trouble sorting it out.

I laid the palm of my hand up against her cheek. She was quiet for several minutes, looking out the dark windows at the passing ghostly trees.

"So he killed that woman?"

"Yes, we think he did."

"And he killed that man you found in the mine?"

"That one was for sure."

"But he wouldn't have killed me," she said. A statement. Not a question. She hadn't heard about the explosion that killed Al Bartholomew and I wasn't going to dump any more horror on her. There was a murderous logic to every thing that happened to that point, I realized, but by the time George Gunther grabbed Cassie, he had to know it was all over. More killing would serve no purpose, except the last one when he took his own life.

"No, he wouldn't have killed you."

When we got home, the familiar old cabin didn't look so enticing, so I laid some blankets and sleeping bags on the floor so we could sleep close to each other. She fell asleep but tossed and turned and moaned a lot. That stopped when Roscoe joined us and laid up against her. She had her arm around his thick neck. At some point, she fell asleep. I got up, called Madeline and took the phone outside on the step to talk. She was calmer than I expected her to be and agreed to leave the next morning.

With the echoes of unanswered questions bouncing around my brain, I called Harlan. Davey, he said, had asked to spend the night in the town hall jail cell because he didn't have any place else to go. Harlan had talked to him when he went back to Jack Springs.

And Davey filled in some big gaps in the story. He told Harlan that Wiley's real father was old man Agnew's brother. The old man suspected something was amiss as soon as Wiley was born and beat the truth out of his wife. They kept Wiley anyway, but he forbade her from holding the child, comforting him when he cried or even cleaning his diapers.

When his wife died, the old man doubled up the abuse on her bastard child, since she wasn't around for her share, with frequent strappings and later vicious beatings.

Harlan reckoned that questioning Wiley's parentage during our confrontation had brought it all back—that, and the humiliation of the beating.

It should have been possible to feel sorry for Wiley, whose future was etched in stone by neglect and abuse with the same chilling certainty of an epitaph chiseled into a headstone, if Lila June's theory could be believed.

I had no reason to doubt it. But that sorrow would have to come from someone who didn't look into the murderous eyes behind that big black pistol. It won't come from me.

As sick as they were, at least George Gunther's motives were clearer. But how did he think he would get away with it?

He almost did, Harlan reminded me. "Remember, we didn't have a clue until Joshua showed us that feller's body in the mine," he said. "After that, I suppose it was just a matter of time. It was just bad luck that George walked in with Joshua in the cell and Cassie showed up at the same time."

After we hung up, the sounds of the mountains at night lulled me toward sleep, and I crawled into the pile of bedding.

When we arose, neither of us was hungry. Cassie wanted to go to Tresha's for the day. I thought that was a good idea—a place that stood for safety with people who weren't likely to get her killed. Tresha was standing on the porch with a basketball under her arm when we arrived. I tossed her the keys to the gym.

At work, Terri was typing and talking on the phone when I walked in. Abigail looked up from the desk in her office, gave me an uncomfortable wave, and looked away. It was clear she wasn't ready to see me after what had happened.

Terri hung up and swiveled in her chair. She, too, was torn, as I could see.

She took the safe path. "How's Cassie?"

"She's still in shock. A little. She and Tresha are up at the school playing basketball."

Terri shook her head in sympathy, acknowledging a kid's ability to bounce back from…what? A day of horror worse than most people will ever experience? Yes. That must be it.

"It'll hit her later, though," I said, then wandered out on the porch.

Harlan pulled up.

"How you doin'?" he wanted to know.

I just shrugged, unable to kid myself any longer but also unable to put words to what I felt.

"Are the girls together?" he asked.

"Yeah, they're up at the gym playing basketball."

"Lordy, lordy," he said and drove off.

Going through the motions of trying to do my job, I called Earl. He told me they found C-4 and a variety of bomb-making material and equipment at Gunther's home, so it looked like he was made for the bombings.

"What about the money?"

"We don't have the bank records yet, but the manager confirmed that George recently made a big deposit in his election account," he said. "And you're going to have to give a formal statement in order to wrap this up."

"Should I get a lawyer?"

"Only if you want to waste a bunch of money," he said. "Davey backed up your version of the events last night."

"I'll be in tomorrow," I told him.

"Be at the Sheriff's Department about 10:00."

"Sure thing."

I called Bob Alexander, the Boulder district ranger. He said the Regional Forester had approved the permit for the Dark Angel Mine. It seems Gottlieb had sweetened the pot with another two million dollars for the reclamation bond. Alexander said he was sorry, off the record.

If I hadn't been on the verge of physical and emotional exhaustion, I would have been angry. But I just couldn't muster that much energy.

I passed the information from Harlan, Bob Alexander, and Earl to Terri, walked out and checked my fishing gear, then drove by the school and asked the girls if they wanted to come. They said no. I told Cassie her mother was coming to pick her up tonight. She didn't seem surprised, but I saw tears wetting the rims of her eyes.

A tangle of emotions too complicated to unravel still overwhelmed me. What would a real father have done? Kept his daughter out of harm's way? Hindsight is 20-20, as they say. What would he be doing today? Lock his daughter in a hospital surrounded by people in white coats and clipboards? Keep her home until her mother arrived so she could be handed off like a football? Stay with her or let her be with her friend? Friends are important at her age. Some think too important. But there it is. Trust her to know her own mind? Yes. Who could know better? Did that make me feel any less a failure? No.

These questions haunted me as I drove to South Creek.

Once there, I fished my 'honey hole' almost automatically, dropping a shiny green cricket in the current over and over. On what must have been my fifteenth cast, a silver flash shot through the current, and the strike almost jerked me forward into the creek.

The fish fought like a dervish, slashing, twisting, jumping and diving, running toward me, then away. But I was possessed, too, and played him hard. My wrist ached, my forearm burned, my shoulder was ready to give out. Each time he rested for a new attack, I reeled him closer and closer, finally getting him into the net.

After pulling the hook out, I held him on the undersides with both hands. He was two feet long if he were an inch. A bright crimson slash as thick as an ax handle throbbed along his side. He was a magnificent trophy, but I could feel the life fleeing his body.

Seeing that wild creature dying was more than I could take, so I lowered him back in the water and pointed him upstream to let the water flow though his gills. He sagged for a minute or so and seemed to want to roll on his side. I moved him against the current, waded into faster water. He tried to wriggle free, rested again and then, with a tail flip, slid out of my hands for the safety of his hole.

Some say you can hear words in the sounds of rushing water. Sitting there by the creek, I could hear something but I wouldn't call them words, exactly; more like a language from a time before words. Nevertheless, the voice of the moving water reached out and cooled the burning ache in my heart.

Something was still bothering me about Stephanie's missing cats. They should have been hanging around when Earl did the crime scene investigation, and four days later, hungry and lonely, they should have been there when Terri went back. On they way back to town, I decided to go by Stephanie's cabin and look around.

After all that had happened, why worry about the fate of some scruffy cats I had never even seen? It seemed like a loose end that needed to tied up, that was all.

The Subaru glided into the driveway and eased up to the house. Before I could get all the way out of the car, a big gray Tom was rubbing against my leg. He looked starved, but when I reached to pet him, he froze and then darted for a nearby tree. I tried to coax him back down, but he'd taken enough chances for the time being.

Walking around the property, I discovered two more cats in the trees, mewing forlornly but showing no indication of coming down. These cats were freaked out. My search expanded into a clearing that surrounded a big ponderosa with low, overhanging branches, where a mound of leaves and pine needles caught my eye. The odor, though faint, was obvious.

I kicked it apart and found a dead calico female. Her head had been crushed. A little ways away there was another tree with a mound and a dead cat. And another.

The best scenario I could come up with is that Stephanie's cats had run out when she was killed. If there were a cat door, it had probably become blocked when the cops were searching the house. A coyote or mountain lion had come across the scene and picked the cats off one by one when they tried to get back into the cabin. No wonder the survivors were freaked.

Inside, the rank smell that had festered in the hot, closed-up building burned my throat and nose and made it difficult to breathe. I flung open some windows, poured a pile of cat food onto the floor and filled the water bowl, then got the hell out of there.

If the survivors were quick enough, they could make it inside to food and safety. In any case, I'd call animal control tomorrow after Cassie had gone home.

I picked her up from Harlan's, where she and Tresha said tearful good-byes. When we got to the cabin, Roscoe, who hadn't wanted to let her go in the morning, sat watching her pack. She went over and hugged him every few minutes. He wagged his tail but didn't move.

When she packed up her basketball, my heart nearly shattered. To find something, someone you cared about more than life itself and then to lose her, was the ultimate irony in a life that made no sense.

Somehow, though, I maintained. We didn't talk much. There just wasn't anything to say. What we had been through didn't lend itself to casual discussion. Madeline showed up a couple hours before dark. When she saw the cabin, she stopped short. "What's all that fuzzy stuff hanging from the roof?" she wanted to know.

"Bird nests," Cassie said, grinning a little.

"Interesting," Madeline said.

As she got closer, she asked, "What about all those holes—" before catching my look. "Never mind, I don't want to know."

We got her stuff and carried it to the rental car, where I hugged her, too hard. Roscoe walked up, and she grabbed him around the neck and buried her face, her tears wetting his fur. He struggled to maintain his composure.

She got into the car with Madeline and sat there talking for a few seconds. Cassie rolled down the window and started to say something. Instead, she waved. I waved back. My tough kid tried to grin, letting me know it was all right.

We waved again, and they drove away.

CHAPTER 31

Five people, not counting the hippie in the mine, were dead. The Dark Angel was still on track, although lawsuits would keep it at bay for awhile. Cassie was on her way home with her mother. And I was home alone, with a big bleeding hole in my heart that I was hoping to plug up with good Kentucky whiskey.

It was a cool night, so I built a small fire in the wood stove, took a couple of healthy swigs of Evan Williams, walked out on the deck and looked up at the moonless sky and the riot of brooding stars in the heavens.

I stood there and contemplated what had happened the past few days; almost been killed twice, put my daughter in danger, rescued her then lost her again. Looking at the limitless night heavens, luck or fate or destiny seemed to have at least as much force in the outcome of events as human will. And what about the primordial tide of unknowable forces that constantly ebb and flow across our lives?

I had a girlfriend in college who believed each of us creates our own fate. But that seemed laughingly absurd, now.

While standing there in cosmic reverie, a car came up the driveway, pulled in and shut off the lights. Not very many people came to visit me, but I was beyond worry. Let them come. I walked through the cabin and sat down on the rear steps and waited.

As soft footsteps came up the path, Roscoe rumbled from beneath the porch.

Then, a little out of breath, Terri said, "Aaron, are you home? Aaron?"

"Terri, what are you doing here?" At the sound of my voice, Roscoe 'whuffed' and settled down once again to resume his moping.

"I couldn't stand the thought of you being alone, not after all that happened," she said.

We stepped inside. The fire in the stove was starting to warm the cabin, and its soft light danced around the room. I faced her and pulled her towards me. We held each other tightly and the confusion, sadness and hurt melted from my body as her warmth came through our clothes. She sighed and put her head on my shoulder. Her hair smelled like a field of spring flowers.

"What about your kids?" I asked, regretting it immediately.

"My mother came over to stay with them," she said. "For the night." Her eyes searched mine to see if the implication struck home.

It did.

"But first, I better tell you," she paused. "Escamilla let you go. And he made me the editor. He said you could work free-lance, that you're too much of a liability to be an official employee. But he likes the work we've done."

I held her again, only back this time so we could see each other. Her hands reached up and cupped my face.

"Will you do it?"

"Maybe."

"But if you don't, what will you do?"

"I don't know."

We stood looking at each other, knowing these questions wouldn't be answered tonight. So she said, "I've got some stuff in the car to bring up."

"I'll go with you. Wouldn't want a mountain lion to get you, just after you've come to your senses."

"A mountain lion?" she asked.

"Just kidding." I thought she was going to pull a Lila June and slug me one in the shoulder there for a second.

We walked down the path holding hands. Terri was bent over, rummaging around in her car when a large, powerful pickup crawled up the driveway and stopped. It had a heavy, black, grill protector, and my heart skipped a few beats until I saw it was Emma. She stepped down from the high cab, started toward me, then stopped. The truck's engine was running, and the headlight high beams were on.

"I'm so sorry about Sunday, Aaron," she said. "My foreman almost lost his leg in a hay baler, so I had to get back. But I was worried about you when I heard what happened. I had to come by and see if there was anything you need."

Just then, Terri stood up. Both women looked at each other—then they looked at me. In the uncomfortable silence that followed, I glanced up on the hillside where Emma's truck lights were shining and thought I saw two big green eyes peering down from the shadows. I could have sworn one eye closed in a playful wink.

I thought about it for another moment and winked back, just for the hell of it. Then I turned to face the music.

The lioness froze, for a moment, in the near-blinding light. She turned away and stepped behind a tree. But something drew her to the scene below. She couldn't resist one last peek and so turned back, her face half-hidden by the tree trunk. She blinked once and then, like a Dark Angel, slipped into the shroud of the night.

3833491

Made in the USA
Lexington, KY
28 November 2009